 Brand, Max, 1892-1944.
The lightning runner

The Lightning Runner

OTHER FIVE STAR WESTERNS BY MAX BRAND:

The Stone That Shines (1997); *Men Beyond the Law* (1997); *Beyond the Outposts* (1997); *The Fugitive's Mission* (1997); *In the Hills of Monterey* (1998); *The Lost Valley* (1998); *Chinook* (1998); *The Gauntlet* (1998); *The Survival of Juan Oro* (1999); *Stolen Gold* (1999); *The Geraldi Trail* (1999); *Timber Line* (1999); *The Gold Trail* (1999); *Gunman's Goal* (2000); *The Overland Kid* (2000); *The Masterman* (2000); *The Outlaw Redeemer* (2000); *The Peril Trek* (2000); *The Bright Face of Danger* (2000); *Don Diablo* (2001); *The Welding Quirt* (2001); *The Tyrant* (2001); *The House of Gold* (2001); *The Lone Rider* (2002); *Crusader* (2002); *Smoking Guns* (2002); *Jokers Extra Wild* (2002); *Flaming Fortune* (2003); *Blue Kingdom* (2003); *The Runaways* (2003); *Peter Blue* (2003); *The Golden Cat* (2004); *The Range Finder* (2004); *Mountain Storms* (2004); *Hawks and Eagles* (2004); *Trouble's Messenger* (2005); *Bad Man's Gulch* (2005); *Twisted Bars* (2005); *The Crystal Game* (2005); *Dogs of the Captain* (2006); *Red Rock's Secret* (2006); *Wheel of Fortune* (2006); *Treasure Well* (2006); *Acres of Unrest* (2007); *Rifle Pass* (2007); *Melody and Cordoba* (2007); *Outlaws From Afar* (2007); *Rancher's Legacy* (2008); *The Good Badman* (2008); *Love of Danger* (2008); *Nine Lives* (2008); *Silver Trail* (2009); *The Quest* (2009); *Mountain Made* (2009); *Black Thunder* (2009); *Iron Dust* (2010); *The Black Muldoon* (2010)

The Lightning Runner

A Western Story

Max Brand®

FIVE STAR
A part of Gale, Cengage Learning

GALE
CENGAGE Learning™

Detroit • New York • San Francisco • New Haven, Conn • Waterville, Maine • London

GALE
CENGAGE Learning

Five Star Publishing, a part of Gale, Cengage Learning.

Set in 11 pt. Plantin.

LIBRARY OF CONGRESS CATALOGING-IN-PUBLICATION DATA

Brand, Max, 1892–1944.
The lightning runner : a Western story / by Max Brand. — 1st ed.
p. cm.
First published as a six-part serial in Street & Smith's western story magazine, under the name John Frederick.
ISBN-13: 978-1-59414-903-0 (hardcover)
ISBN-10: 1-59414-903-8 (hardcover)
I. Frederick, John, 1892–1944. Lightning runner. II. Title.
PS3511.A87L47 2010
813′.52—dc22 2010024666

First Edition. First Printing: October 2010.
Published in 2010 in conjunction with Golden West Literary Agency.

Printed in the United States of America
1 2 3 4 5 6 7 14 12 11 10

The Lightning Runner

Chapter One

Marshal Neilan had slept eight hours a night for two weeks. He had eaten three square meals, and had a full hour's *siesta* after each lunch, and yet the marshal was tired. He looked tired, and he was tired. He had a battered face and he had a battered soul. He was mortally weary, and his weariness came from walking constantly in danger of his life.

They were all out for the marshal. The drug-runners and the smugglers of Chinese across the border, the yeggs and thugs of the river towns, the horse thieves and the cattle rustlers, and all those clever internationalists who occasionally drifted in the direction of El Paso and points east and west of that cheerful city, all of these and many odd items had it in for the marshal. He was tireless, he was unforgetting, he was unforgiving, and he was incorruptible.

Men said that Steve Malley, the great smuggler, once laid a stack of a thousand $100 bills on the marshal's desk and got it back the next day. After that, they gave up trying to bribe him. But everyone wondered why he kept on at the job. Certainly it was not the money involved. His salary was beggarly small; if he wanted to turn back to his law office, he could make ten times as much with the greatest ease. Neither did he enjoy great fame; he was rarely in the papers.

In fact, what kept the marshal at his post was an odd thing, a sense of duty so pure and noble that his labors rewarded themselves. Still, he could be tired, and he was especially weary this morning, as he wrote on a slip of paper:

Dear Bill, will you send Lawrence Grey over to my office?

He dispatched this note by his office boy. Then he turned and looked out across the roofs and listened to the murmur and the rumblings of the city, until the sound took on another character and seemed to him like the drumming sound of bees in the sunshine and the still, ominous purring of the mosquitoes in the river flats. He looked at the yellow sands of the desert beyond the town and the rock faces of the hills that made his horizon. That was where he wanted to be—anywhere out there, in the open. But his work was too great and spread over too wide a field. Electricity had to carry his thoughts, and this was the center of power. He had to sit here in the center and send out emissaries to spin the farther margins of his web.

He was in the midst of these melancholy thoughts when his office boy returned and opened the door for an excited man who came with him, Deputy Sheriff Sam Tucker, late of Tucson and other points west where trouble was in the air.

Sam Tucker said: " 'Lo, Marshal Neilan. Look it here, Marshal, is it a joke?"

The marshal, by painful degrees, dragged his thoughts back from the great open places and turned his tired, battered face toward the other. "Is what a joke, Sam?" he said.

"You wrote a note. You sent it over, and you say that you wanna see Rinky Dink. Is that right, or is it a joke?"

"It's not a joke," said the marshal. "How many people know that you've got young Lawrence Grey?"

Sam Tucker looked uneasily over his shoulder toward the door. He looked toward the ceiling, and he looked toward the floor, also. It seemed that he suspected everything around. Then he stepped closer and laid a brown hand on the edge of the marshal's desk. "Not a living soul," he whispered, "and thank

God for it. Nobody knows, and nobody's gonna know till we have to let it out. That'll be the time. The fool newspapers, they'll blow the word around. They'll be shoutin' out loud, and his friends will hear. It'll be harder and worse to hold him then, than it is to hold freezin' nitroglycerin."

"How did you get Grey?" asked the marshal curiously.

"Didn't the chief tell you?"

"No. I haven't heard. You fellows have been very close-mouthed."

"Smythe and Ridgeby and Allen and Fulton and Meggs, they went out. They all went out to make the plant," said the deputy sheriff.

"About the five best men you have," suggested the marshal.

"Not about . . . they are the best," said Sam Tucker. "They're clean and away the best. Who else would we be sending for *Don* Diablo?"

"I suppose so," said the marshal. "And what happened?"

"Well, they got a good start. The greasers had framed him," said Sam Tucker. "They took most of the punching, too."

"How bad was it?" said the marshal.

"A couple of Mexicans will never eat *frijoles* any more," said Sam Tucker carelessly. "Meggs is in a pretty bad way, but they say he'll pull through. Smythe and Allen, they're laid up, but they'll be reporting back for duty in about a month, I guess. The whole bunch was lucky, any way you take it."

The marshal half closed his eyes and seemed to be dreaming. "Yes," he said, "they were a lucky lot."

"About that note, now," said Sam Tucker with a forced laugh. "The chief, he just wanted me to drop over and find out what the joke was."

"There's no joke," said the marshal. "I want to see him. I want to see him here."

The jaw of the deputy sheriff dropped. "You don't mind if I

ask again, sir," he said. "It's Rinky Dink that you mean, all right? It's *Don* Diablo, is it?"

"Yes," said the marshal. "It's Lawrence Grey. Tell your chief that I have to have him here, and your chief along with him, if that's possible."

Sam Tucker left. He slid through the door with an alarmed glance behind him, as though he were departing by the skin of his teeth from the presence of a madman.

And the marshal turned back in his chair and continued to stare out the window, blankly, sadly for nearly an hour.

In the meantime, there were many calls on his telephone and many taps at his door. But he refused every one. He was saving himself. He was too tired a man for more than one interview such as he intended to have that morning.

Eventually they came.

First, two guards came through the doorway. Each wore revolvers; each carried a sawed-off shotgun. They entered, stepped half a pace to either side of the door and faced inward, holding their shotguns at the ready. Behind them appeared the sheriff, who came in, nodded briefly at the marshal, and, taking up his position in the center of the room, faced the door in his turn. He allowed no weapons to be visible, but the bulges under his coat were not made by packages of candy.

When these preparations had been made, two more men appeared, assisting between them, as it seemed, a third, whose wrists were held together by heavy irons connecting through a powerful double chain with other manacles that fitted over the ankles. He was bundled through the doorway. The door was then closed, and the key turned in the lock.

"Well, Neilan," said the sheriff, "here he is. I've known you close onto twenty years, Neilan . . . and so I've brought him when you called." He was panting. He took out a handkerchief and wiped his forehead. But the movement was furtive, and his eyes never left the face of the prisoner.

And the guards looked only at the man in chains, and so did the marshal. Yet Lawrence Grey was no abysmal brute in face or body. He was a slenderly made youth who might have been twenty-one when he smiled and twenty-five when he was serious. But generally he was smiling. He had one of those pink-and-white complexions that refuse to be tanned by the fiercest sun; it merely becomes pinker—and whiter. His blond hair, to be sure, seemed rather sun-faded at the outer margin.

When they got Lawrence Grey, he was dressed in neat flannels, a white shirt with a soft collar and black tie of silk tied in a big flowing knot, such as Bohemians and artists are so fond of affecting. He wore a jaunty slouch hat, with the brim turned up on one side. In general his appearance was that of a pleasant, casual young man. Now, his appearance was altogether different—there was no coat, no slouch hat, no black tie.

"Thank you for bringing him," said the marshal. "You might introduce me to him, though."

"As if this *hombre* didn't know you," growled the sheriff. "But you tell him, Rinky Dink. You tell him if you know him."

"Of course, I know Marshal Neilan," said Lawrence Grey. And he smiled at the marshal, as if to say he was honored to meet him, and that he was also, perhaps, honoring the marshal just a little. In fact, he seemed a modest young man, and yet he gave a second impression of being rather sure of himself, in a quiet way. Young Englishmen often give the same effect.

"And I know you, Grey," said the marshal, "although this is the first time I've seen you. One hears about one another."

"Yes," said Grey, with another of his charming smiles. "One does."

"Listen to him talk," said the sheriff, half grinning and half snarling. "Sweet, ain't he? Butter'd melt in his mouth, all right."

"You don't need to point him out," said the marshal. "Now

that you've brought him here, I want to ask another favor of you, old fellow."

"Go on," said the sheriff. "You know the sky is the limit, between you and me . . . only don't spring another like this one."

"I want you to send your strong boys back home, and I want you to go and sit in the outer office, yonder, and leave Grey in here alone with me."

The sheriff started to speak, and then stared. But he stared at the prisoner, not at the marshal. He still looked at Grey as he answered: "Leave you alone with Rinky Dink? You're crazy, Neilan. You know that you're crazy to ask that."

"I'm asking just that," said the marshal. "He's loaded down with iron, and I'm well-armed, you know."

The sheriff shook his head, as a man does when he cannot offer a logical objection, although he feels resistant still. "I don't like it. Fact is," he said, "I hate the idea of it."

"I want to be alone with him," said the marshal quietly.

At last the sheriff looked at him. "You're never wrong, old son," he said at last. "And I hope that you're right now. I'll be sitting out there on springs. Make it as short as you can."

Chapter Two

The sheriff and the rest of his men had withdrawn from the office, with the exception of the second of the two bearers of the riot guns, and this worthy fellow, with a sour look at young Lawrence Grey and a wondering one at the marshal, now blurted out: "I don't wanna be botherin' you, sir, but suppose that I was just to stand here in a handy corner with this here gun . . . it might be tolerable useful."

The marshal nodded seriously at him. "Thank you, Jerry," he said. "It's fellows like you that make life easier for us. But I'll have to trust myself alone with our young friend."

So the guard went out, shaking his head and closing the door slowly behind him, with a long, long look of doubt cast toward Lawrence Grey.

When he was gone and the door at last closed, Neilan pointed to a chair. "Sit down, Grey," he said. "Make yourself at home while I open the window."

He spent only a moment, loosening the catch that held the window down and then lifting it with some effort, for it was a trifle wedged at either side. When he turned around from this work, he found that Rinky Dink was sitting with the shackles and the double chain piled neatly beside his chair, his knees crossed, and his hands locked lightly across one of them.

The marshal, looking at him without surprise, dusted his hands, for the under edge of the window had not been quite clean. After that, he merely said: "Don't you want to smoke,

Rinky Dink?"

"I'd like one," said the boy gratefully. "They're rather careless about the details over there in the jail."

"Here's some tobacco and wheat-straw papers," said the marshal, taking them from a pocket. "But, hold on. You have a fancy for Turkish blends, I think." He opened a drawer of his desk and took out a package. "Here's a sample parcel of Turkish stuff sent over the border for the hands of a small, select American manufacturer. But it got to the wrong address, Rinky Dink, the way things will. Want to try it?"

"Of course," said Grey. He made his cigarette with the leisurely speed of one whose fingers need no watching; they guided themselves and solved their own problems.

The marshal, however, made his own cigarette of an American blend. He lighted both smokes from one match, and afterward tossed it onto the pile of steel shackles and tool-proof chain. "That was rather a fast bit of work, wasn't it, Rinky Dink?" he asked.

Lawrence Grey tilted a little in his chair and regarded the gleaming heap. "The locks are rather old-fashioned," he said. "No, that wasn't a very fast job."

"A very neat one, though," said the marshal. "And I heard nothing. You must have wrapped the links with flannel."

"More or less." Rinky Dink nodded. "I just held the chain between my legs."

"So there's no mystery at all," remarked Neilan, going back to the chair behind his desk.

"Oh, none at all," said the boy. "This is grand tobacco," he added. "Someday I want to get over to the section of the world where they grow this stuff."

"Well, you'll get there one day," answered Neilan.

"Not if the sheriff has his way," said Grey.

The marshal smiled, very faintly, and his battered face seemed suddenly younger. "Why did you let them keep you a whole day?" he asked.

"Why? Oh, the jail has very strong bars. Tool-proof, and all that," answered the youngster.

"But it has to depend on locks," remarked Neilan.

"Very complicated new ones," said Grey.

The marshal shrugged his shoulders, apparently not convinced in the least. "I suppose that you wanted a rest," he suggested.

"Don't underrate the sheriff," warned Grey. "He's a formidable fellow. Every honest man is dangerous to people like me, you know." And he opened his eyes and nodded. He looked like a child, for the moment.

"I don't underrate the sheriff," said Neilan. "But something tells me that you're not likely to end your career in this town. It will have to be in a much bigger place than this, Rinky Dink. By the way, who gave you that new name the sheriff is so fond of using? Who called you *Don* Diablo?"

The boy sighed. "You know how it is," he said confidingly. "If someone has a bit of bad luck, let's say, and takes quite a fall, he's apt to call the other fellow the devil. It was only that."

"Well, Grey," said the marshal, "or Rinky Dink, or *Don* Diablo . . . I'm glad to have you here under any or all of those names. I've been waiting for years to see you face to face."

"Thank you," said the boy. "You'll understand if I cannot say that I've been hoping for the same thing?"

The marshal chuckled. "Now I'll tell you why I've sent for you, Rinky," he said. "I have on hand just the job for you . . . the very thing that's made to order for you."

A shadow came over the eyes of Grey, a mere suggestion of disappointment and disgust. "Well?" he said slowly.

But the marshal had read the meaning of that passing shadow and he said: "It's not a graft, Rinky. It's not likely that you could make much money out of it. It's merely a good chance for you to go and break your young neck."

Lawrence Grey regarded him earnestly. He drew in a breath of smoke; he touched his throat with femininely sensitive fingers. "Yes?" he said.

"Here's the rest of that tobacco," replied Neilan. "You smoke away at that while I talk. I begin by reading you a letter that I got four years ago . . . it runs like this." He spread a paper on the desk and read:

Dear Marshal Neilan: You may remember me from the old Brownsville days. The boys called me Brick then. It may help you to identify me if you recall the fellow who was accused of stealing Jay Saunders's bay gelding. I was the Brick Forbes of that episode.

Yes, I stepped a little too high and touched the ground not often enough in those days. Since then I've turned respectable. And I want to tell you the cause of it.

I was down in old Mexico at San Vicente. It was running high, wide, and handsome in those days. I understand that it still is. I had washed out some gold in the hills behind the town, and I came down to San Vicente to have a bust.

I had it, all right. Before I finished, I'd spent my money and got into a fight. Two greasers had me cornered and they were about to let the light into me when a fellow came by and slammed one of them over the head with the barrel of his six-gun, and kicked the second one into the street.

This stranger who rescued me was around middle age and about five feet nine or ten in height. The peculiar point in his appearance was a divided beard. It split in the center, parted outward, and ended in two points. He had dark eyes. His beard was gray. That's all the description I can give him, except that he was well-dressed.

He took me by the shoulders and brought me out into the light. He said: "I've been watching you. You've played the fool, but you're not as much of a fool as you pretend to be. This nonsense doesn't amuse you. Go home and be a good boy. This will take you back to the States."

He dropped a whole wallet into my pocket, and afterward I counted a shade over $1,000 in it. I sat down with that money and had a think. I saw that the stranger was right. I had been chasing a good time all over the West, but I never had found it. I had blown my pay every month, but I always cursed myself on Monday morning. I was sick of the life, and I hadn't known it. I had been at the door of the jail twenty times, and all for nothing. So I decided to pull out.

First, I asked for the name of my benefactor, and I was told that he was called John Ray. He was a high-stepper and a great spender, and everybody's friend in San Vicente. I tried to see him and thank him and tell him that I was going to follow his good advice, but he was out of town.

So I packed up and left San Vicente and went back to Pennsylvania. I had been raised in the country there, and I went right back to the old ground and sank the rest of my $1,000, after railroad fare was subtracted, to buy some land at less than $20 an acre. I got about fifty acres for what I thought a bargain, but I found out that it was the worst ground in the world. It was covered with outcropping soft black stone, and about one sheep to three acres was enough to keep the grass cropped short.

I couldn't live on that fool place. I went to work in the town as a carpenter and kept at that for nearly five years. Then, all at once, along came a fellow with a pink face and a foxy eye and wanted to buy my land. He offered me my original price. But I held on for more. He came up with $1,000, and finally I bucked him up to $3,000 cash. When I had that offer from him, I simply told him to go to the devil. The land wasn't worth that much on the face of it and it never would be. I decided that I would find out what was under the face of it.

Well, when I learned that that fellow was a coal miner, it gave me my lead. You won't believe it—the outcropping on that wretched ground was coal. I'd bought fifty acres of as good anthracite as a body could find in the world! And that was in Pennsylvania, where even the worst old fools and the smallest kids know all about coal. But I had spent five years cursing my black rocks.

That made me rich. I didn't have to use any intelligence. I simply sat by and let a company work the mine and took a big fat percentage for myself. I got so much money that I could afford to sit back and just pick up the good things that offered themselves, here and there. So I've stacked money on top of money for ten years and lived the softest sort of a life. I have somewhere between five and six millions today.

Now comes the rub. I got a dizzy spell one day. "Indigestion," I said.

"Hardening of the arteries," said the doctor.

"What does that mean?" I asked.

"Make your will. I'll explain later," he said.

I go to make my will, and there's another rub. I've been raising money, not a family. I have no wife or children. The nearest relations are a batch of second cousins, as hard as steel and as small as conies. The tightest, meanest lot of people I ever knew. If I pass out tomorrow, they get my whole fortune and split it into fifty parcels—just enough to make them all mean and self-satisfied the rest of their days.

Then I look at the charities. But what do I care about charities? What did charities ever do for me? No, I want to give my cash to a human being. But, mind you, all I've made in the past fifteen years have been business acquaintances. You can't call them friends.

Now I come to the point where I appeal to you. I think back to the old Western days. Those were the times when I found people that I loved around me. But they were a harum-scarum lot. Pretty worthless, a lot of them were, as worthless as I was myself. Only one man ever really did me any good. He gave me hard cash; he gave me good advice; and with his money, I'd bought my fortune, so to speak.

I remembered John Ray of San Vicente.

Considering the pace he was going when I last saw him or heard of him in San Vicente, he was probably dead long years since. A man can't be the friend of everyone in town very long. It spoils the digestion first and empties the pocketbook second. But if John Ray is dead, at least he may have left some descendants, possibly sons or daughters.

The moment I think of that, I get a flash of inspiration. I feel pretty good inside and out. And, straightaway, I send a registered letter to San Vicente, addressed to John Ray.

I'm not surprised when it comes back, the addressee not having been found. And next I send down a special messenger all the way to San Vicente, a good, solid fellow I can trust, a fellow with a pair of hands and a head, too. He goes down to San Vicente. I get a wire from him saying that he thinks he's on the trail. And the next thing I know, there's a small item in a Pittsburgh paper referring to the death of my man down there in San Vicente. His body had been found in the lake among the lily pads. He must have drunk too much tequila and fallen into the water; there's no signs of foul play.

That's very good. But Sam Bowman never tasted a drop in his life and never made a misstep. He was straighter and more careful than a certified accountant. So I send down a private detective, name Richard Burton. I wait three months and never hear a word from him.

After that, I say to myself: Something's rotten in the State of Denmark. Those two men have been bumped off because I sent them looking for John Ray.

And here's the point where you enter, Neilan. If I can't get men from out here to locate John Ray in San Vicente, you can. I'll pay five times any reasonable fee. John Ray, or one of his blood, is what I want to find. I pass along the job to you. Whatever money you have to spend on the job is all right with me. I'll send you the checks for it.

Only you got to work fast. According to the infernal doctors, I'm walking a tightrope that's likely to break under me any minute. And, if I fall too soon, $6,000,000 will tumble into the hands of about fifty hard-fisted, miserly, mean-souled scoundrels, all because there happens to be a slight taint of their blood in me.

Chapter Three

At this point the marshal paused in his reading. "That was four years ago," he said. "There's two things worth noting down. One is that John Ray hasn't been located. The other is that Brick Forbes is still hanging onto his life out yonder in Pittsburgh. At the last report, he had been living on graham crackers and water, or some such diet, for three years. And now they've put him to bed and only give him the air for an hour a day in a wheelchair that they take over the bumps with special care.

"But still Brick Forbes is fighting like a Trojan, and he won't leave off fighting until the last breath is out of his body. He doesn't want his money to get into the hands of his relatives. They're a little too distant to suit him, and they're too unlike the type of man he respects. They've never been West to thaw out . . . they've never learned to spread their elbows at the board."

"How many men have you sent to San Vicente?" asked the boy.

"I've sent three in the four years. The first fellow got tired of the job and came back, having accomplished nothing. The second was a sound man, and he stayed down there for months, using up my money and faking reports to me. Then I learned that he was too canny to be honest. He'd been prospecting on the side . . . he'd struck it rich, and finally he threw up the job and stuck to his mining claim. These fellows, between them, had used up two years. And poor Forbes was sending me pathetic letters from Pittsburgh. He was getting worse and worse.

"So I picked out one of the best men I had. Perhaps you know him. H.J. Broom."

"I know Dolly Broom," said the boy. "We met one evening in the Big Bend."

"The Big Bend is quite a place to meet in," observed the marshal, with a wrinkling about his eyes.

"Well," said the boy, with a similar smile, "that evening we both needed plenty of room. But Dolly was all right. I liked him . . . outside of his profession. What happened to him when he went to San Vicente?"

The marshal shook his head. "Broom worked for well over a year and got nothing. But at the end of that time, I had a short note from him saying that he was on the right trail and that it would prove to be a surprising one. Then all communications from him stopped. I thought nothing for a month or more. He might be working out the last details in silence. But then his continued silence began to worry me. So I sent down to investigate the silence of Broom. To put the report curtly, he had been seen and known in and about San Vicente, but some time before he had disappeared. From that day to this, I've been looking for the right man to send to San Vicente. And at last I've found him."

Lawrence Grey looked at the marshal in candid astonishment. "You're not serious?" he asked.

"Of course, I am," said Neilan.

Grey shook his head. "Tell me why I should do it?" he asked.

"For the simplest reason in the world. Three people have already died or disappeared on the trail. So the job is made to order for you."

Lawrence Grey said nothing for a moment, but finally he

leaned a little forward and eyed the marshal with eyes as straight as ruled lines. "I don't make it out," he said.

"You do, though," said Neilan. "Already every muscle of you is twitching to be off to San Vicente. Confess I'm right." Then he added: "Don't pretend that you're a dyed-in-the-wool criminal, Rinky Dink. I've watched your career. It's been a bright one. I didn't need to take a lantern with me, because you supplied your own illumination. But . . . you've been in the game for the fun you get out of it. Come, come. Tell the truth . . . confess. I won't repeat it."

The boy sat back in his chair. He said: "Well, what am I to do? Break jail and ride south?"

The marshal smiled. "You won't have to break jail," he said. "Wait a moment."

He called in the sheriff, and the sheriff came with a hand beneath his coat. When he saw *Don* Diablo unshackled, his hand flashed out with a gun in it.

"Now, steady up," said the marshal. "I've brought you in to ask for a two months' parole for this boy."

"Parole?" said the sheriff. "Neilan, say that again. Parole for a murderer?"

"Stuff," said the marshal. "You mean the two Mexicans? You know about them, I suppose?"

"I know they're dead," said the sheriff.

"Dead on the other side of the border, for one thing. For another, one of them was Francisco Vittorio . . . the other was Juan Cappano. And old Mexico offers a price for either of 'em, dead or alive. As for your own agents, tell me what they meant by making an arrest on the other side of the river?"

The sheriff blinked at this startling array of facts. "Neilan," he mourned, "it was right on the edge of the river. The lights from the house made a path right across to our side. There'll never be a state complaint about that arrest. Mexico doesn't care who catches *Don* Diablo, so long as he's caught!"

"I care, though. You go ahead and arrange the parole, like a good fellow," replied the marshal. "Or else, just turn your head at the jail. That's the better way. Let the boy take care of himself. Is that agreeable to you, Rinky?"

"That's all right," said Grey.

"Who unlocked the irons?" asked the sheriff angrily. "Did you take it on yourself to do that, Neilan?"

"Come here to the window a moment," said the marshal. "Grey, you might as well get ready to leave, if you don't mind."

He drew the sheriff to the window, and there he said to him quietly: "Don't be a fool, old son. The boy can land you in all sorts of hot water because of the place you arrested him. I know that it's been done before. I know there's such a thing as railroading fellows who deserve it. But this is an exceptional case. Grey has too many brains."

The sheriff groaned. "Well, then . . . ," he began. And so, turning back toward the prisoner, he was amazed to see him sitting once more invested in the full weight of the manacles and chains. He strode to the boy and tried the irons on wrists and ankles. Both were securely locked. Then he stepped back with a scowl. "I don't understand any of it, Neilan," he said. "All I know is that it's a bad business. I don't understand it and I don't like it."

He called loudly, and his four men rushed in eagerly, like a dog pack expecting to be fed.

"Take him back!" commanded the sheriff.

And, leaving last of all, he glowered over his shoulder at the marshal and shook a solemn head.

Chapter Four

When Rinky Dink, alias Lawrence Grey, alias *Don* Diablo, found himself at last inside the jail, he carried with him from the office of the marshal the remainder of that pound of curiously good blended Turkish tobaccos, good as only a sample can be. It was put away in his pocket. He carried also the memory of something that was almost a promise. On the way, he considered it. It was not exactly a promise, either. It was something more and something less. He had not given his word to the marshal, and neither had the marshal striven with threats to induce him.

Without a bargain made, the marshal had threatened the sheriff with the power of the federal law unless he turned young Grey loose.

This Rinky Dink most seriously considered.

His morality was that of a man who always had taken whatever appealed to his eye. It was also that of a man who, whether from strength of nerve or strength of will and honor, never had found it necessary to break his plighted word. In short, he felt that he lay under an obligation to the marshal, and he was one who loved to discharge an obligation generously. If it were a blow, his custom was to return ten for one. If it were the graze of a bullet, a shot through the heart would be about the proper recompense. If it were the loan of a horse, the gift of two good ones would about make things equal.

These were the ways of Rinky Dink, not simple, but exceedingly clear, so far as light could be cast upon them.

When he came back to the jail, the big sheriff stood for a while at the door to his jail.

"You know, Rinky," he said. "You know how it is."

"Sure I do," said Grey.

"You know that a man, he's gotta have something to say where his say don't belong, even."

"Sure I know that," said Rinky Dink good humoredly.

"That's the way with the marshal," said the sheriff. "It don't mean nothing, what he had to say. There ain't no sense to it. Old Mexico, what would it be wanting to say, just because you got arrested on that side of the Río Grande?"

"Sure," said Rinky Dink. "Old Mexico wouldn't have much to say. She'd be glad."

"That's what I said," replied the sheriff. "She'd be glad. You settle down here. You ain't going to have anything to complain of from me."

"No," said Grey. "I think you'll give me the right kind of a hanging."

"With last statements, and pictures, and everything," said the sheriff. "I wouldn't let you miss any tricks."

"I'll bet you wouldn't," said the prisoner.

He smiled at the sheriff, and the sheriff, nodding solemnly, went back to his office. There he was taken with a certain uneasiness in the afternoon of the day. He summoned a jailer and asked him to look to the star prisoner.

"See if he wants anything," he said dubiously.

The jailer came back. "He don't want anything," said the jailer.

The sheriff shook his head. "That's funny," he said. "Mostly they all want something. They wanna chew of good tobacco, or something funny like that. But it ain't nacheral. I mean for a prisoner not to want something, is it?"

The assistant jailer was amazed to hear himself thus appealed to. He almost swallowed the plug of cheap tobacco that was stowed in the corner of his cheek. "Sure, it ain't nacheral," he said. "I never heard nothing like it." And he hurried away. Even a close approximation to swallowing a plug of tobacco is slightly nauseating.

The sheriff went home to his dinner. On the way, he found that men had heard, albeit rather vaguely, that he had done something eminently worthwhile. The moment the sheriff was aware of this, he gathered his blackest scowl and strode along the streets without noticing even his oldest friends.

He knew that a sheriff is expected to appear as a man of dark humor and martial bearing. He knew that, on this day, he was collecting at least two thousand votes. He felt that he would draw his salary perennially. He was a good man and a brave man, but, after all, he was only an elected officer.

When he got home, he kicked his favorite hound out of the front path, scolded his favorite daughter, and snarled at his wife.

She was a buxom woman, over-gifted with teeth that made her always smile. This had endowed her with a rather false reputation for good nature. She still smiled as she lingered in the doorway, but her words were: "You can flash your big, brawny bluff downtown, but you stow it away before you get inside this stall. You hear?"

The sheriff heard. But he shook out his evening newspaper with a noisy rattling, as though he had not.

His wife understood perfectly. She was a woman who continually made her point, but never pressed it. At dinner she was even a little worried when she saw her husband merely toying with the excellent steak she had put before him.

"Listen, honey," she said, "that ain't chops, you know."

"I know," said the sheriff absently.

After dinner he went into his office, a small room that was

his sanctum. He never worked in it, but he fortified it with certain time-yellowed files from downtown. He always kept a blotter on the desk, scribbled a few words every evening, and blotted them on the blotter, so that it looked as though he were transacting fresh business every evening. He told himself that he needed seclusion, and that the harmless pretense of his office gave it to him. In reality, the office was his sand pile, in which he played at various imaginings, such as a second marriage and fewer teeth in the house.

This evening, he had just passed through an imagined divorce case and was selecting a wife from an imaginary file of applicants, when a shadow fell across him. Not figuratively, across his mind, but actually across his blotter.

He looked up into the eyes of Lawrence Grey. There was no leveled revolvers, no mask, nothing but the youth himself. But the sheriff, although he was a valiant man as men go, did not attempt to snatch out his weapon from the open drawer beside him. Instead, he stared fixedly at the boy.

"It was that sucker, Jones," he said. "You tell me the truth. It was that hound, Jones. You fixed him, didn't you?"

"It was those sucker locks you use. Birnham and Bixbee locks are the only kind to have in any self-respecting jail," said the boy.

"I went and recommended them in my last report," said the sheriff. "But look at what I've got to put up with in a jay town."

"I didn't come here to talk about the town or the town cops," replied the boy. "I came to talk about the county and the sheriff of it."

"All right," said the sheriff. "What have you got to say?"

"I thought that you were on the up and up," said young Lawrence Grey.

"I'm on the up and up, Rinky," said the sheriff

"You call it that . . . going body-snatching to the shady side of the Río Grande?" asked the boy.

"Aw, you know, Rinky," said the sheriff. "That's all in the game."

"It's not in my game," said the boy softly. "I'm on the up and up, too. Only I'm straight on it. I came here to tell you something. The next time you try a double-cross, I come and get you."

The sheriff felt an inward qualm, but outwardly he maintained his face. "I hear you talk, son," he said.

"You won't hear me talk the next time," said the boy. "What's the price of that five-year-old bay mare that you've got in your corral, back there?"

"Eight hundred dollars," said the sheriff.

"Here's six hundred," said the boy. He took it from a pocket with his left hand, and he counted it out on the desk. It was all from the left hand. The right hand remained divorced from occupation, as the careful sheriff noticed.

For he knew that overconfidence will sometimes make even the wisest relax, and he was watchful to take advantage of such a moment. On the other hand, he was very well aware that Rinky Dink was inwardly praying for some overt move on the sheriff's part.

"Six hundred," said the boy, "and that's worth a hundred more than she is. Am I right?"

The sheriff did not dispute the point. He said: "Where did you get it, Rinky? You didn't have a bean when we got through with you at the jail downtown."

"I rubbed the lamp," said Rinky mysteriously, and yawned. "That's the way I get everything."

"Yeah, you get a lot of light," said the sheriff. "There's no doubt about that." He fingered the money with some satisfaction. He had paid $280 for the mare the year before. She was worth more now, but hardly this much.

"Which way, Rinky?" he asked.

"Oh, south," said Rinky Dink. "Why?"

"We'll be sorry to lose you," said the sheriff.

"Will you?" asked Lawrence Grey. "Well, that's all I wanted to say. This, besides . . . if you start any gab about a stolen mare, you know, it won't go down."

"Look here, Rinky. Don't you underrate me," said the sheriff.

"I'll try not to," said the boy. "But that was pretty raw . . . I mean, going over and trying to slam me on the south side of the river. That was the worst."

"I made a mistake," said the sheriff.

"Nothing but," commented Rinky Dink. "Well, just turn your head a minute, will you?" He had stepped back to the window.

The sheriff turned his head.

"So long," said a voice outside the window.

The sheriff looked. He had expected it, but still he had to rub his eyes.

"So long," he said.

Chapter Five

Young Grey went out behind the house and to the barn. There he took a bridle. He lighted matches until he was sure that it was the oldest bridle in the lot that hung along the wall. Then he stepped into the corral and went, as though he had marked down the spot before, to an extreme corner where he roused a sleeping horse.

She stood up, without a start and without fear. She stretched herself, one hind leg at a time, shrinking her back. Then she poked her soft muzzle into the face of Rinky Dink.

"You come with me, sweetheart," he said, and passed the bit into her mouth as she tried to nibble his fingers.

He jumped on her, unsaddled, and, instead of opening the corral gate, he tried her at the bars. She winged her way across them and landed running, as only a hot-blooded horse will do.

"I knew it," said the rider softly.

Then he jogged the mare down to what could only be called the underside of town. He went through several twisting alleys. Once he had to dispose of a yapping dog, a big fellow. This he did by catching the dog by the scruff of the neck and throwing it across the neck of the mare, and over a fence adjoining. The dog landed in a pile of tin cans, made a vast metallic racket among them, and then fled with a whine.

Rinky Dink went on smiling. He did not court trouble, he told himself, but, when it presented itself, he could not help admiring the virgin's fair face.

He came to a small house with a large back yard in which two cows were tethered. At the door of the house he rapped, and, when the proprietor came out, Rinky Dink murmured a few words that caused the man to disappear and come again, bearing a saddle. This he strapped on the back of the mare, while Rinky Dink stood by and smoked some of the Turkish tobacco, admiring its taste and admiring the line of the mare, and admiring himself just a little, also, if the truth must be told.

"You know," said the man as he finished the saddling, "I'd take this to be the sheriff's bay."

"It is," said Grey. "I bought her from him."

"Bought her from him?" said the other. "Yeah, I'll bet you did. So long, Rinky."

"So long, Boz."

Rinky Dink rode out from town and went down to the river. He stood the mare on the bank and looked down at her image and his own in the water, overshadowing the reflection of a star or two.

On the far side lay Mexico, like smoke. On this side, a rider approached him, with the pale sheen of a carbine laid across the pommel of the saddle.

" 'Lo," said the new rider.

" 'Lo," returned Grey.

"What's the news?" said the other.

"Tamales," said Rinky Dink.

The rider laughed. "I mean, what's on your mind?"

"I'm telling you," said Rinky Dink. "Tamales, and *frijoles,* and tortillas thinner than lace wheelwork, cold as a fish, and better than Easter Sunday."

"Is that what you're thinking about?" said the other.

"Yes," said Rinky Dink, "and beer, *pulque,* tequila, mescal, hot peppers, and cold wine. You know?"

"Yeah, I know," said the other. He laughed again softly. "I

guess you're going south," he said.

"Yeah. I'm going south," said Rinky Dink.

"You go around by the bridge, then," said the stranger.

"That water looks like wading mostly," said Grey.

"Not while I'm looking," said the rider.

"You're a border guard, are you?" said Rinky Dink.

"You can call me that," said the stranger. "You sashay back through the town and hit the bridge, old son. It's all right . . . only, you go over by the bridge. That's all I gotta say, right now."

"The bridge is hard," said Rinky, "and this mare has tender feet." He reached across. His hand was a little faster than the paws of a cat when it flicks out at the already captured mouse. He laid it on the barrel of the carbine. With the other hand he laid the muzzle of a revolver on the man's big chest.

"Oh," said the guard, "somehow I didn't seem to recognize you at first."

"That's too bad," said Rinky Dink. "Which way are you going?"

"Away," said the guard, with the proper emphasis.

"Go right on," said Rinky Dink. "I'll watch you travel. I've got good eyes in the dark."

"What's your name, brother?" said the guard. "I mean, what's your working name?"

"Most people call me Rinky Dink," said Grey. "And some forget the Dink part. You can call me either . . . or both. I'm not proud."

"Sweet little piebald Saint Mackerel!" said the guard. "Is that who you are? So long, brother. I never really seen you, taking how dark the night is."

"Of course you didn't," said Rinky Dink. "So long, partner." And he watched the guard drift softly down the bank, the mustang that bore him stepping high and light like a horse that still has all its running inside it.

When the man was a dim thing to be guessed at among the distances, Lawrence Grey rode the mare down the bank. When she was belly deep, he let her drink one swallow of the muddy water and felt her shiver.

"She's been raised high," said Rinky Dink, "but she's going to be raised higher." Then he turned and looked back at the lights of the town, streaming over the water. They ran tiptoe, flashing over the ripples of the current. They made the boy think of small flags, streaming and flashing in wind and sun. And the flag he thought of above the rest saddened him a little.

"Someday I'm going to change," said Rinky Dink. "I'm going to get me a brand new name, and settle down, and be a clerk or something." He made a sour face in the darkness. Then he put the mare at the water, which she took eagerly, bravely.

They climbed the farther bank, the water dripping down from them noisily, and the river moving with a soft whirl and murmur in their rear.

Out of the brush before them a voice said cautiously: "Pedro?"

"No," said Rinky Dink. And he rode straight up the bank and past the brush, paying no heed. He heard voices murmuring inside the shadows.

"That Pedro, he is always late, and he never brings enough. He drinks whiskey. We are fools to keep a man who drinks whiskey so much."

"A man who did not drink a lot of whiskey," said the other, "would never do Pedro's work."

Rinky Dink passed on through the night. He put the mare to a canter and judged her as she handgalloped and then ran. The horse was so full of herself that she began to buck as she raced along. Rinky Dink laughed gently, and with the edge of his heel he ground into her ribs. The mare flinched, bending in a half bow, and then remembered her good manners.

They went on to a small village, which opened out its gathered lights into a wide scattering. He rode through the streets, turning several corners. The warmth of the day still lingered there, fenced in from the cool night winds. The lazy voices of the gossips murmured here and there, and men and women sat on doorsteps with the light from within flashing on moist brown faces. There was a smell, partly sweet and partly pungently aromatic and sour, the characteristic odor of a Mexican town.

He felt that he had ridden not miles, but centuries south of the border. At last he came to a house where the door was unlighted. He halted his horse and leaned. He called: "Margarita! Margarita!"

A woman ran out from the nearest house, panting with excitement. "Be still, fool of a man!" she gasped. "There has been a death."

"Margarita . . . Margarita!" called Rinky Dink softly.

He felt rather than saw the woman in her trailing black as she appeared on the threshold.

"Hai," she said. *"¿Sí, señor?"*

He waited a moment, taking in the taste of the wooden, wretched voice.

"Margarita, reach out your hand," he said. He could see the hand, dimly, by the help of the starlight. Into the hand he put a sheaf of bills. "There are some *pesos,*" he said. "There is enough to keep young Manuelo honest for two years, and by the end of that time he may stay honest forever."

"Who are you?" said the woman, gripping suddenly at the paper as though the meaning of it were nothing until she had his name. "Who are you?"

"You call me several names," said Rinky Dink. "But I'll tell you this. Whatever they say, Francisco was wrong. He tried to sell a man who never had harmed him, and he deserved to die."

"You liar, you sneak . . . now that he is dead," said Margarita. "Take back your dirty money."

"Hush, hush," said Rinky Dink. "I am the man who killed him, and who would kill him again. I am not giving you this for his sake, but for the sake of the younger boy. Remember me for what I tell you. Remember me and my words, because enemies always tell the truth." He heard the great intake of her breath. He reined back the mare into the street, and, taking off his hat, he saluted her. *"Madre, adiós,"* he said. And he rode off into the dark of the street.

There were children playing in the warm dust, and he had to make the horse weave deftly among them, picking her way with dainty steps.

His thoughts went backward, to the bereaved mother of Francisco Vittorio and the brutal words he had spoken to her. He thought of the young Manuelo, also, and his bright face, and the fine width between his eyes. He might be saved to the world, after all.

He rode on until, when he glanced back, he saw that the lights of the town had gathered together once more into an armful, then into the breadth of a hand, finally into a single broken ray.

Chapter Six

Not in the Mexican newspapers, not in the conversation of the cultured classes which is permeated with French, but in the chatter of the rabble, in the folk songs, and in the tales that live from mouth to mouth rather than from page to page, one hears much of San Vicente.

It is usually referred to in phrases like this: "white as the walls of San Vicente", or "shining far away, like San Vicente among its green fields", or "rich as the golden-hearted water lilies of San Vicente", or "cool as the cypress shadows of San Vicente."

One gathers, too, so often is it mentioned in the songs and the tales, that youth in San Vicente is gayer, younger, more beautiful than in other places in this world, that the peon has more leisure and the farmer more profit and kindness to spend. One feels that music, over its river, sounds sweeter, that the tremor of strings is never quite still, night or day, about the town. One knows that in San Vicente the hour is never too early for ambition and never too late for love.

The Mexican poet begins charmingly: "When the Creator of all saw San Vicente, He loved its beauty, and He cast his arms about it, and ever since it has lain within the embrace of the green mountains."

In all of San Vicente there was no more favorite gathering place than the Casa Bianca. Up from the river, the cypresses rose in a double row, reaching the tips of their branches in a friendly fashion to one another, and beyond the cypresses there was a ragged and rather weedy lawn, and beyond the lawn there was an open-armed building of whitewashed adobe, like most of the others in the town. In the day, that whitewash looked rather flea-bitten and it peeled away continually in patches, showing the dull gray of the mud walls beneath. The lawn seemed a trampled and half-dying thing, and under the cypresses, among the tables, there was generally a flutter of paper here and there on the ground, with a disorderly sprinkling of cigarette stubs, more or less smoked. The poor woman who cleaned up the place swore that the cigarettes grew out of the ground of their own accord, just as rocks grow in the fields of the poorest and most unlucky peons. But at night the Casa Bianca was quite another place.

Then the lawn seemed a glimmering sheet of velvet-soft grass. The house was dignified and large and ancient in its look. By the light of the lanterns scattered among the lower branches of the cypresses, it always seemed that the nobility of the nation had gathered to drink, smoke, and gossip, and to eat tamales and other dishes so hot that they curled the membrane on Nordic tongues.

On this night the scene was a little more brilliant than usual because General Miguel O'Riley was present with most of his suite.

The general, in another land, might have been called Mike O'Riley. But since the family was three or four generations old in Mexico, he had become well nigh as Spanish as all the rest of the land. His skin was as dark. His eyes were as black and had the same hint of smoke in them. He wore a waxed mustache, two double chins, and a large stomach. In the bursting red of his cheeks, however, and in the sparkle of his eyes, there was the hint of a more northern race.

He was as gay as the rest, and he was dressed in his uniform that sparkled with the greatest amount of gold braid. But the twinkle in the general's eye seemed to say that he smiled a little at his own magnificence.

General Miguel O'Riley, which might be called long for Mike O'Riley, was the chief potentate of San Vicente. He owned the largest stretch of lands. He had the greatest number of peons attached to his estate. He possessed a larger share of San Vicente town real estate than any other. So he became a general without ever having drilled a company, marched a regiment, or handled a brigade, whether in the field or barracks. He was made a general because his adherence was most valuable to the regime that was then in power.

The difference between him and a good many of the other generals was not an important one from many viewpoints. It was simply that he had a sense of humor that three generations of life in a passionate southern land could not quite wash out from his brain and his blood.

On this evening, Miguel O'Riley sat under the largest of the cypress trees. Around him were grouped four tables. He sat at one, with a friend on either hand. Others were grouped in larger numbers at the other tables. And all faces, at all times, were turned toward the general.

He had recently returned to the land of his forefathers, and, since he already spoke English very well, he had come back with something of a brogue, of which he was very proud, and a good deal of the latest slang. The general was one who wished to keep abreast of the times and, his blood being what it was and his name what it was, the only times that sincerely mattered to him were the times in Ireland. Secretly he nursed a longing to amass sufficient coin in Mexico to return to the land of his forefathers, buy a castle and a dozen hunters, and settle down to a life of fox hunting and the serious drinking of good Irish whiskey.

All that kept him from selling his fat estate instantly in Mexico was the size of his stomach, which did not sit well on the back of an Irish hunter. Every Monday he determined to reduce. Every Tuesday morning he started the painful process. Every Tuesday afternoon he gave up the task until the following week. He was always full of good determinations, but he found it hard to reduce them to cold facts.

The rest of the general's party was equipped with gold lace in plenty, very much like himself. Most of them held commissions that they had derived through his influence, and they knew as much about military affairs as he did himself, no more and no less, the total being zero. But they were all fond of the general because he was the affluent sun that shone upon them, and he was very fond of them because he knew of their dependence. No Irishman can be unhappy when he is the center of influence.

These people were drinking red wine that was a little acrid but pleasantly cold, and they were eating sandwiches of good white bread, filled with red fire.

The next group worth consideration was a set of five men with gloomy faces who sat one tree beyond the general's cypress. They were drinking tequila out of little green-tinted glasses, which harmonized both with the slight green-white color of the liquid and the raw green fire of its taste. They smoked, one and all, Mexican cigarettes, made like cornucopias, large at one end and pointed at the other.

They allowed the cigarette ashes to fall where they might, on their own clothes or, windblown, on the clothes of each other. After a time, the shower of ashes began to turn their shoulders and the lapels of their coats white, but the whiteness was never dusted away.

As they talked, they leaned a good deal toward one another and spoke very softly. If anyone came too close to their table, he was sure to be received with a silence and two or three black looks, as dangerous as the glinting of bared knives.

These five looked all of a pattern. They were all young, between twenty and twenty-five. They all wore small mustaches, some less successfully than others. They all had on broad, gray hats, and they all wore tiny white camellias in their buttonholes. It was easy to see that they belonged to a club. It might be a club of thieves, of night roisterers, or gamblers, of indigent younger sons of poets, of news writers, or of revolutionists. Each and all of these classes might have turned out a group dressed in exactly the same fashion, talking in the same deadly earnest. The theme might have been where the next throat could be cut, the next purse taken, the next scandal picked up, the next poetic meter introduced, or the next bomb thrown.

They did not attract much serious attention, but, since they so obviously wished to be left alone, the other patrons of the Casa Bianca, on this night, chose tables at least one remove from the table of the five ardent talkers.

The third point where the eye should rest on this occasion was the quietest table of all. It was rather near that of the five youths. The reason it was so extremely quiet was that it was occupied by only one man. He was very young, sprightly, elegant, and handsome. He was well-dressed, seemed to have plenty of money—for he ate and drank of the best—and he had been coming to this particular table for seven nights in succession. He was now recognized in the place and the right to that particular table was established. He did not have to tip the waiters exorbitantly, for in Mexico the rights of habit are recognized almost before any other rights in the world.

No one offered to sit down at his table for the reason that he never spoke a word of Spanish. And he seemed incapable of learning anything. Although the same waiter, on five successive nights, had successively pointed out the same dishes, named them, sweated over them, gesticulated, brought samples, crowed like a rooster, flapping his arms, quacked like a duck, made the horns of a deer upon his head, and imitated a cow chewing her cud, still the young man from the North seemed unable to understand, and he was always surprised when he saw what he had ordered. He was always surprised, but he was also delighted. The waiters put him down as a fool, but that was to be expected from one with hair so yellow, eyes so blue, and face so pink and white. They put him down also as a good-natured fool, and that made all the difference. He tipped them just well enough to keep them expectant.

This youth might have been a mere traveler, but he was probably attached to one of the mining companies that operated with foreign capital more and more near San Vicente, combing out the ores in the great veins of its mountains. He was probably rich. He was the sort of a patron that one wants to see more of at a place like the Casa Bianca.

No one in all that place, head waiter, lounging detectives, or scrawny news reporter looking for a story, would have suspected that the table of the general, the table of the five young men, and the pink-and-white youth from the Northland were all to be connected, in another moment, with the worst scandal that ever had occurred in the Casa Bianca. But such was the case.

Chapter Seven

At 11:00 P.M. punctually, the circle of five gloomy young men always dispersed. So they did on this night, walking off toward the path that led down the river, and most people watched their going with relief. It was only the young Nordic with the yellow hair and the blue eyes who appeared to notice nothing, but with a covert side glance saw one of the five turn back from the rest of the group and return along the margin of the river, where the lights from the lanterns shone with only the faintest light. It was so dim that only the best eyes in the world could have perceived the youth, lost as he was in shadow from time to time, and then half appearing again. But the lad of the yellow hair had eyes as keen as the eyes of a hawk, and he followed that progress.

Then he put on the table enough money to cover his bill and leave a tip of just the right size. Afterward, he arose and stretched himself a little, although without raising his arms. And, since the night air was turning damp and very cool, he pulled across his shoulders a jaunty cloak, and took a pair of gloves out of the slit side pocket of the cloak.

The orchestra, a little before this, had received from General O'Riley a request for a certain piece, and now, the more to honor him, they approached and struck up the tune near him, all smiling in his direction. The general liked such compliments. They were not particularly delicate, but the general had not great taste for delicacy.

The music was in full swing. It was not of the sort to appeal to a connoisseur, but General O'Riley chose to lean back in his chair a little and half close his eyes, nodding his big head in rhythm with the beat of the piece. This pleased everyone, the musicians, the waiters, and the others who were dining or drinking and gossiping under the cypresses.

But this idyllic pause was interrupted by a wild, half-choked cry that shattered the music and brought it to a jangling pause. One of the men at the general's own table rose quickly from his chair, his face distorted, one arm stiffly pointing.

Those whose glances flashed in the direction of the gesture saw a tall, dark-clad youth, with a somber look and a pair of short mustaches. He was not five yards from the general, his arm raised, his body bent back a little and tense as if for throwing, and in his hand a round, black ball, the size of a small melon.

But it was not a melon. They all knew what it was, and men simply cast themselves backward and rolled from their chairs—all saving the general. He also had seen, but he did not stir. There was no time to save himself. And he preferred to meet death leisurely.

This instant in which the cry was heard and the assassin seen lasted the sixteenth part of a second. Then, as the bomb thrower started to fling his missile, a revolver cracked sharply. The would-be murderer twitched half around and clutched at his ruined right shoulder with his other hand, while the bomb, dropping to the ground, rolled slowly on toward the general, as though it had a volition of its own, to complete the work that the gloomy youth had commenced.

Now, he of the cloak and the gloves and the blue eyes and the yellow hair, slid deftly back beneath his clothes the gun that he had drawn and, running forward, while waiters and guests and musicians were scrambling for their lives, many of them on all fours, he picked up the rolling bomb and tossed it with an underarm throw far out into the river.

As it touched the water, it exploded with a roar that made the flame leap in the throat of every lantern chimney, set the table services jingling, and sent through the trees a gush of noise like one blast of a powerful gale. Far above the surface of the river arose a great fountain that stood like a broad-shouldered ghost for an instant, then melted away into the water once more.

In the meantime, he of the cloak and the general faced one another. Of all within the grounds of the Casa Bianca, only those two had confronted the danger without flinching—the general motionless in his chair, the stranger in action.

Now General Miguel O'Riley stood up and made a gesture. "Seem to be plenty of empty chairs near me," he said. "Won't you sit down?"

The blue-eyed youth bowed. "I was just going, General O'Riley," he said. "Some other evening I hope to see you again."

And he walked off with a careless saunter beneath the cypresses. He left the general behind him with bulging eyes and a discolored face. For O'Riley had so long been the Zeus and the disposer of all graces and favors in San Vicente, that he could not imagine a service performed except for the sake of a reward.

Now he could only gasp to the gendarmes who were coming up on the run. To one of them he said: "Have that fellow . . . that American who did the shooting . . . have him followed . . . find out about him. And you there," he roared to the police who were manhandling the wounded bomb thrower, "don't tear that man to bits. He's a fool. That's all. And he's been punished already for part of his folly. Bring him here."

They brought the youth before the general. They had guns pressed against the small of his spine and against his sides. He was white with the torment from his shattered shoulder; all his right side was crimsoned with the flow of blood.

The general looked straight into his eyes. "Who are you?" he asked.

"A man who hates tyrants!" cried the boy, and he stiffened himself as though he were facing a firing squad that instant.

"Oh, the devil," said the general with a groan of boredom. "Another patriot, eh? Take him to the hospital, not to the jail. Give him the best care at my expense, and then turn him loose. He won't throw bombs again."

"Set him free? What? The murderer!" cried the lieutenant of gendarmes.

"Do as I tell you," said the general. "Every young man is a fool, and this one is the youngest I ever saw. Take him away, and take him quickly. Call Doctor Matazzo. He's the best bonesetter. Take him quickly. The boy is losing blood fast. Gentlemen, it is time to sit down again. Music, strike up once more. The evening is spoiled for only one of the people tonight, I take it."

Within two minutes, he had restored the Casa Bianca and its grounds to a perfect tranquility. It was one of the characteristics of General O'Riley that he could be less angered or upset by physical danger than by a badly cooked meal or a poor wine. The music started, the people returned to their tables, and fresh crowds poured in from the streets, first attracted by the roar of the explosion and then by the report of what had caused it. They thronged in and got tables as close to that of the general as possible.

He enjoyed the scene. The tale of his calmness was repeated on all hands. He was stared at and idolized. And General O'Riley felt that this was one of the few perfect nights of his entire life.

Chapter Eight

It was not alone that the general's life had been saved; it was that in the same scene he had showed himself as a good deal of a hero. For the first time, in a way, he felt that he could put on his gold-braided and silver-shining uniform coat with the feeling that he deserved to wear it.

He stayed up late that night, sunning himself in the public esteem. When he went home to his big, rambling house, one of the few in San Vicente that were made of stone, he found there a little man with pouchy eyes, stained purple all beneath, far down his cheeks, and with claw-like hands, the first fingers of which were deep yellow-brown from the fumes of the cigarettes that never left them. The general was glad to see him. The man was his own private investigator.

He took him up to his own sitting room, which served him as an office for his many affairs. Without even sitting down, the general thrust his fat hands into his coat pockets and said: "Now, Ortuga, what have you found out?"

"Nothing," said Ortuga.

"Impossible," said the general. "You're like a bird . . . your eyes have to see more than those of other ordinary men."

The general believed in flattery and always used it. He loved it so much that he knew how to apply it to others.

Now Ortuga flushed just a little and almost smiled. "I only had an innkeeper to look at. That was all tonight," he said. "Tomorrow, it may be a different story. I got at everything the innkeeper knew. He was anxious to tell everything twice over, when he learned what his guest had done for your excellency."

"Tut, tut," said the general, relishing the honey taste of this. "But go on. What did you learn?"

"Only that this seems to be a model young man. He rises at eight every morning. He goes to bed at twelve every night. In the morning he stays in his room, studying Spanish, in which he appears to make no progress. In the afternoon, he goes to a restaurant and sits for a long time over his meal. In the evening, he walks at the usual hour in the plaza and then goes to the Casa Bianca. He does these things every day. He is always home not later than eleven-thirty, and he always is in bed by midnight. He seems to have no business except the study of the Spanish tongue. The innkeeper suggests that he is a very good but a very stupid young man. His name is John Lawrence."

"English blood!" hissed the general with a scowl. "I hate that English blood. Taciturn, dull-witted, regular. He saves my life and goes home . . . not to avoid my thanks and embarrassment, but because it is his bedtime."

The general walked up and down the room and swore several times. Then he dismissed Ortuga and went to bed. In the morning he rose early—that is to say, at 10:00 A.M. While he sipped chocolate frothed with hot milk and ate handfuls of sweet bread, cut transparently thin and toasted dry, he received his secretary and went over the probable business of the day.

The assassin of the night before was now resting easily in the hospital. The doctor declared that his right arm was not necessarily ruined, but that it would be stiff for years, and that he might feel the changes of weather in it through his entire life.

"Whenever he lifts a glass of wine, he will be reminded of the clemency of your excellency," said the secretary.

The general smiled. Then he turned to other work.

A peon had lost his wits and run amuck the day before, knifing three of the general's other tenants, but none fatally. The man was now raving in the jail and telling the keepers of the jail that debt was a weed that grew two *pesos* for every one that was paid off. There was an American who had come up from Vera Cruz. He was in haste. He looked like a man worth seeing, but with precautions. Governor Ilvarado was coming to San Vicente in three days' time and sent his special respects. There were five letters begging assistance of one kind or another. *Señor* Huerta wanted a hundred and ten *pesos* a hectare for his grazing land, but for cash the secretary thought it could be bought for ninety.

"That American," said the general. "Where is he?"

"Waiting now in hope of seeing you."

"Why do you think he is worth seeing?"

"Because he will not tell any of his business to me."

"How much did he give you in cash?" asked the general.

The secretary looked straight back at him. He knew the general exactly from of old and exactly how to deal with him in all matters. "He gave me ten *pesos,*" he said.

The general was not offended. He knew that his servants all accepted bribes. He felt that the bribes were a direct tribute to his importance as a man and as a master. All he objected to was lying and concealment of what his employees took in. He did not ask them to keep their hands clean. So he smiled at his secretary.

"If he's as liberal as that," he said, "I'll see him here and now. Give me the blue slippers, there, with the feather-work on the toes of 'em. Help me into that dressing gown. So . . . now I'll go into the office and see the *gringo.* You go to Ortuga and learn from him what new things he has found out about the young American, John Lawrence. Then go yourself to the inn at once and give the young American my compliments. Tell him that I trust he will do me the honor of entering my carriage at one o'clock and coming to my house for lunch. Hurry! Until I know something more of that young fellow, I shall not have a moment's quiet in my mind."

So he walked into his office, and by the time he was settled at his official table, taking the rubber strings off a few important-looking sheaves of papers, the American entered. His name was Dickon Jarvis. The moment he came in, the general recognized the type. For Jarvis was one of those lean, long-drawn-out Southwesterners who speak with a drawl and wear clothes that always have a suggestion of dust in them.

He shook hands lazily; he smiled on one side of his face, and he was no more impressed by the general than he would have been by a beggar boy on the one hand, or the Archangel Gabriel on the other.

He said: "I've come to talk to you about a man."

"What man?" asked the general. "Sit down and rest yourself." He was proud of every Americanism he could bring into his easy flow of English.

"He calls himself John Lawrence," said Dickon Jarvis.

The general showed not the slightest interest. There was a genuine prickle up his spine, but he knew how to control his face. "I've heard the name," he said.

"He's poison," said Dickon Jarvis. "I'm here to tell you about him."

"What are you going to tell me? And why are you going to tell it?" asked the general.

"Because the people who sent me down here from the United States are afraid of him."

"What people are they?"

"People that know a thug when they see one," said Jarvis. "This lad is really *Don* Diablo, if that means anything to you."

"Is he called Mister Devil somewhere in Spain or Mexico?" asked the general.

"He is. All up and down the river, and a lot of points farther south, too."

"What else is he called?" asked the general.

"On our side of the river," said Mr. Jarvis, "we call him Rinky Dink. Some people call him Larry. He has other names. He has more names than coats. He's really Lawrence Grey."

"Then he's wearing one half of the truth down here," said the general. "Before you go any further, I want to tell you that this same *Don* Diablo, this Rinky Dink, saved my life last night."

"Of course, he did," said Jarvis. "And that's why I'm here. He'll use you as a lever now. It's not you he wants. Dead men are nothing in his young life. He's had plenty of them sprinkled along his trail. He broke from jail with a murder charge against him. He's wanted here in Mexico, too."

"Instead of coming to me," said the general, "I should think that you'd call in the gendarmes, if that man is wanted, and you wish to get him out of the way."

"Gendarmes would never get him," said Jarvis calmly. "Gotta have special operators to handle him, or he'll burn his way right through the fingers of twenty men."

"You know where he lives, I suppose," said the general.

"He lives," said Jarvis, "in a tavern room that looks over a kitchen roof. The roof runs out to a stable that has three loft windows he could get at. Then he could get out of two windows from his room, or he could run down the hall and try the cellar exit, or run through any one of half a dozen other rooms and slide for the street."

"You know all the exits," said the general, "and I suppose that you could get plenty of men."

"I'd need three good men, at least, at every possible exit," said Jarvis. "And suppose that I march up thirty or forty fellows and start to surround the place . . . do you think that would work with a fox who never sleeps except with one eye open and one ear cocked?"

The general smiled.

Jarvis briskly continued: "Rinky Dink's sure a bad one. You never know where he'll be. You never know what he'll do. I've come here and shown you my cards. . . . And this is what I suggest. A man in your position, General, can't afford to get himself messed up with a man like Lawrence Grey. After what he happened to do for you last night, he's sure to try to use you. And you're pretty sure to see him again. All that I want to do is mighty simple."

"And what do you want to do?" asked the general.

"Let me slip three men into your house staff. They'll give you security."

"And what will they give you?" asked the general.

"A chance to check up on him, wherever he goes and whatever he does."

General O'Riley smiled faintly. "He saved my life, Mister Jarvis," he said. "Now you want me to sell him."

"I want you to save your reputation from him. That's all," said Jarvis. "And your skin, too, perhaps. I tell you, if Rinky Dink filed notches for every man he's put out of the way, his gun handles would be half notched away. I know the story. He wouldn't stay last night when you asked him to. That's because he knew that you'd send for him today. Haven't you?"

The general shrugged and admitted that such was the case. "I have to think this over," he added. "I can't make up my mind all in a moment. Will that do you, Jarvis?"

"That'll have to do me," said the other. "But if I could have my way, I'd load a dozen men into your house and catch him when he comes."

"You know, Mister Jarvis," said the general, "that I don't use this house for a trap. However, I'll think things over. Perhaps you're right, but I must have time. I still can see the youth with the bomb raised. And there's still a roar in my ears . . . the noise it made when it exploded."

Jarvis seemed to see that he had covered as much ground as possible. He said his *adieu* briefly, and left the house at once, leaving behind him General O'Riley in a more amiable frame of mind than he had been in for months. For there was nothing that he loved with a passion equal to his love of trouble. An air like this, with plots and counterplots, was his ideal atmosphere, and he guessed now that this was the air that he might breathe for some time to come.

He thought of the dapper form of John Lawrence, alias Lawrence Grey and several other titles, and he thought of the big, loose-jointed frame of Dickon Jarvis, with his cold, straight eyes. When such men as these entered, a good deal of warmth should be generated before long. And the general loved action when it was hottest. He sat back in his chair and actually rubbed his hands together and began to chuckle.

He was fond of saying: "The bigger the net the more it catches . . . and San Vicente is my net." Now it was entangling fish that were likely to break the meshes, to be sure, but they would be all the more sport to land.

For one thing, he had not the slightest intention of taking the broad hints of Jarvis and betraying the young man. On the other hand, he did not wish to betray Jarvis to Grey. This appeared to be a gentleman's game in which a new pack needed to be broken open for every hand. But the general had sat in at just such games before, and he loved them above all others.

So he went off, whistling, to take his bath. Whistling would not do for him. He began to sing.

As the sounds were heard outside the door, the servants passed the word along from one to another. They passed the word with gloomy faces and with frightened eyes. It reached the gardener and made him pause and gape. It reached the cook on the lowest level of the big house and he hissed through his teeth and blinked both eyes.

Although all of his domestics were fond of the general, and although his smile was familiar to them all, they were well aware that smiling and humming did not have the same connotation as singing and laughter. When General O'Riley sang and laughed, there was almost certain to be a storm in the offing that would shake the house of O'Riley to its foundations.

Chapter Nine

When Jarvis left the house of O'Riley, he went in his buggy with his span of horses, spinning down the street, raising a good thick cloud of dust behind him as he kept the horses at a brisk pace. As he came to a little shop where morning chocolate and lunches were served cheaply out under the patchy shadows of a number of umbrella trees, Jarvis pulled up his team, tethered them at the hitching rack, and sat him down at one of the little iron tables.

The proprietor was also the cook and the waiter. His kitchen was no more than a stall. And he never had, as a rule, more than three things to serve. But his *frijoles* were famous, and they were so tempered that even an unpracticed tongue could enjoy them without being scalded; his bread was cooked at home by his wife, and she kneaded and hammered and beat it until it was as brittle as pastry. Also, when it left her oven, it was a deep, uniform brown, which she secured by coating the surface with just the right amount of butter.

The beans, the bread, and the coffee of this little eating place were all matchless. On those three dishes the proprietor managed to keep himself above water. He had under the trees four small tables. When they were full, with four at each table, it was a pitiful thing to see him trying to run with his wooden legs, pale with haste and with fear of giving offense by being slow. At the end of such a meal, he used to lie back on a little bench in his kitchen and wipe his face with a clean dishcloth, whisper to himself, and shake from head to foot.

Yet he was a man of experience. He had sailed thrice on wooden Yankee clipper ships in the old days of his youth, and he could speak very good English. He was clean, gentle, and honest, one of those men whose lives prove that justice in this world is a blind goddess and fate a rooting pig.

Jarvis had chosen his hour well. For it was before noon, and there was not a soul sitting at the tables in the cool of the trees. He took the table nearest to the kitchen and he gave the kindest smile he could summon to the proprietor. He did not waste time beating about the bush. He said: "Well, *Señor* Murcio, I came here hoping that I'd see the famous young man who saved the general's life."

Murcio smiled, a little sadly, and shook his head. "He will come here no more," he said. "This will be a good deal too simple for him, now that all the doors in San Vicente will be open to him. He never came, you see, except that he liked to sit under the trees and study Spanish. Besides, I could speak English to him. That was why he used to come here."

Jarvis blinked. He had heard the purest Castilian ripple from the lips of that same young scoundrel, Rinky Dink, in days of yore. He muttered, rather choked: "He can't understand Spanish, then?"

"Not a word. Hardly a word," said Murcio. "He has not the gift of tongues. Some men have it, and some have not, but God knows that the language makes no difference, so long as the thought is good."

"That's true," said Jarvis. "I can smell those beans. It's a little early to eat, but I have to have a plate of them, and some bread and butter."

These things were brought, and afterward Murcio stood at a little distance, smiling in hope, but ever anxious until the verdict was given.

"The best beans," said Jarvis, around a mouthful, "that I ever had between my teeth. The very finest, the best cooked and the best flavored. You ought to be in Mexico City. You'd be rich there."

"Do you think so, *señor?*" said Murcio. "Once a year, some kind *señor* says this to me, and for a month I have dreams, but, after all, it is a great distance and a great chance. And then, even beautiful Mexico City is not San Vicente, you know."

"True," said Jarvis. "But tell me about that brave young countryman of mine. Everyone is talking about him today."

"And why not?" said Murcio, extending his right hand to demand the same question of all-pervading space. "Is it a little thing to draw a gun and shoot a man? And is it a little thing, then, to pick up death, like a child's ball, and throw it away?"

"No," said Jarvis, "he must have courage. But they say that he doesn't look the part."

"He looks"—Murcio smiled—"like a child that has grown up suddenly. He always seems a little afraid. He used to sit there, at that back table, his back to the street, rumpling his hair, and poring over his book, poor young man, and saying to me . . . '*Señor* Murcio, say again for me *"hombre."* I never can roll the r.' And that was true, for he never could learn it, though he tried for seven days."

"Just sitting there and studying, and talking very little, I suppose," said Jarvis.

"Not for two or three days," said Murcio. "But then I was lucky, for I struck on a theme that was after his fancy. A theme like a fairy story . . . the tale of Juan Ray, the great American rich man, the millionaire, who lived such a life here in San Vicente and ended so strangely."

Jarvis suddenly looked down, lest his eyes should betray him. "I've heard a good deal about John Ray," he said, "who you call Juan."

"Who has not?" said Murcio, again asking the question of all the world. "Who has not heard of *Señor* Ray, except this young American, so brave, so gentle, so charming, and so modest. I felt for him, when he used to sit there with his book, a certain pity, as though he were a little child and in a terrible world. God knows that it is a cruel world, *señor*. But now the great general, he will take care of him, of course."

"I suppose," said Jarvis, "that if the boy never had heard of John Ray, he asked a good many questions, eh?"

"Questions? No," said Murcio, "I don't think that he ever asked questions, but he used to shake his head and exclaim, and his eyes would become dreamy as I talked. That was the way with him. He forgot his book. He forgot everything, and sat there, *señor*, like a child and listened. When I told how *Señor* Ray scattered his money, and rescued his friends when they were in trouble, how the good man would never say no to any who needed help . . . when I told him those things, he used to sit there almost with tears in his eyes. Yes, and then he would ask me the names of the people who at the last turned their backs on poor *Señor* Ray, after his money was all gone. He used to ask me their names, and shake his young head, and say that they were bad people."

"He asked their names, did he?" murmured Jarvis.

"Yes," said Murcio. "He used to ask their names and frown, as though he were trying to remember them . . . as if one day he would like to do justice on them."

"One day, perhaps he will," said Jarvis.

"What did you say, *señor?*"

"Nothing," said Jarvis. "But John Ray makes a good subject for talk, well enough. Everybody refused him help, in the end, when he lost his fortune, they say."

"All except Miguel O'Riley," said the restaurant keeper. "He . . . God bless him . . . with his great heart, he would not forget such a man as Juan Ray, though he had had very little from that wild, rich man. But they say that he took Juan Ray into his house and showed him the sum that he had in the bank, and asked him what part of it he would use. And Juan Ray would not take a penny, but swore that, since the rest of the world had been untrue to him, he would not give the world the satisfaction of paying him money through a single one of his friends. There was only one exception, he said. That was just before he died."

"In the river?" asked Jarvis.

"Yes. In the river. His body was found there."

"But I've heard," said Jarvis, "that the body that was picked up never was proved to be his."

"One hears a good many things," said Murcio, "but, after all, what was more like Juan Ray than to curse the world and throw away his life, after his money was entirely gone."

"That might have been like him," said Jarvis. "Then, again, one hears that he may have gone up into the mountains."

"What would he do there, a man like him, used to twenty servants always about him?" asked Murcio gravely. "What would he do up there among the rocks? No, he would live and die here in San Vicente, I think. When I remember him, it is as he was one day when I saw him riding a stallion at full gallop, bareheaded, under the cypresses. His long hair was blowing, his strange divided beard was whipping across his shoulders, and he was laughing as he galloped. When I think of a strong man . . . though he was not very big . . . I think of Juan Ray . . . when I think of a happy man . . . though he had his sorrow in the end . . . I think of Juan Ray, and always as he was that day, galloping under the cypresses." He paused, shook his head, and went hurrying and hobbling off to the kitchen.

At the same time, a slender young man stepped in from the street under the shadow of the trees. He carried a thin stick that glimmered like a rapier, and he picked his way among the tables until he came to the rearmost table.

"Why, hello, Rinky," said Jarvis.

Lawrence Grey turned and seemed to stumble. At least, he moved suddenly back so that the trunk of a tree was between him and the speaker for an instant. Then he came straight to Jarvis and held out his hand.

"Hello, Dickon," he said. "I'm surprised. This is a long way off your beat."

"I had to move," said Jarvis. "That last deal in Denver caused too much comment. It got breezing through the newspapers. People are getting too excitable these days. A little safe-cracking, and they're all in a buzz. What's brought you down here?"

"Oh, same idea," said Grey. He sat down at the table.

"I never knew trouble to make you budge before," said Jarvis. "And you've had plenty of it buzzing around. But you've gone and made yourself a hero since you arrived. I've heard about last night."

"The fool stepped right out in the light," said Grey. "He made a picture of himself. Half-witted, I'd say. Or romantic . . . or something like that. Good beans, aren't they?"

"The best. I've been talking to Murcio about you. Seems you eat here?"

"Every day. By the way, I don't understand a word of Spanish."

"I follow you," said Jarvis, and he nodded to Grey, but also his nod covertly included two men who were drifting by in the street. They immediately turned straight in among the trees.

Chapter Ten

Murcio came out with a pot of chocolate for Grey and waited until the latter had poured out a cup, sipped it, and smiled his appreciation. Then he went back to continue with his anxious cooking, for a thousand successes were never quite enough to reassure him.

Said Grey: "It's a queer thing, Dickon, that people like to look at themselves while they're eating. Ever notice that?"

A warm content filled Jarvis, for his men were approaching nearer and nearer each moment. Two good men they were. He had brought them a long distance and he preferred their calm brains and their sure hands to twenty ordinary gunmen. He began to taste victory in the very beginning; a sudden foreflash of distant results sweetened the mind of Jarvis.

"I've noticed that," he said. "You take restaurants, the way they line the walls with mirrors. . . ."

"Even a little dump like this," said Grey. "Murcio's pretty clever. He's put a mirror on every tree facing the tables."

"I didn't notice that," said Jarvis.

"They take some noticing, they're so small," said Grey. "There's one on the tree, there, right behind you, and just in front of me. Every time you move your head, I can see myself behind you."

"Can you?" said Jarvis, bored a little.

"So I can see in the mirror everything that you see," said Grey.

Jarvis blinked suddenly.

"Can you?" he murmured.

"The other trees and flashes of the street, looking pretty blinding bright under the sun," went on Grey.

"I suppose that you can see that," said Jarvis.

"And the two fellows who are sauntering in," said Grey.

"Yes. There's a couple of them over yonder," said Jarvis.

"If you made a sign to them," said Grey, "I wonder if they'd fade away to the street again?"

"If I made a sign?" said Jarvis. "What d'you mean? What have I to do with 'em?"

"Oh, not much," said Grey. "Not any more, at least, than I have to do with the gun that's on my knee just now."

Jarvis shook his head. "You've got a wrong steer, old son," he said. "I'll tell you what . . . I'm by myself down here."

"Word of honor?" asked Grey.

"Yes. Word of honor."

"Look at me and say it again," said Grey.

Jarvis looked him straight in the eye. It was hard to do, but he managed the trick.

"Good," said Grey. "I always knew that you were a good, first-rate liar, but I didn't know you were as good as this."

"I tell you, that couple doesn't mean anything to me," Jarvis assured him again.

"Well," said Grey, "you try a sign on them anyway. Try a sign that'll send 'em back into the street where I can see 'em go. Don't let 'em come a single step nearer," he added, his voice lowering.

This new note in the voice of Grey was something between the croon of a child and the purr of a cat, and the eyes of the youth wrinkled a little at the corners as though he were tasting some keen physical pleasure.

Jarvis leaned back in his chair and for the tenth of a second he tried to weigh chances. But his brain refused to work. He made an apparently casual sign, and the two who had come in from the street drifted just as carelessly back toward it.

"That's a good deal better," said Grey. "And since I don't want to have anything on you, I'll put this away."

Jarvis saw just a glint of steel as Grey's hand disappeared under his coat. Then admiration warmed the voice of Jarvis. "You never carry 'em on the hip, Rinky Dink, do you?" he asked. "It's always under the coat?"

"It's harder to get at 'em under the coat," said Grey, "but they come away more easily. There' some chance of the flap of the coat getting in the way, of course, but not much chance, if you practice. Practice is what it takes, though."

"Yeah. You've had the practice," said Jarvis. "You're slick, Rinky Dink. You're by far the slickest that I ever saw."

"I'm sorry you had that trouble in Denver," said Grey.

"Yeah. That was a bust," confessed Jarvis. "I made some cash out of it. But not enough. You never make enough, in our game. There's always too many ways to split everything. A few thousand to a night watchman and a percentage to a cashier, and then your backers and the boys that do the deal with you. Well, we took in two hundred and twenty-five thousand up there in Denver. And what d'you think that I pulled down out of it?"

"How much, Dickon?"

"Forty grand."

"Is that all?"

"Yes. It's pretty thin."

"It is thin," agreed Grey.

"Then out of the forty, I gotta slip five to an old partner of mine that's on the low-down. And there's another five that I slip to a state senator that's been on the board of pardons for a long while. You know. I never may need to use him, but when the time comes, that's when it pays to have your string hitched onto the bellwether."

"That's right, but you take almost a quarter of a million and you only get thirty thousand clear," said Grey. "That's a pretty big percentage against you."

"Big? It's rotten," said Jarvis.

"And then," said Grey, "you slip, every now and then, and the house rakes down all bets."

"What do you mean?" asked Jarvis.

"I mean, the zero or the double zero comes along, and then the house cashes in. I mean, the cops grab you and shove you in the pen, for five, fifteen years, or so."

"Oh, yeah," said Jarvis, "I guess that happens now and then."

"Take you," said Grey. "You're thirty-two. And you're about as smart as they come. But since you were fifteen, between reform school and prison, you've been put away ten years."

Jarvis looked at the other from under lowering brows. "You know quite a lot," he said.

"I have to know a little bit, here and there," said Grey. "I was just figuring out the rotten percentage that you work on. You got twelve percent of what you make, and you only are in the open for forty percent of your time to enjoy your twelve percent."

"Look here," demanded Jarvis darkly, "are you trying to reform me?"

"I'm not that big a fool," said Grey, and his smile was a caress.

"I hope you ain't," said Jarvis. "And where do you get your easy money, Rinky?"

"It's a lot different with me," said Grey.

"Is it? I don't see where," said Jarvis.

"You don't think, Dick," said the boy. "Look, for one thing, at the way I've kept out of stripes."

"You're young. You'll have your turn," said Jarvis. "Oh, you got the fat head, for a while, but, when they plant you, it'll be

Salt Creek for you, sweetheart."

Grey brooded upon him, almost tenderly. "You don't understand, partner," he said. "You're all wrong and up in the air . . . they'll never have me in prison."

"Aw, I know," said Jarvis. "You'll croak yourself sooner. That old gag."

"No, I won't croak myself, either. I've never done anything much."

Jarvis gaped at him. "Rinky," he said, "d'you think that I'm weak-minded, or something?"

"Good old Dickon," murmured Lawrence Grey. "I like to see your eyes pop. But that's the truth, Dick. I'm an honest man."

Jarvis suddenly grinned. "Go on," he said. "I like to hear you. Go on, Rinky Dink. I never heard nothing so good as this, before. You're straight, are you?"

"Practically," said Grey.

"That's why the cops chase you so much, I guess," said Jarvis.

"That's exactly it," said Grey. "My business wouldn't be worth anything if I didn't have the police working for me. They give me a run all the time, and that makes the thugs and the yeggs like you, Dickon, think that I'm one of you. But I'm not. I fill my hooks out of the tenderest flesh of you yeggs, Dick. I always have, and I always will, unless I get tired of the game. You're my meat . . . you and the crooked cashier, and the fake bankrupt, and the smart boy who runs opium and chinks over the line. I dine on you fellows. You look back. Fellows like you are always the ones I've plucked."

Jarvis looked back. His mental glance unwillingly seemed to be confronted with a series of facts that testified to the truth of the last statement. "You wouldn't spill the beans to me, if it was true," he said.

"You won't believe," said Grey. "And if you tell any of the

others, they won't believe. That's the way with them. That's the way with all of you."

Jarvis reddened slowly, to the cheek bones. His eyes glowed fiercely, also. "What do you get out of shooting off your face like this, Rinky Dink?" he asked.

"Nothing much," said the youth. "But just for the moment it made me a little sick to be sitting here with you, Dickon. It turned my stomach to think of what a hound you are and that I'm sitting here, drinking chocolate, at the same table with you."

The flush became blotched with white, the white of rage, on the face of Jarvis. "I'm not good enough for you, Rinky?" he asked.

"Not good enough to lick my boots," said the boy. "Tell me who sent you down here?"

"Who sent me down here? Nobody sent me down here. I sent myself down here. Even if I didn't, would I blab to you, because I like your handsome face so much? You got such a fat head, it's a shame, Rinky Dink."

"You'll tell me though," said Grey.

"Will you put money on that?"

"A dollar to a dime," said Grey, "that you tell me everything you know inside of five minutes."

Chapter Eleven

Jarvis leaned back in his chair and smiled with an honest amusement. "You're wonderful, Rinky Dink," he said. "I mean the face you got, the way you put it over . . . that's what's wonderful. You've got me all heated up, son. All about nothing. Just talk. What do you think you're kidding me into?"

"I'd as soon kill you as kid you," said Grey. "And you know I can do it. I'm a tenth of a second faster than you are, Dick. And I'm a little straighter, too. Besides, you're the stuff that I like to go after."

"You tell me why, Rinky?" asked Jarvis, his voice suddenly altered.

"Well, I'll tell you," said Grey. "It's because you're a thug and such a dirty thug. You look clean, but you're not. I know something about you, Dick. You cheat your friends. I know about the flatty in Silver City. He was a friend of yours. He'd given you a hand a lot of times. But you bumped him off, and I know how."

"Hold on," said Jarvis. "I know who you mean . . . Wash Roberts, the fellow that was burned to death, the poor devil. Are you laying that to me?"

"Yes, the fellow who was soaked in coal oil and a match dropped on him."

"Anybody says I did that lies," said Jarvis.

"It was Dago Mattis told me," said Grey. "He told me while he was dying. He told me how Wash Roberts screamed all the while the coal oil was being poured over him, because he knew what was coming. He told me what Wash said, and how he begged, and how you worked slow, so you could hear more of the begging. Yes, Dick, you're exactly the kind I like to go after. I'd like to shoot the eyes out of your crooked head."

"But you don't like hanging, Rinky Dink," said Jarvis, now pale and coldly alert, on the defensive.

"Oh, I wouldn't hang," said Grey. "Oh, no . . . because in another moment, I shoot, and they come running out and find you dead. You've already got a gun in your hand, and, when they search you, they find other guns on you . . . and in your wallet a stack of hard cash, more than an honest man would be carrying around instead of leaving it in a bank.

"You see how smooth my case will be? You're just another anarchist, like that poor boy the other night who tried his hand at the general. That's what they'll say. The people down here will give me a vote of thanks. That's all I'll suffer for knocking you off, if you look the job in the face. But you won't let me shoot, Dick. Because you're going to talk. You're going to tell me who sent *you* down here after me."

A fine sweat beaded the forehead and the upper lip of Jarvis. At last he took his eyes from those of the boy, and, drawing a handkerchief from his breast pocket, he scrubbed his face dry. "You win, Rinky Dink," he said. "I guess you always win." He said it bitterly, sneering at the table, as though he despised himself for making this admission.

"Go right on, Dick, while you're in the humor," said Grey.

"You know Pop Swan?" asked Jarvis. He did not wait for the answer. "Pop always had it against you because he said that you knew too much about his business. He said that he lost out in that deal in Santa Fe because you tipped off the elbows. He said that you had tipped off others, and spoiled everything for him. His brother is up for ten years already. He blames it all on you, and he put a lot of pressure on me to go after you. I didn't want to. I had nothing against you. But he offered a bale of cash. So here I am."

"You trailed me all the way south, did you?" asked Grey.

"Yes. It was a hard job. But here I am. It's old Pop you really want, and not me."

"That's a good lie," said Grey. "But, still, it's a lie. Now try the truth."

Jarvis stared at him. "You beat me, Rinky Dink," he muttered.

"Begin," said Grey. "Begin with Pittsburgh."

"You know!" exclaimed the other.

"Go on," said Grey. "I want to hear it from you." He added: "I've spent too much time. Start with Pittsburgh, and wind up with John Ray, or Juan Ray, as they call him down here."

Jarvis fairly collapsed in his chair, sinking low down in it. "All right," he said. "I guess you know. They sent for me. I went all the way to Pittsburgh and saw that fellow Brick Forbes. You know."

"Well?" said Grey.

"They'll pay anything. It's kind of in futures, but they'll pay anything to keep John Ray from being turned up. Why, I don't just know. Do you?"

"Yes," said the boy. "But go on."

"They knew that trouble was likely to start from the border. I was sent back to wait in El Paso. I wait there for orders. Pretty soon I have them, to get to San Vicente fast, and, when I get there, to pry you apart from General O'Riley, or see that you never get to him. I'm to put you out of the way, if I can. If I can't, at least, I'm to trail you, because you may get on the way to John Ray."

"They want you to handle me and Ray, too. Is that right? If you can find Ray, he goes west, too?"

The other shrugged his shoulders. He was disturbed, troubled. "You know, Rinky Dink," he said, "they offer pretty big money."

"How big?"

"It's fifty thousand to me if I turn the trick. All expenses, without any questions asked."

"That's a lot," murmured Grey. "And I think I've had fifty thousands' worth of talk out of you already."

"Are you through?" asked the other.

"I suppose I am."

Jarvis stood up, but he lingered a little, his jaw working, his teeth gritted. "You've won this trick of the game, Rinky Dink," he said. "But the game's not over. Mind you, I'm going to take another whirl at you."

"Are you the head of the other side?" asked Grey.

"Of course I am," said Jarvis.

"They have less brains than I thought, then," said Grey. "So long, Dickon." He turned a little in his chair. "Take care of yourself," he said after the retreating figure of Jarvis.

Jarvis turned a little and halted an instant. "What's that?" he demanded.

"I said, take care of yourself," the boy repeated.

Jarvis shrugged his shoulders. "I'll do that, all right," he said. He walked on from the restaurant to the street, and, turning down, he stepped off with a brisk pace.

The sun was very bright and hot. The white dust in the street reflected both the heat and the rays until he was half-blinded. He was not at ease, but his brain was working fast and hard. It had been a serious blow, this trick that the boy had taken from him, but he was glad that all the cards in his hand had not been drawn out by Rinky Dink Grey. There were still a good many items, the knowledge of which would have been of profit to Grey, had he known them.

From the first, it had been clear to Jarvis, as an intelligent man, in spite of the instructions he had received, that the really important point was not the destruction of old John Ray, even if that man still were alive, but the murder of Grey. That murder he was grimly determined to accomplish.

He had felt, at first, rather a twinge of conscience because he had always admired young Grey so much, and because that youth flashed across the minds of the lawless in the Southwest as a sort of superior genius and a guiding star. They loved to talk of him, to recount the narratives of his exploits, and to sun themselves in the brilliance of his superior adroitness in all things. But now the death of Grey was a passionate determination in the mind and in the heart of Jarvis.

He was turning over gradually in his thoughts various plans for the destruction of the youth, and, in the meantime, he walked slowly on, taking various turns and short cuts to get to his destination.

A voice spoke behind him, calling him by name. "*Señor* Jarvis!"

He turned and saw a man with a fat, smiling face, a very rosy-brown skin, and slant eyes, almost like the eyes of a Chinaman. He walked with a stick in his right hand and a little package of brown paper in his left. It might have been a small bundle of sausages—the brown of the paper was a little stained with oil, or grease, in one place.

"Well? Well?" said Jarvis impatiently.

"You are *Señor* Jarvis, are you not?" said the brown-faced man, who was always smiling.

"Yes, yes," said Jarvis. "What d'you want with me? I'm in a hurry, my friend."

"Are you in a hurry?" said the other, lifting his eyebrows.

"Yes. In a big hurry."

"Would you tell me where you are going?" asked the stranger.

"Why, I'm . . . well, what makes you want to know where I'm going?" asked Jarvis. He looked closer at the other to see whether or not there was the blank look of drunkenness in his eyes. But he could not make it out. It was a smiling eye that he encountered.

"Because I had an idea," said the other, "after you had talked to *Señor* John Lawrence, that you might be about to take a long trip,"

Jarvis suddenly started and then frowned. He looked about him. It was a narrow alley in which he stood, with blank, windowless walls of massive adobe rising loftily on both sides of him. Elbow turns shut off the view from either street and there was no other person to be seen except this rather elderly man with the brown face.

"Not behind you," said the stranger. "Look at *me,* Jarvis."

Jarvis looked back at him with a start and an angry exclamation. As he turned, a thin tongue of fire darted from the end of the brown package that was held in the left hand of the stranger, and a heavy report struck the ear of Jarvis, a pain shot like a finger of ice through his breast, blackness struck in one solid wave across his eyes, and he dropped face down in the dust, dead.

Chapter Twelve

At 1:00 P.M., the carriage of the general came to the inn where young Grey was living. He had returned from the chocolate shop before this and mounted to his room, and he was found by the *moza* who summoned him, still busily poring over the Spanish-English grammar and shaking his head, as though in patient fatigue.

He was not easily made to understand that the carriage of the general was waiting for him in the street, but at last, after many gesturings, he nodded, and then washed his hands and dried them with care. When they were dry, the fingernails did not seem to him properly groomed, so he returned to give them a fresh scrubbing with a brush.

Then he brushed his hair, brushed the shoulders of his coat, pulled it down at the back, hunched up his coat collar until it fitted a little higher, adjusted his necktie a trifle, took his walking stick, thin and supple as a rapier, a pair of gloves, and a soft gray hat, the brim of which furled a little along one side. With a last critical look downward at his shoes, he left the room and went softly down the stairs, tapping the edges of the steps lightly with his stick.

The *moza* and her husband both attended him to the carriage. It was driven by a liveried coachman, with a footman likewise attired in the most correct livery, ready at the door of the carriage to hand in the guest. Opposite the footman was the secretary, giving to Grey his brightest smile and his most graceful bow.

Grey got in. He put on his hat, settled his stick between his knees, and, folding his hands upon the top of it, he directed his gentle, child-like smile straight before him as they drove through the streets of San Vicente toward the general's house.

The general's coachman drove with a dangerous speed. That was partly to show off his skill as a driver and partly to show off the quality of his horses, now that he had a passenger worth impressing.

They never turned a corner upon more than one wheel. Yet, when they reached the house of the general, the pale secretary was forced to admit that Grey had not changed color and had not altered his gentle smile for one instant.

The nerveless, cold Nordic, said the secretary to himself.

Then he showed Lawrence Grey into the house and into the presence of the general himself. The general received him with much courtesy, and, as soon as the servants were out of the room, he said: "We can dine in the garden or in the house, Mister Grey."

Grey observed the general with a smile, but with eyes that wrinkled just a little at the corners. "Jarvis called on you, I suppose," he said.

The general started. He had used the name Grey without malice aforethought. He had not the slightest intention of revealing at once what little he knew of this seemingly innocent and blandly indifferent young man. Then he remembered. Lawrence was the name under which the American chose to pass. "I've said too much," said the general.

"No," answered Lawrence Grey. "You've said too little."

O'Riley was miserable. He told himself that he was a fool, and that he had shattered the web, at the first touch, of what might have proved to be the most charming little mystery.

"Jarvis was here," he said frankly. "But whatever he said is unsaid, exactly as you wish."

Grey smiled at his host again. He relaxed just a trifle in his chair. "Let's eat in the garden," he said. "In the open air, there's always a little wind blowing, or a rumble from the streets, and one can have real privacy. I need privacy for what I have to say to you."

The general rang, gave the proper directions, and sat down near his guest. "Whatever brought you to San Vicente," he said, "I am not one to ask you questions. I am simply at your service in every way. Only"—here his Irish eyes flashed—"I'd like pretty well to be into it. However, it's your affair. Use me as you see fit . . . just so far and no further. I ask no questions." However, it was plain that the effort to keep the questions under cover had raised O'Riley's temperature to the boiling point.

"I can tell you almost everything," said Grey. "I can tell you, for instance, that I sat for seven nights under the cypresses waiting for the time when I could introduce myself to you."

"Why didn't you come at once?" asked the general. "Why didn't you frankly come and speak to me at once? Why did you wait, my dear young friend?"

"Because," said Grey, "what I had to say was pretty odd. I needed the introduction."

"Tell me, then," said the general, "did you think that sitting there for seven evenings would get you closer to an introduction? Are you as patient as that?"

"I had to establish myself as a deaf man," said Grey. "Deaf to Spanish, I mean. After that . . . it was about the third day . . . I began to hear things. Especially I began to hear them from the table where the five young men were always sitting."

"Hai!" cried the general, light breaking visibly upon his mind. "You could speak Spanish all the while?"

"As well as English," said Grey. "So I sat there and overheard a good deal. The table at which I sat was a little distance from the other, but, when the wind was down and the music was still, I used to pick up some interesting words, such as dynamite, death, the general, the idle rich, and such things. The more I heard, the more I determined to wait. Finally, on the seventh night, I found that it had been worthwhile."

The general listened, gasped a little, and swore for a full minute in rapid, expressive Mexican curses. There is no language more gifted in this respect. "You guessed that they were going to try their hands at me, and still you waited? Until that last instant?" he demanded.

"I drew it a little fine," said Grey. "I didn't figure on the rolling of the bomb. I hadn't thought of that. If the bomb had not rolled, I would have had three or four more seconds to get rid of it, and then everything would have been perfectly safe."

The general said nothing. He merely surveyed his guest with added attention. "Do you usually calculate your margins down to three or four seconds?" he asked.

"Sometimes one has to," said the young man. "At any rate, everything turned out well, and there won't be anarchists flourishing in San Vicente for some time."

"True," said the general. He hesitated, and then he added: "It seems that Mister Jarvis must have used small margins, also. But he was unlucky. You know about his bad luck, I suppose?" He looked narrowly at the boy.

"Bad luck?" said young Grey. He leaned a little forward. "I know of one bit of bad luck that he had this morning, when he was talking with me," he commented, "at Murcio's little restaurant. Anything else?"

"One more thing," said the general. "After he left you, he was shot through the heart. The murderer has not been found. No trace of him has appeared."

This word of his brought Lawrence Grey suddenly to his

feet. "Jarvis dead?" he muttered. "Jarvis really dead? And this morning." He snapped his fingers impatiently, angrily. "I might have known. I might have guessed it."

"You might?" asked the general.

"He was too small for his job," said the young man. "Of course, they would have had a better brain over him."

"I don't quite understand," said the general.

"Understand this then," said Grey sharply, "that if you will help me, now is the time."

"As far," said O'Riley, "as money or influence or men can help you. Command me."

"I will, then," said Grey. "My life and another life depend on what I can get out of you. I don't want your money. I don't want your influence. This is what I want." He hurried the general to the window, and with a gesture he indicated the sweep of mountains that arose outside of the town.

O'Riley waited for the explanation.

"I want," said the boy, "the two hardest things that any man can ask for. I want a guide who knows the country really well. And I want a man to whom I can trust my life. I want a guide who understands those mountains as though he had made them, and with whom I'll be perfectly safe, a fellow to whom you'd trust your own life, your house, your friends, your money."

The general prided himself upon quick decisions. "I know the very man," he said. "I'll have him here in half an hour. He has been acquainted with me for years. He has mined and prospected in person every inch of those mountains. He has made and lost such fortunes that money would mean nothing to him, and he is, in addition, the most honest man I have ever seen. I have known him for years, and there has never been a breath of scandal against him. He is a Rock of Gibraltar." He rang for a servant and sent the *mozo* away on the errand.

He would have taken the boy into the garden, but Lawrence

Grey said curtly: "I have to sit here in a corner and think. Let me be alone. Every second that runs by me now, General, is spinning me into deeper water and worse danger. You can't help me. Nobody can help me . . . only that honest guide you speak of, the man who never has done a wrong to anyone."

The general retired to the window without a word, for he recognized necessity when he saw it. He waited while the long minutes slowly dragged away.

At last, a servant opened the door and announced a name, and the general, turning in haste, exclaimed to Grey: "Here is Mister Oliver Slade. Here is the man I told you of, my friend."

Grey rose and faced the door, through which he saw entering a man of middle age, with a good, strong, light step, although he seemed rather heavy of body, with a fat face that was continually smiling. His skin was extremely brown—Mexican brown, in fact—and his eyes were set slanting and seemed opaque, like yellow ivory and green-black jade.

Chapter Thirteen

The Oriental blankness of the eye of Slade and the oddity of the whole cast of his countenance were not exactly prepossessing to Lawrence Grey, but the vigor with which the general recommended him outbalanced any predispositions on his part. He shook hands with Slade and felt a soft, reluctant hand in his.

Said the general: "I could never recommend a man as I do you, Slade. And I have never asked you so sincerely for help as I ask you now. Now, tell me, Mister Grey, in what way I can help you further?"

"Let me ask Mister Slade if he can give me a month of his time," said the young man.

"But you have my time, already, because I'm unable to refuse anything to General O'Riley," replied Slade.

"Good fellow, Slade," said the general. "I knew that I could count on you. Whatever you can do for Mister Grey, is done directly for me, I give you my word."

"Very well, then," said Slade. "I'll go with you, whenever you say."

"There's one last request," said Grey to O'Riley. "Let me take Slade away at once."

In two minutes they were on the street. As they walked, Grey explained: "The moment we leave this town, perhaps from the very fact that you're walking along the street here with me, you're in danger of your life, Slade. The general says that you know these mountains as if you'd made them. I want to climb every height that overlooks San Vicente. Do you know the way?"

Slade looked down at the sidewalk and canted his head a little. "Nobody knows those mountains as if he'd made them," he said. "I'll tell you. I've walked them, prospected them, mapped them, and studied them for years. Still, I don't know them. Old trails break down every winter. New ones are made every summer. There are landslides and cloudbursts and flooding rivers that keep writing new wrinkles into the face of the land up yonder. But I can take you about from place to place fairly well, I think. Only, I can't say that I know every line in the face of those mountains. No man does . . . not even the shepherds in their own districts."

The youth nodded. "By the way you speak," he said, "you show me that you really know 'em. Very well. You're the guide for me, if you'll come. Will you tell me what you want as wages?"

"I've never worked before for daily pay," said Slade, without false pride. "But I'm flat broke now. I'm glad to pick up money wherever I can. You can set your own price."

"I don't want to underestimate things," said Grey, "and I don't want to make you nervous, either. Suppose we say twenty dollars a day?"

"And I find the animals and the food?" suggested the other.

"No. I'll find those."

"Twenty's too much," said Slade.

"If it suits you, it suits me," said the boy. "We're starting on a trip that may take a month, but I've an idea that it will take less time. What animals do we need?" asked Grey, in conclusion.

"Riding mules," said the other. "They're the best in those mountains."

"Mules are slow movers," answered Grey.

"The surest mount is the fastest one," said Slade. "I tell you, it's mostly straight up and down, and you go zigzagging on trails a foot wide most of the time. Mules are the thing. They have good ones here that can raise a gallop, too. Spanish mules from Andalusian stock . . . the best in the world."

"There's one horse that we take along with us," said Grey. "A bay mare.

"Let the mare stay behind," said Slade. "She'll only be in the way."

"She won't be badly in the way," said the boy.

"She'll have to be led over trails that will take the heart out of her."

"She's used to mountains," answered Grey. "And she won't have to be led, because she'll follow."

"Two mules for riding and two for packing would be the best," insisted Slade.

"Two mules for riding, because the packs we'll carry will be light," said Grey.

"Whatever you want, then," said Slade. He submitted without sulkiness, but it was plain that he was disappointed.

"You know these mountains," explained Grey, to take the edge from his own stubbornness. "But I know that light luggage makes a safer skin when it comes to a pinch. Less to pack in the morning and less to unpack at night. Can you handle a gun?"

"I can do a man's share of hunting with a rifle," said Slade.

"And a revolver?"

"Revolvers?" said Slade, smiling a little. "I've worn them and I've used them, but I don't take much stock in all the six-guns."

"Very well," answered Grey. "Let the revolver work go. We may need rifles for something more than deer, though. You understand that, Slade?"

"I understand that you're afraid somebody may bother us," said Slade. "You know you haven't explained."

"I don't intend to," said Grey. "All you have to know is that every man that comes within sight of us is likely to be an enemy, and an enemy that would as likely as not take pleasure in shooting the eyes out of our heads. You keep awake, and I'll keep awake, and watch every rock for a head popping out behind it and every bush for someone peeking through at us."

Slade merely nodded. "You have to do that, anyway, in the San Vicente Mountains," he assured Grey. "You know the mountains up yonder are spliced together with outlaws and thieves of all kinds. It's a hole-in-the-wall country. They've always been up there. Every revolution sends another sprinkling. And every thug in the country, sometime or other, hides out from the law yonder. If you have special enemies, well, that means a little more trouble. But you have to keep your eyes open, anyway, hobble your cattle at night, and act as though you were in Indian country when the tribes are on the warpath."

Grey nodded. "You're going to be just the hand to see me through this business," he told Slade. "You get the mules, will you? What price does a man pay down here?"

"A hundred dollars a head for good riding mules. Two hundred for animals that will go where the mountain goats go."

"That sounds high."

"Not for what you get."

"Then get the best. Here's the money, and enough over for two small packs . . . blankets, saddles, and whatever men need, traveling skeleton light. You know the idea."

"I know," said Slade. He took the money that the boy extended toward him, counted it, and put it carefully away in a wallet. "I can have this stuff in an hour," he said.

"Can you make it half an hour?" asked Grey.

"Time means as much as that, does it?"

"Yes. Every minute counts, particularly to get us out of this town."

"Ready, then," said Slade. "Very well. I'll work fast. Where do we meet?"

"At my tavern." He gave its name. They parted at once, and Grey went to a store where everything from a stiletto to a fine shotgun could be bought.

He selected two fifteen-shot Winchesters and a brace of Colt six-guns, together with an ample stock of ammunition. He returned to his tavern, made up his pack, got the bay mare of the sheriff from the stable, and brought her saddled to the front of the tavern in time to see Slade come up with two mules. They looked like any other mules, at the first glance, with narrow shoulders and long ears. But a second glance showed that their legs were perfectly straight at the knees and hocks, and they had not the hanging belly of the usual heavy-feeding mule. Their eyes were bright and big and they had an unusual air of alertness.

"I paid six hundred for the pair," said Slade. "Where one goes, the other will follow. They've been worked together for two years. And they know these mountain trails around here. They'll hear a landslide begin long before our ears will catch the sound of it. They'll stay fat on thistles, and they'll never give up their work."

"You've learned a lot about 'em in a short time," said Grey, smiling.

"I learned it from the Mexican who owned them. He looked as though he cut a throat a day," said Slade, "but he cried when he saw me take that span away from him. Real tears. Those mules will be right."

"We start now," said the boy, and straightway the packs were made up and they started off.

Each of them rode a mule. Behind them, without a rope to lead by, wandered the bay mare. She followed them closely and faithfully through the streets of the town.

Said Slade, looking back with amused interest at the mare: "You've spent a long time teaching that mare, I suppose?"

"She learned everything in ten days," answered Grey. "A horse will learn when it has to, like a boy cramming for an examination."

"And how," said Slade, "did you make the horse understand that it has to?"

"By talk," said Grey, "when you're alone in the middle of the desert, or the heart of the mountains . . . just at the time when a horse begins to listen to the noises of the wolves and the caterwauling of the mountain lions. That's the time when the ears of a horse are open, you know. It hears things then."

Slade smiled again. He never seemed critical, but only amused.

So they left San Vicente, and began the long climb to the mountain heights.

When they had gone to a little distance, Slade looked back toward the town, which was growing together, smaller and smaller, and Slade said: "Well, whatever we're up against, we're between the two troubles now, I suppose."

But the young man shook his head. "The trouble may be under our feet, right now," he answered.

Chapter Fourteen

They advanced, as the afternoon wore on, through the rolling foothills. The sun, now that the wind was shut away by the mountains, beat down with great force. They had mounted above the level of the green plains, and here they were in a world of rocks and cactus. Now and then came a scattering grove of limes, but they were mounting to a region naked and deserted.

They had talked very little. Grey had told his companion frankly that he did not intend to discuss the object of the expedition. He wanted a guide, simply, and the guide was to know that they were likely to be riding constantly in the face of danger. That was all.

But now, as the strength of the sun diminished a little, Slade opened the conversation. He did not speak of the goal of their expedition, but merely remarked: "Tell me, Grey, did you ever get much use out of a revolver?"

"Some," answered Grey.

"I've never seen them do much execution. I've been long enough in the West and in Mexico to see all sorts of barroom brawls, and plenty of Colts in the air at the same time. But what was smashed was chiefly crockery and windows. The ceiling and the walls were pretty well ripped up, as a rule, but I can't say that I've seen more than chance wounds."

"No?" said young Grey quietly.

"No," said Slade. "The point, as it seems to me, is that a rifle is slower, but a lot surer."

"Yes, a lot surer," admitted Grey.

"As for the revolver," said Slade, "I've heard a great many tales about fellows who can knock a hole in a tin can, or break a rock when it's thrown in the air. But I've never seen it done. Have you?"

"Yes," said the young man.

"Have you, really? Who did it, then?"

"I've done it myself," said Grey.

"Come, now," said the other, still smiling in his usual good-natured manner, but obviously doubtful. He leaned out from his saddle and picked up a few small stones that lay on the top of a boulder, abutting on their trail. Water freezing during the cold of the winter had splintered the upper surface of the rock and left these smaller fragments. "Let me see it done, will you?" asked Slade.

"You're a doubter, are you?" answered Grey. "Well . . . throw the stones up."

"There's one," said Slade. He tossed it into the air some ten paces in front of them. It was of a good size, and one could see it turning slowly over and over in the air.

"That's too big to make a test," said Grey. As he spoke, he fired almost without giving his target a glance. The gray stone disappeared into a puff of dust.

"Good," said Slade. "Very good, indeed. Nothing much for a rifle, but I'd hardly believe it of a revolver. However, shooting at a man is not at all like shooting at a helpless rock, even if it's falling through the air."

"You have three more," said Grey, smiling in his turn. "Throw 'em all."

"Will you pick 'em out of the air . . . all of 'em . . . before they hit the ground?" asked Slade.

"Yes."

"Without fail?"

"Yes, without fail."

"Well, then, here you are," said Slade, and, rising a little in the saddle, he hurled the stones high into the air, and well before them.

Grey did not fire in haste. He waited until those trembling little targets were at their highest. Then he fired. One stone disappeared. He fired again and missed. The third shot snuffed out the second stone, and a fourth blew to bits the third rock before it touched the ground. A small bird, aroused by the clamor of the shots, flew out from the rocks and darted away. Grey smashed it with the final shot from his gun. Then he commenced to reload, paying no heed to his work, the fingers operating quite independently.

Slade, in the meantime, was nodding his head and frowning seriously. "I've been a fool," he said. "I've lived too long in Mexico. I've begun to doubt everything. I see that the thing's possible, right enough." He shook his head again. "I'm almost willing to believe in the ambidextrous fellows who can do these tricks right- and left-handed, according to the storytellers. Can you, Grey?"

"I can't hit stones as small as those," said Grey. "But at the same distance I could hit stones, say, the size of a man's heart, every time." He did not speak with pride. It was a simple fact. He had proved it too often. His life had depended upon that skill.

"I won't ask you to demonstrate," said Slade. "I take back everything that I've been thinking on the subject." He fell into a study. Then, a little later, he said: "Why, Grey, you could give half a dozen men a hard argument at revolver range."

Grey shrugged his shoulders. He put away his revolver. And then he asked his strange companion how long he had been in Mexico. He wanted, really, to learn something about Slade's life, and the latter seemed to understand.

He said: "I'll tell you. I've been one of those fellows who have a stroke of luck every third year and lose their luck through the next two. I've made my million twice and I've puffed it away. I've mined from Alaska south. I've made a strike in the Klondike, and I've raked out some rich diggings in Montana. I dug up silver in Nevada, and I've had my luck down here, too, in the San Vicente mountains. But then I went mad, as most prospectors do, on the subject of the mother lode. So now you see me flat broke, and working by the day, and glad to work that way, too. I've collected nothing. I haven't a wife or a child. I haven't a house or any sort of a home. I hardly have a friend, acquaintances only. I'm the true and typical rolling stone . . . I've gathered no moss." He said this in his quiet voice, with a smile of deprecation directed toward his companion.

"But," suggested Grey, "you don't regret your life, do you?"

The latter laughed softly. "Not in the least," he said.

They fell silent, and Grey was wondering if there were some hidden reason that had made his companion so extremely interested in the matter of revolver play. It might have been a purely innocent doubt and curiosity, but Grey was in a cynical humor. He decided, then, that he would watch his guide as a hawk watches the mouse in the field far below it.

They were too busy, from this point on, to do much conversing. The trail was now climbing steadily up into the mountains, and the early evening found them, about sunset time, well up on the face of the San Vicente range.

There young Grey turned in the saddle, and, as they breathed their mules, he looked down over the scene behind them. San Vicente lay small in the distance, like a white chalk mark on the green of the lower fields, and the San Vicente River was a dull, red gold, twisting through the fields, until it reached the town and there was lost to view.

Somewhere, on the heights, he suspected that old John Ray might have taken up his abode. That was the odd thought that had come to him, like an inspiration, that day in San Vicente. The man who had squandered the last of his money upon ungrateful friends might well have withdrawn from the town, but it would be strange if he had gone too far to have it within sight.

At least, that was his theory—that somewhere upon the mountaintops that surrounded the town—he would come upon the old man, some place where he could live simply, like Timon, the misanthrope, but in view of the place where he had lived the happiest and the richest years of his life. From such a place, every day, he could curse humanity and San Vicente's population above all others. There was an odd certainty in the youth's mind and that was why he was determined to scale the heights about the white city.

After that view back into the plain, at the town and the river, they went down a narrow, darkening gorge and came out into a fairly pleasant valley, where the ground was strewn with many rocks, but plenty of good grass grew for grazing and cattle and sheep were dotted about on the landscape. A crossroads village lay before them, the lights beginning to wink like bits of gold through the twilight.

"There's an inn down there," said the guide. "Do you want to try it?"

"An inn?" said the boy. "Inns are good places to get one's throat cut."

"That inn?" Slade laughed. "Why, they're the most honest, stupid people in the world," he said. "These mountaineers around here are a solid breed. They don't dig for gold with knives. They try to clip it off the backs of their sheep. Money that doesn't come out of wool or mutton, they wouldn't consider real. You'd be safe enough there."

So Grey consented, and they rode straight on down to the town, with the bay mare still following cheerfully behind them. They found the inn as it had been described. It was an adobe-house type, with the same ponderous, massive walls and clumsy arches. Since stone was the readiest building material at hand, however, it had been used in the place of mud and grass, and the inn was a great mass of masonry, the blocks fitted together with the nicest precision.

Here they dismounted.

Chapter Fifteen

There was a great bustle to receive them. Everyone in the inn turned out for such distinguished foreigners as guests. There were the host, his wife, his eldest son, and three or four younger children. There was the one *moza* of all household work, besides a boy who attended to the stable and was at once porter, messenger, wood chopper, and general roustabout.

These people first unsaddled the mules. Then they crowded about the stalls where the animals were placed, and held up a lantern to admire the points. They knew mules with a shrewd and practical eye, and the consensus of opinion was that one mule was worth two horses for such a district as they lived in.

Grey was glad to get this unsolicited confirmation of Slade's opinion. In fact, when he looked at the towering, rocky slopes that hemmed in that little valley, he could not help feeling that the feet of a horse were much too big for any real service. Yet he took good care of Doll, the mare. She had carried him on such a long march that she was more than a horse—she was a friend to him. So he rubbed her down with a few wisps of hay—not that she greatly needed such attention—and he himself saw that her portion of hay had few weeds and no moldy spots in it. Then he sifted out for her a good clean portion of oats and poured it into her feed box.

The stableboy, gaping at this care bestowed upon a dumb animal, stood by, holding the lantern, and Slade also watched.

"She's sort of a mascot, I suppose," he commented. "Or like a dog, eh?"

"Well," said Grey, "if ever I need one burst of blinding speed, I can get it out of her. Out of the mule I never could. I may never need her here in the mountains, but I would almost as soon be without a gun as without a horse that has plenty of foot."

They went into the inn. It was like most Mexican taverns. On the first floor there were storage rooms where vegetables, corn, peppers, and all the other standard edibles were stocked away, along with all the accumulated lumber of broken-down carts, wagons, and stripped running gears. On the second floor were the kitchen, the dining room, and several bedrooms. But the best rooms, to which they were now shown, were on the third floor of the building. The landlord was very proud of his star chamber, into which they were ushered. It had on the floor two big skins of mountain sheep, washed as white as snow. There was a bed on either side of the room, topped off with similar skins. Goatskins were on the three chairs. Against the wall hung a little wooden carving of some saint with a gilded halo about her head. She was represented in a peasant's dress, walking down a mountainside, with a train of goats in bas-relief following behind her, and one in the foreground upon whose horned head her hand was resting. It was a charming thing, and young Grey stood a moment before it.

The host was delighted by this attention. His great, great granduncle, it appeared, had been the carver of the little square, he whose father had built this whole inn, except the stable wing, which had been done a mere seventy years ago.

Then in came hot water, borne by the panting *moza.* Finally the bare feet padded and slipped and whispered out of the room and went down the corridor. Once more voices sounded beneath.

"You like it?" said Slade, seeing the smile with which the other continued to enjoy the room.

"I like it a lot," said Grey. "All that I dislike is the fact that we have a roof over our heads. Stars would be safer . . . a lot safer, Slade."

The latter shook his head. "Mind you," he said, "if trouble comes our way, you have that pair of ambidextrous guns."

It seemed to Grey that the other was smiling a little, as though he still failed to take the matter of revolvers very seriously, in spite of the shooting exhibition that he had witnessed on that day's trail.

They went down to the little dining room. It was as good a meal as Grey ever had tasted, although he had had many a counterpart of it in Mexico. It was roasted kid, tenderer than any fowl, with excellent tortillas, which were thin as paper and could be wrapped around fiery *frijoles* cooked with garlic and peppers as fierce as flame. There was a rough red wine to wash it down, a wine made in this same valley. It had an acrid aftertaste, but it fitted in harmoniously with the meal.

Afterward their host came in and timidly offered cheap Mexican cigars.

They preferred cigarettes, but they had their host to their table with them to finish off a half bottle of wine. He was a little man with a shovel face and a mustache that contained not fifty hairs, widely separated by a part in the center of the upper lip. But like most Mexicans, he had good manners.

He inquired after their health, their voyage, and their animals. He declared that the mule with the starred forehead was the second best in looks that ever had been in his stable. He knew Slade, it appeared, because the latter had once before stopped at this same hotel. And he declared that the time could not be far off when Slade would once more part the rocks and take out gold as a cook parts the froth on the pot of stewing beans and takes out rich ladles full. Slade thanked him for that prophecy. But he said that now he was merely the guide of this gentleman.

Guiding, said the host, was a sacred profession, and in those mountains nothing could be more respected.

After that they went up to bed. The night had turned cold, with a strong mountain wind whining through the chinks of the shuttered windows, and moaning near and far. They went to bed, snuggled down deep under the goatskins, and young Grey was soon asleep. But he slept lightly, as he always did. There was some truth in the saying that one eye was always open and one ear was always cocked.

It was shortly after midnight when he wakened, with all of his senses instantly alert. There had been a mere whisper in the room. He waited.

"Grey," said the faintest of whispers from the farther side of the room.

"Yes," said Grey in a low voice.

"Did you hear it?"

"What?" asked Grey.

"Voices down there . . . voices from the stables. Whispering voices, by thunder. Why should people be out there murmuring at this time of night?"

Grey bent his ear. The wind had fallen dead away. There was not a breath, there was not a touch of a breeze. Utter silence weighted down the old inn, and yet the cold of the night had increased steadily until it was freezing.

"Do you hear?" asked Slade in a cautiously lowered voice.

"Nothing," said Grey.

"There's something down there, though," said Slade. "I'm wondering if someone may have admired those mules a little too much. I think I'll go down and have a look."

"I don't think they'll steal the mules," said Grey. "Go to sleep, man."

"No," insisted Slade. "I'm going down." There was a loud rustling of bed clothes being thrown back.

"Nonsense," said Grey, springing from his bed. "If anyone's to go, I'll go down." He could not let a man so much older go out into the bitter chill of that night. But he cursed silently the nervousness, so unexpected, in this fellow.

"Don't you do it," said Slade, protesting. "I'd as soon go. My skin is as thick as yours."

"I'm up already," answered Grey. "Where's the light?"

"There on the small table, nearer the foot of your bed than mine."

"True," said Grey.

He found matches in his pockets. Next he fumbled with a cautious hand until his fingertips touched the icy cold of the lamp chimney. He laid hold on it with his left hand, and with his right he struck the match. The flame began to spurt, and as suddenly died. So, with a mutter of complaint, he picked up another match.

"Cheap things, these Mexican matches," commented Slade from the other bed.

"Mighty cheap . . . no good at all," said Grey. Then, with the second match ready in his fingers, he paused.

In that single spurt of fire from the first match he had had an odd impression that the door of the room leading into the hall was wide open. It could not very well be, because he had both locked and bolted that same door when he went to bed. Yet there was that strange feeling that the door had been ajar just now, like the open mouth of a great beast silently gaping at him. A little chill ran up his spine, and it was not all the effect of the icy air of the night.

"I've got some Swedish matches over there," said Grey. "I'll get hold of them in a moment."

"They're the best," agreed Slade.

But when the boy moved, it was not toward the bed and his discarded clothes, but in the direction of the door. His bare feet felt the way. They found the warm surface of one of the goatskins. His outstretched left hand followed the line of the table, while he cast his mind back upon the picture of the room as it had been when he entered. He remembered that as he stood in the door, looking at the little wood carving, that the very corner of the table had been before him. From that corner he judged his way. It should be about three strides. So he made nine small ones, and then, with the revolver that he carried under his left arm night and day grasped in his right hand, he reached out for the threshold of the door.

His bare foot struck cloth—cloth warm, as if with the heat of a human body.

Chapter Sixteen

A gun spat fire in the very face of Grey. He struck a sweeping blow with the revolver in his hand, but, instead of managing to reach the head or the arm of this man in the dark, he felt the stroke taken on a cushioning of soft flesh. At the same time he threw himself forward and grappled with a writhing form on the floor of the hall. They whirled over and over. The revolver, striking the wall, was knocked from Grey's hand. He had no advantage of strength. This fellow who wrestled in the dark was as powerful as a bull, but the slight weight of Grey was reinforced by all that the science of wrestling could teach him. In an instant he had located the other by touch as though a light were cast upon him, and a second later he had clamped on a neck-breaking half-nelson.

It was broken. By the only maneuver known to wrestling it was broken, and with amazement he realized that he had a trained athlete on his hands. Where could the bandits of these mountains have obtained such schooling in catch-as-catch-can? He was so bewildered that he made no sudden move to regain his grip, and with a wrench and a fling the under man twisted from him and spun to his feet, running. At the same time he heard the hoarse shout of Slade, and felt, rather than saw, his roommate rush past him and down the hall.

Leaping to his own feet, he was in time to see, by the dull night-gray of a window that opened on the hallway, the form of the fugitive swaying as the fellow struggled to get under way at full speed, and behind him Slade, his hands empty, rushing as fast as he could run.

He could have cursed the stupidity of Slade in dashing down the hallway without a weapon, at the same time that he felt a thrill of admiration for the bulldog courage of the man. He could understand, all in a flash now, why General O'Riley had been so willing to trust everything to the hands of Slade.

As Grey sprinted in pursuit, he saw the pair whip out of sight at the head of the stairs. He saw Slade apparently leaving his feet in a headlong dive. There was the sound of a dull, heavy blow, and then Grey, taking the same turn, stumbled over a prostrate form that stretched across the stairs. He saved himself with hands and feet as he turned over in the air. He landed on the platform where the stairs turned, and down he went, for he could hear the fugitive before him.

The house was up now. He heard voices shouting everywhere, and, as he raced down the lower hall after the dim shape before him, a door opened and the bulky form of his hostess stepped out in her nightgown. Grey could not help the collision. It cast the poor woman headlong back into the chamber, screeching at the top of her lungs, and it sent Grey staggering back against the wall. By the time he regained his balance and could start, he heard the heavy door in the front of the tavern slamming.

He did not pursue any farther. He waited one instant, and the noise of hoofs went rattling off up the valley. The night murderer was gone.

Lanterns came tossing in the dark of the corridors like bright ships in a stormy sea. And lamps came swaying. When the *gringo* guest was recognized, they swarmed about him. They laid their hands upon him and all asked questions at the same time.

He picked out the host. "Send these people back to bed," he commanded, "and come up the stairs with me. My friend has had a fall. He may be badly hurt, for all I know. This whole thing is nothing but a little attempt at murder."

The host yelled half a dozen orders, but he was totally unable to command his frightened, babbling family. However, he ran with his lantern up the stairs behind Grey, and together they found Slade.

He was lying head down along the steps, with blood running fast from an ugly gash along the side of his skull. When they picked him up, he groaned a little; by the time they had stretched him out on his bed once more his wits had returned.

"Dived for the rascal on the stairs," he said, "and I missed him. Confound him. Cracked myself up a bit, but I'm all right, except that there are some cathedral bells ringing in my brain. Otherwise, there's nothing wrong with me at all."

Grey murmured a vague reply and looked carefully at the wound. Perhaps it should be sewed. Perhaps a mere bandage would be enough. He asked the host hopelessly if there were any sort of a doctor in the village.

"There is better than a doctor," said the host. "There is *Padre* José." And straightway he sent his eldest son scampering to fetch the man.

"A priest," said Slade, sitting up on his bed suddenly, "is not likely to know much of these things."

But the host smiled with a calm conviction. He said: "*Padre* José is not a priest. He is not a doctor, either. He is everything. When he comes, you'll understand!"

"He's their local medicine man, I suppose," said Slade to Grey. "Every village community generally has one or two around. They'd rather go to them than to accredited doctors. They're cheaper, for one thing, and they give you a lot more folderol for your money. However, we'll let this *Padre* José have a look at the cut. Some of the rascals know herbs very well . . . things that help along the healing of a wound."

Padre José came in the course of an hour. He was very brown, but his complexion was rather that of a white man who has been tanned by exposure than a Mexican born dark. He had an ugly face, smooth shaven, with a thin, eagle's nose, and eyes buried beneath very deep brows. His distinguishing feature was a bush of white hair that fell as far as his shoulders and was kept out of his face, Indian style, by a band of cloth tied about his head. In his dress he might have been the poorest shepherd. The gray woolen cloak that hung over his shoulders was turning green with age; every atom of the nap had been worn from it.

He spoke to Grey and the hurt man curtly, in extremely good Castilian Spanish, then he looked to the wound. It would close, he said, if the patient remained quietly in one place for a few days. If he continued to travel, the lips of the cut should be sewed together, and he was willing to undertake the task.

Slade looked to Grey, and the latter, with a wry face, declared that it was better to wait.

"Time counts with you, man," protested Slade. "I can't let you waste it on me in this way. Let the old chap sew up the cut. I'll be able to ride as well as the next one."

But Grey was firm. He felt that the event of this night had proved the mettle of Slade down to the ground, and he was unwilling to allow him to take any risks. After all, as he pointed out, the sewing might cause an infection, and they were far from a place where an infection could have the proper care.

They communicated this decision to *Padre* José, and he nodded.

He had a broad sheepskin belt about his hips with several pouches attached to it. One of these he opened and, unfolding it, showed several small parcels inside, wrapped in thin tissues. Of these he selected one and dropped part of the contents into a small portion of hot water. A strong, pleasant aroma spread through the air of the room. Then, washing the wound carefully, he pressed the lips of it together, laid over it a compress soaked in the liquid he had prepared, and then skillfully wound two bandages about the hurt, one crossing it longitudinally and the second at right angles to the first. It passed under the jaw of Slade.

"You can talk," said the healer, "without parting your teeth. And you can eat once a day, when the bandages are changed."

"Who will change them?" asked Grey.

"I," said the shepherd, "if you will come out to my cottage to live for three days. At the end of that time, if he is careful to do what I say, the wound will be sufficiently closed so that one bandage will hold it. And he can wear a hat and begin to travel."

The host plucked Grey by the arm. "Go with him," he said. "There is more wisdom in an hour of his talk than in a year's schooling under good teachers."

"Where do you live?" asked Grey.

"A mile from this place," said the shepherd, "among the hills. It is a beautiful place. You can be quiet there, and at peace."

"Peace is what we want," said Grey to Slade. "And I'd rather be away from this place than in it. They've followed me closely enough to this point. They'll have less of a chance at me if we're in the open air."

Slade said, shaking his head a little and speaking without difficulty through his teeth: "You'll have to get that idea out of your head. It was simply some mountain bandit, old fellow. Nobody from San Vicente tried that trick."

"No mountain bandit is likely to know how to break a half-nelson," said the boy. "And no mountain thief is liable to understand the workings of a lock as well as that fellow did. Have you looked at the lock? It was either opened from the inside, which it wasn't, or else there was a master hand at work on the outside. That man in the hallway was a genius. He was an exceptional chap. Witness the length of time that he took entering the room. A crude bungler would have been well inside long before that. But the master waited. No, no, Slade. That visitor of ours was an expert in his business. I know enough about it to recognize the signs of the proficient. He came from San Vicente, and soon we're going to have them buzzing like mosquitoes around our heads. You mind what I say."

Slade seemed only half convinced. He even smiled a little. Smiling was the habit of this man. It amazed the boy to notice that nothing in life seemed very important to Slade. He had made and lost so many fortunes that he was in the habit of taking all mortal events very lightly. So he smiled now at an adventure that had nearly cost him the fracturing of his skull.

But they accepted the shepherd's proffered hospitality and made their preparations to remove to his place in the morning.

Before they left, another event took place almost as strange as the attempted assassination in the night—the host absolutely refused to take a penny for their food and room. His guests, he said, were as his family, and, since they had suffered an attack while in his place, a debt was owing from him to them instead of vice versa. They could not prevail upon him to accept a penny.

Chapter Seventeen

When they got up to the camp of *Padre* José in the early morning, they found the roughest scene imaginable. The land on which he grazed his sheep was the mouth of a gorge that opened upon the main valley. It was broken land, being partly covered with great rocks and partly with a straggling growth of trees, big pines that formed dense groves in places, and again stood in twos and threes. The grass grew where it could, and the sheep and a few goats grazed on it, wandering high upon the sides of the steep, rocky walls that enclosed the cañon.

This ravine looked north, and, since it was comparatively narrow and the walls were high, it received little sunshine during the course of even the longest summer day. Among the shadows, therefore, the shepherd had built his house. It was made of untrimmed stones picked up at random, more or less, and only chiseled on the surfaces that lay one upon the other. There was little mortar used. The stones were big at the base of the wall and small at the top, so that they required very little cementing. And they projected outside and in.

His hovel consisted of one room only. It had not even a window, only a door—that is to say, an aperture closed by a flap of skin, like the teepee of an Indian. There was not a chimney; the cooking was done among some stones just outside the entrance.

The inside of the house, if it could be called a house rather than a mere cave, contained a mattress of straw laid in one corner over an Indian willow bed, one stool obviously homemade, and a table hardly larger than the stool. From pegs on the wall hung some garments of the rudest sort. One corner contained a corded heap of firewood, or, rather, kindling with which one could be sure to start a strong flame, after which there was plenty of green timber around to supply the fire for cookery. Another corner of the place contained a few implements for cultivating a little garden of herbs and vegetables, a small pack saddle for a burro, and a fishing rod. This was practically everything to be found in the house.

What was inside the shack the two strangers did not make out at once. For as they came up to the place with their host, a young fellow jumped up from the doorway, where he had been sitting cross-legged, and came running to meet them, his bare, brown legs flashing as he ran. He began to wring his hands and wail when he was still at a distance, and, when he came up to *Padre* José, he was fairly dancing in impatience and sorrow. He was a handsome lad, except that his hair grew down rather too close to his eyes, but now his good-looking features were distorted with grief.

Lawrence Grey knew Spanish perfectly, and every species of Mexican argot and slang, but he could make out of the tumultuous uproar of the boy nothing except that a devil, or *the* devil, had come to him the day before and told him that he would eat his heart if he married María.

Padre José replied merely: "Go find him if you can, and bring him here. Bring María, too."

And the wailer ran off hastily down the gorge. *Padre* José looked after him, shaking his head. But he offered no explanation of this scene, and they now went into the house, where its barrenness was only too evident.

Said *Padre* José: "You"—pointing to Slade—"will sleep in here, because the cold night air might be bad for your head. You better lie down now and be still. Your friend and I will sleep outside on beds of pine boughs."

"I won't turn you out of your house," answered Slade.

Padre José smiled at him with singular sweetness. "The whole valley is my house," he said. "What you see here, of course, is only the most miserable room in it." And he waved his hand to indicate all that was in the place.

"Take it," said Grey in English to his traveling companion. "You may as well. This fellow is a sort of an anchorite or a saint. The more you can take from him, the more reward he thinks that he'll get from heaven. What do you eat here, *Padre?*" he asked, for they had started without breakfast.

"I have a great many vegetables," said *Padre* José. "Then there is goat's milk, and some good cheeses that I make out of their milk, also. I sell the cheeses in the village. Now, let me tell you something," said the simple man with a smile of pride. "One of the carriers took six of my cheeses clear down to San Vicente, and a rich man there bought them. When he tasted them, he said they were very fine, and every summer, during the month he lives in San Vicente, he sends a mule specially to this distant valley, and the muleteer stays until I have collected many of the cheeses. Then we pack them in ferns from the creek, put them in big fish nets, and they are taken clear down to San Vicente."

He waited, with a gleaming eye, for their applause. Grey congratulated him. Slade was already in the corner of the shack, poking at the mattress with a tentative forefinger. There was always something intensely practical about that man. Grey liked him for his frankness.

So they arranged to stay for three days—three of the strangest days that ever were spent by human beings. In the beginning, however, nothing could have been more peaceful.

The first thing that Grey did was to go off up the valley with his rifle. He went a quarter of a mile when, stepping from the woods into a little open hollow, he saw half a dozen deer grazing. They lifted their heads and looked at him as though they had been cows, and he, with his rifle at his shoulder, hesitated. He did not know whether to take the towering buck, or the plumper doe, or one of the little ones. He wound up by lowering the rifle again, for they had lowered their heads and begun to graze again. Only one of the little ones romped to a distance.

Tame deer? In this wilderness of mountains? Grey thought, and stretched out his hand and approached. They would not quite let him touch them. The stag shook his head threateningly when he came too close, and held his ground like a hero.

So he turned and went thoughtfully back toward the house. He shot two fat mountain grouse as he went, picking off the birds without any trouble. These he brought home to the hut of the shepherd, and asked the man if the deer were really tamed.

Padre José shrugged his shoulders. "No one shoots the animals in this valley, my son," he said. "You see, there is a curse on killing. If I had seen you take your rifle with you when you started walking, I would have warned you. However, since you've killed nothing but a pair of wretched birds who often do damage in my garden, I think it's no great matter. But shall I tell you the story of the curse?"

Grey sat on the doorstep; Slade lay sprawled at ease inside. The lower bandage was loose enough to permit him to hold a pipe between his teeth, and therefore he was smoking comfortably.

Old *Padre* José, in the meantime, was rubbing soaked corn into a fine meal for the making of tortillas. He had the rough stone slab and the heavy stone mortar for the work, and he went at it like a washerwoman on a Monday morning, very heartily.

"There used to be a very rich family up there at the head of the gorge," he said. "You go up to the head of it, and then climb rocks that are like a giant's stairway. When you come to the top of the stairs, you see a broad plateau all covered with shrubs and with rocks. In the near distance you see half of a great house. The other half is gone. It has been knocked down. You will notice another thing," went on *Padre* José. "That the house is backed against a high cliff that shuts away the heat of the south wind. And this is the story.

"Once there were two brothers, the sons of that house, and they loved the same woman. The elder one married her . . . but the younger lived on in the house where they were and hated his brother more every day. At last they went off hunting, riding their fine horses. When they came back, only the younger brother was alive, and he carried the body of the older brother strapped across the saddle. He said it had been an accident with a rifle while hunting. They laid out the body, and that night, while the widow was praying beside the corpse, a storm blew up, and an avalanche of rocks and earth shot down from the cliffs and smashed in one half of the house. It broke the roof over the head of the praying wife and buried her with her husband. That was a judgment of God, they say."

"A pretty hard judgment," said Grey. "What had the young wife done?"

"Well, who can tell?" said the shepherd. "Perhaps she had not always looked straight ahead. But I know nothing of that. But the younger brother, Fernando Garcias, who loved hunting more than he loved life, from that moment gave up guns. And he forbade any shooting in any part of his estate. If he knew that you had killed these two birds, he might do you some harm, except that you are my guest. However, from that time on no rifle has been shot at the deer. They have learned to know that this is friendly ground."

"I suppose that poachers break in now and then?" suggested Slade.

"Something bad always happens to them," said the shepherd. "So now the people all say that there is a curse on the head of the man who uses a gun here in the valley and the lands above it. That is what I wanted to tell you."

"That fellow Garcias," said Grey, "still lives up there?"

"He lives a strange life," said the shepherd. "After the death of his brother and of his sister-in-law, he swore he would never marry. But to give the world a woman as lovely as the dead girl, he went away and found a pretty little child and came back and adopted it, and now he raises her like a daughter. He has lost his money. Bad weather kills his crops. His tenants steal from him. He lives like a beggar. But he is raising the girl. She is a woman, now, and there is no other like her. You see, my friends, how evil may bring forth good from the mind? So Fernando Garcias has turned evil into good."

"Did he murder his brother?" asked Grey.

"Who can tell?" said the shepherd with a strange indifference. "And now there is a little work for me to do. Do you see them coming?" He pointed down the valley where three people were coming toward them.

Chapter Eighteen

There was a man on a small horse, a girl riding a mule, and, leading the others on, that same fellow who had been there before, appealing to the shepherd. He explained the matter to Grey.

"That man on the horse," he said, "is a wild youth called Cordoba. He has done a good many bad things, and he knows too much about guns and knives. You can see the glimmer of the gold on his sombrero. On the mule is little María. And that is Juan Gil, who you saw here before. Juan Gil was to marry María, but after everything was arranged, then in came Cordoba and told Juan the other day that he would cut his throat quietly if the marriage took place. Now they are coming to me, so that I can arrange it for them. I must be the judge."

Grey chuckled. "You'll have to give a hard lesson to Cordoba," he said.

"Perhaps," said the shepherd.

"Do they all come up here for your judgment?" asked Grey.

Slade, filled with interest, got up and came with his bandaged head to the door of the hut.

"You see how it is," answered *Padre* José. "Suppose that a man goes to a court of law? Then it is a long journey. There are lawyers to be hired. The poor people sell half their land to pay for the costs, and they break their hearts for two years before they know the decision. But if they come to me, it costs them nothing, and the thing is settled one way or another at once.

This is a thing that I don't wish to do. How can one man act as a judge over another and do it wisely? Why, it is impossible. Still, it seems to be a burden that is prepared for me, and so I accept it. If I cannot say what is good, at least I try to say what is not bad."

He spoke so simply, so utterly without pride in his position that young Grey looked on him with a new eye. The dignity of *Padre* José seemed to grow every moment. He took on a priestly character without having been ordained.

The three now came up, the man dismounted, and Juan Gil took María under the elbows and swung her to the ground. She made a curtsy to *Padre* José and blushed for the benefit of the two Americans.

"These are two very wise friends of mine," said *Padre* José. "Speak before them as you would speak if we were all alone. Who is accusing? You, Juan Gil?"

Cordoba was a man like a hawk, thin, narrow-shouldered, with a bright, cruel eye and a very dark skin. He was a man of some dignity as well as splendor, and he wore his flashing clothes as though he had been accustomed to them from birth—as an ancient king would wear robes. He now turned his eye with an instant's flashing regard to each of the three faces before him, and finally looked aside at Juan Gil. The latter was staring at him defiantly. Cordoba pointed to him.

"He wants to talk," he said. "Not I. Go on, Juan Gil."

Juan got himself into a passion without any more ado. He pointed out that he had fixed upon pretty María five years before, when he was fifteen and she was twelve, and that, at that time, he had told her parents he would, on a day, with the grace of God, marry her, and that they had smiled and shaken their heads. For he was as poor as a beggar, and his parents before him. He, however, had not been discouraged. He had worked patiently. Also, he had studied hard. For María had been taught to read and write, and therefore he went to the good priest and had learned from him, going once a week, and in the day spending his spare time learning how to form letters.

Here Cordoba, the fighter, began to make a cigarette. His glittering eyes never left the face of Juan Gil, but his face remained immobile.

For five years, continued Juan Gil, he had worked practically day and night. He had denied himself everything. He had lived on roots and corn practically, and gradually he had built up a good round sum of hard cash. With this money, after three years of penury, he had bought some sheep. He had bought weak, sickly ones, because they were a quarter the price of the sound ones. He had bought them in the winter, when it seemed that they would hardly live through to the spring. So he got them for almost nothing, and he got them through to the next year by breathing some of his own life, as it were, into their trembling nostrils.

So for two long years he constantly had added to his flock, and now it was a very good one, as anyone in the country could tell you. In the meantime his industrious hands had erected a good house. He himself had worked to help the mason in the village, and had learned from him how to trim stones and how to mix the right, strong mortar. And so, taking time when other men were drinking wine or else idling on holidays or sleeping in their beds, he had built a house. It was a very good house, too. It had two rooms, a chimney, and two windows. He had broken ground behind it and planted a vegetable garden.

He had done all of these things, and then he had gone to the parents of María and taken them out to see the work he had performed. He had allowed them to count his flock. He had shown them his receipts for ready money now in the bank. In exchange for all of this, and, looking with a good deal of wonder and admiration at the patience with which this almost Biblical young man had labored for their daughter, they had broken down at once and sworn that he should have her. That was six months ago. The matter had been arranged. Everybody knew that he was to marry María. Every second Sunday he had walked all the eight miles to the village in order to spend an hour with her, and then had trudged all the way back to his cot.

In the meantime, his condition had not become worse, but much better. And he had bought a good span of bullocks and had made part payment upon a section of good land where they could raise crops of corn. In short, he had built all the foundations for a future happiness in married life. And then fell the stroke of black danger and misfortune.

This man, this scoundrel, this known taker of purses and cutter of throats—deny it if he dared!—this same Cordoba, here, had come and promised to kill him the night of the marriage. This was the truth and the full truth.

Padre José turned to the defendant. "Now, Cordoba," he said, "tell me, is there any truth in all of this?"

"Yes," said the other calmly. "It is all true."

"You threatened to cut the throat of Juan Gil?"

"Yes."

"You want María, is that it?" asked the shepherd.

"Yes," said Cordoba. "I want María, of course."

His calmness sent a tingle through the spine of Grey.

"Have you got a herd of cattle, or a flock of sheep to support her?" asked *Padre* José.

"No," said Cordoba.

"Have you any land, either?" asked the *padre*.

The answer was remarkable. "My hands are not very strong," said Cordoba. "I could not work as a farmer. Besides, I cannot stand wet feet and cold winds, the way a shepherd must stand them. I could not do any of those things."

"Have you money saved?" asked *Padre* José.

"No, I have no money," said Cordoba.

"Then why do you covet this girl, when you're in no condition to support her?"

"Well, I could support her," said Cordoba.

"Tell me how?"

"With this, for instance," replied the calm bandit. And he touched with a light, yellow-brown fingertip the haft of a knife at his belt and, again, the handle of a revolver.

Padre José turned to the girl. "This man, Juan Gil, loves you and wants to marry you," he said. "So does Cordoba. What have you to say about it?"

She had stood like a doll, wooden-faced, during the accusation and the pseudo-defense. Now she opened her great eyes at *Padre* José. "What have I to say?" she said. "My father and mother have already spoken. I am to marry Juan Gil."

"Then why have you done this to Cordoba?" asked *Padre* José.

"I? What have I done to him?" asked the girl.

"Look at him," said *Padre* José.

She turned her head, but just as her eyes met those of Cordoba, those gleaming, uncanny eyes, that ugly and impassive face, her glance dropped. She grew crimson.

Padre José said: "You want a wife, not María, Juan Gil. You love your sheep and your house and your land, not María. And if you married her, she would run away from you inside a year. Then you would have all the expense of a new marriage. Would that be any good to you?"

Juan gaped, but could not drink in this news.

Said *Padre* José: "Look at her blushing. She loves Cordoba."

"*Padre* José!" shouted Juan Gil. "Cordoba is a bad man!"

"That's why she loves him, of course," said *Padre* José. "You go home and forget about her."

"I shall die!" cried Juan Gil. "For five years. . . ."

"You'll have one night of bad sleep," said *Padre* José. "Then you'll remember your sheep and your fine new span of oxen. You'll go to work again."

Juan Gil wrung his hands. "I have sworn to her father . . . ," he began.

"Oh, Cordoba will take care of all that," said *Padre* José. "Now go away quietly. You have said enough. Everything will be as I said."

It amazed Grey to see the boy take this judgment as though it had fallen from the sky. He turned and went with an uneven, fumbling step and a fallen head.

From the hand of Cordoba the fuming cigarette dropped. He was pale, and he trembled. "*Padre* José," he said, "do you believe in me?"

"I do, my son," said the *padre.*

Cordoba looked to the sky, stunned. "Sacred God," he whispered. He did not thank *Padre* José. But he helped María into the saddle on her mule. He took the reins of the horse over his arm, and down he went along the ravine, walking at the side of the mule.

"See," said *Padre* José, "what children we all are."

Chapter Nineteen

When *Padre* José had taken his spade and gone out to work in the vegetable garden, his two guests talked together a little apart from him.

Said Slade: "Is that old fellow real or all fake?"

"What do you think?" asked Grey.

"All fake, except that he's shrewd and knows herbs," said Slade.

"What makes you say that?" asked Grey.

"Because nobody's as wise or as good as that," said Slade. "We're all partly fakers, and he's a faker like the rest of us. Look at him living like a hermit up here. As a matter of fact, when his face was fat he was a lover of good living. Look at the wrinkles around his eyes. They're not all there from worrying and praying, I tell you. He's got some of 'em in the small of the morning."

"Stuff," said young Lawrence Grey. "He's a saint. What will happen between Cordoba and María? That's what I wonder."

"Do you?"

"Yes . . . how will it turn out?"

"Cordoba will have good resolutions for a week. He may even get a job. But the first time that there's a pinch, he'll go off robbing again."

"I don't think so," answered Grey. "I have more faith in people than you have, I think."

"You're young and good-natured, that's all," said Slade. "Men all think the same when they're on the shady side of forty-five."

But the young man shook his head.

Slade went on with a certain tone of malice: "How long will it be before you go up the valley to see Garcias and this pretty daughter of his?"

"I'm not interested in old freaks and pretty girls just now," said Grey.

"No? But you'll go there, and old *Padre* José knows that you will."

"You think so?"

"Why else should he have rung in all that story?"

"Because he'd seen me go hunting and come back with a brace of birds," suggested the boy.

"You're simple," said Slade. "You need a few years. That's the chief part of your needs, Grey. You'll see through people a good deal better later on."

"What do you think was in *Padre* José's mind, Slade?" asked Grey. "Why do you think he wanted to tell me about Garcias especially?"

"Every fellow like that," answered the other, "who has set himself out to be a doctor of souls, wants to see the weak points of the people around him. No use being a doctor until the other people are ill, you know. So he's dropping the acid on you and wondering when it will work. He's wondering when you'll go up the gorge and visit the Garcias family."

"As a matter of fact," said the boy honestly, "I never thought of it till this moment."

"Oh, you'll start thinking of it pretty soon," said Slade. He smiled as he spoke. "I'm interested myself," he said, "in seeing what happens when you get to the Garcias house."

Young Grey left the house a little later and looked behind the house, but his host was not there. He went down toward the creek, sauntering idly.

The sun was in the middle of the heavens now; they had not been offered food, and his appetite was as keen as a hawk's. So he went to the place where the creek, as it ran chanting and singing through the valley, at last widened out and formed a comfortable pool. The images of the big pines that surrounded it fell into the clear water, and there was one gleaming point of white—the body of a man who stood on the margin and scrubbed himself thoroughly with soap and a rough horse brush. It was *Padre* José himself, who was having his bath, and the young man, having given him one glance, looked again with increased interest. For all the body of *Padre* José, except his arms and neck, was a bright rosy-red, as though it were breaking out in a rash.

Young Grey watched with interest, keeping in hiding while the old man got out of the water and dried himself with a scrap of rough cloth. He was as meager as a half-starved crane. But what was the red discoloration on the upper part of his body?

The solution presented itself in another moment. As old *Padre* José began to dress, the first garment he put on was a dark-colored shirt of a shapeless make, and, as the youth scrutinized it incredulously, he tried to make up his mind as to what it might be. It was not worn for the sake of warmth, that was certain. But it could hardly serve any other purpose. Then it flashed into the mind of Grey as the explanation of the reddened skin of the upper body of the old man, and a little shudder ran through him.

There had been martyrs of that sort in the olden days—men who wove for themselves with clumsy hand rude horsehair shirts that would cause a constant and maddening irritation, as though ten thousand mosquitoes were constantly biting the skin. There could be no careless and casual comfort for a man clad in such a garment of torment. And that might be the explanation of the hermit's discolored skin.

Grey, turning suddenly, like a guilty eavesdropper, walked back to the little hut. He had to speak to someone of what he had seen, he felt, but, when he came to the shack, he was amazed to find that his companion was not there. Slade had vanished, in spite of the fact that he had come to this place particularly in order to rest and be quiet. It seemed impossible that he could have gone off of his own volition. Who, then, could have compelled him?

He set about the task of hunting for signs, and he found them almost at once. The shoes of Slade were almost like moccasins, that is to say, the sole was of soft leather and sewed on flat, without any allowance made for a heel. He said that in his work, prospecting among the rocks of the mountains, he usually found it much safer to walk and climb in shoes like these. Some twenty yards from the door of the hut, in a bit of softer earth, Grey found the mark of such a shoe pointing outward. He went straight ahead, and fifty yards off he found the mark again, pointing definitely up the gorge.

Up the gorge, accordingly, went Lawrence Grey. But after a time he lost the trail. He thrust forward boldly, cutting from side to side, but the trail went out under his nose, and he could not locate it again. He kept on, however, although very soon he could guess that he had gone farther than Slade would have walked. He continued until he found the gorge pinching together, with more naked rocks and fewer trees, and so he came to what had been described to him—a sort of giant's staircase down which the creek plunged with a great roaring, dashing its waters into fine, flying dust. The trees on one side of the walls were drenched with the flying spray, and Grey went up the other side.

Even there the rocks were slippery enough, encrusted here and there with green mold and mosses. It was a stiffish climb, but at the top he had a reward, for he found a broad, flat plateau, with only a hint of a valley through which the upper waters of the creek flowed. Rocks and trees grew out of the bosom of the land, and far away he saw the front of the house of Garcias.

He could see the wrecked half of it from which the gigantic rubble of stone had been only partly cleared away. He could trace the slide above the house that had fallen upon the lost wing. The thing looked as though it had happened but a moment before, as though the dust had barely settled and the rest of the *casa* might be wrecked the following second.

There was a well-marked trail leading up beside the creek that wound directly toward the house, and this trail he followed. Upon this upland he found everything brighter and more cheerful after the narrower gloom of the gorge. The sun fell through the scattering of trees and made a random yellow pattern upon the ground. So elusive was the effect of these shadows that he hardly saw a doe and fawn until he had practically stumbled upon them, they were so thoroughly lost in the mingling of bright rocks and of dun shadows. They were not frightened, although he was close enough almost to put out a hand and touch them. They merely turned their pretty heads toward him. When he walked on, the fawn actually followed him a few steps, and then bounded back in a sudden foolish fear toward its mother.

Even Lawrence Grey smiled to find such trust and such idle fears among animals. There were city-dwelling people who lived as peaceably and with as much trust of one another, like sheep in a pen. Such a life was not for him. As well, he thought, be bred, raised, and forever work in a kindergarten. So thought he as he stepped lightly along, growing more and more alert to the things about him—the bird life that slipped through the sunny patches and the shadows, the creek with its waters sliding along with hardly a murmur, and a whisper and stir of four-footed life here and there in the shrubbery.

Slade had been right after all, and he had come straight up toward the house of Garcias as though led there by a line. He had to find out what manner of people were there.

In spite of his alertness, he nearly blundered into and spoiled a pleasant picture a moment later, for, as he rounded a great boulder near the edge of the water, he saw in a little clearing beyond a girl sitting on the ground and a swarm of fully twenty squirrels about her. One sat upon either shoulder, and, stretching their heads out, they scolded one another. Others were in her lap. And a big fellow stood up on her knee and ate something that he was holding between his paws, taking a bite, and then seemed to lecture the girl silently to her face.

Lawrence Grey felt that he had come to the end of the world; he remained transfixed and staring.

Chapter Twenty

She was dressed almost like any peon's daughter. She had on the plainest of dresses, unstockinged legs, and she wriggled her toes in the straps of the cheapest sort of sandals. There was only one note not in keeping with her attire—a heavy golden chain was thrice looped around her neck like a narrow collar.

She was in color warm ivory and black—ivory that has a tone of rose in it when the light looks through a translucent slab of it, and her hair was night dark, not glistening and thick, but fluffy and smoky as late twilight. It seemed to be puffing out of the band that gathered it at the nape of her neck.

She was feeding the squirrels. He watched her slim hands moving among them very slowly. The downward cast of her eyes and her solemn, unsmiling lips gave her a melancholy and thoughtful air. A Renaissance Italian would have painted her so and called his picture "The Madonna of the Squirrels".

Lawrence Grey grew a little giddy, and a fine, rosy mist spun before his eyes.

He hardly knew that she had looked up, when he heard her saying: "It's all right. You can walk along. They won't run away from you."

He canted his ear to the voice; it was so low and husky, rather as though she were recovering from a cold. He had a definite and physical sense of pleasure from her speech. Then it occurred to him as strange that she should speak English. He took off his hat to her in greeting.

"That's taken a lot of time," he said, coming slowly around the rock.

"I like it," said the girl. "They're such a vicious lot."

"Vicious?" he said. He came closer. Her attitude, her readiness to talk, gave him an excuse to halt.

"Yes, vicious," she said. "They're a regular breadline . . . pine-nut line, to be accurate. I have packs of pine nuts every time I come down here. That's why they seem to like me."

"Come, come," he said. "They like you. They're fond of you. That's why."

"You'd think so, to see the way they come dropping out of the trees like little monkeys when I appear," said the girl. "But they don't care a rap about me really. There's no more gratitude in 'em than there is in men for the mine out of which they dig the gold."

This casual air of hers delighted him. From the picture, he had expected the exquisite naïveté of a child. Instead he found a keen cynicism that braced his nerves and started his blood like the touch of a mountain wind.

"Have you tried 'em without the nuts?" he asked.

"Of course I have. Then they come flocking, just the same way. Sometimes a sick one will crawl into a pocket and lie there, glad of the warmth, but pretty soon the rest of them leave me and stand around in a circle and make speeches to me, and tell me that I'm no use and that I'm letting everything rip, and that they won't stand it. Oh, they're a precious lot."

"If they're like that," he said, "why do you feed them?"

"You know," she answered, "it's like living in cities. People don't live in town because they like other people, but because they're amused looking at the foolishness of the lot."

He nodded.

"It's a lesson, too," she said. "Look at Graybeard, here on my knee. He's the biggest of the lot. And that pretty little red thing over there . . . you see her by the chip? . . . she's his wife. This pig comes here and gorges. He eats till he bursts. And he never takes a thing away to store up. But when his poor little auburn-haired wife comes along, he jumps at her and gives her a terrible scolding. Only the men vote in his family, you can be sure. There's nothing advanced or modern about him. He's a cave man, a wife beater, and the king of the whole tribe. That's the reason for his kingship, I suppose."

"The beating of his wife, you mean?" asked Grey.

"Of course. The other squirrels wish they could do the same thing, and they feel that he's a great fellow because he manages to do what they don't dare."

"Why don't you give him a fillip and knock him out of his place of honor?" asked Grey.

"Why should I?" said the girl. "As long as he suits the squirrels, why shouldn't he suit me? He's the strongest, and so he wins the best place, and I pick out the biggest pine nuts. If I give him a partly spoiled one, he gets into a frightful tantrum. You watch." She presented Graybeard with a nut between tapered thumb and forefinger, and the big squirrel took it, tasted it, and at once spat it out, using his paws to knock it away to a distance. He ran straight up to the girl's shoulder, knocked from his seat a brother who was already there, and on that elevated platform Graybeard did a little dance of rage, barking and chattering in her ear.

"You see?" she said. "He's telling me if I dare to do that again, he'll bite me and put his mark on me. I won't dare to try that trick on the king again, I can tell you. He means business from now on."

Lawrence Grey sat down on a stone. "Well," he said, "to see you with 'em, one would think that you loved 'em all."

"I do, in a way," she said. "You know, we like things about that are smaller and weaker than we are. That's why we like children, I suppose. That's why we let children bully us . . . because we like to feel that it's all a sham and amounts to nothing, and that a brush of the hand would upset the king and change the whole squirrel state. Well, that's the way with us. It's not very admirable, but it makes us feel strong. And that's the best way to feel."

"You've been in the States," he said. "You talk like it."

"No. I haven't been in the States. But I had a rare good stroke of luck a few years ago," she said. "A good, handy gunman was run out of Texas and got down to San Vicente, and he heated up San Vicente, too, until it was about boiling, and so they gave him a run that landed him at our house. He stayed on for a long time. He almost lost a leg from an infection that set in. In fact, if it hadn't been for *Padre* José, he would have lost his leg. As it was, he had to stay long enough with us to polish up my English a bit. But as soon as he could hobble, he borrowed a mule from us and rode north again."

"Stole a mule, you mean?" suggested Grey.

"We thought so, at first, but after a while he sent us down three times the price of the mule. After that, whenever my birthday came around . . . and Christmas and Easter . . . he used to send down big sums of money. He said he was doing very well at his trade. We never knew any address to write to him, though, and tell him that we couldn't take his money. It's all laid away and waiting for him."

"What's his trade?" asked Grey.

"Bank robbing, mostly," she replied calmly. "And sometimes he does a little counterfeiting. But he says that counterfeiting is a bore, because it takes so much time and one has to have such a plant. Perhaps you know how it is?"

"No. Not exactly," said Grey, smiling. "What's the name of this fellow?"

"He called himself Leonard Smith when he was here," she

said. "I don't know his name. He was red-headed, and he had a good, hearty laugh. He was wild to get back to his own country again."

"To hunt for more money?" asked Grey.

"No, not that. But he was a king, d'you see, like Graybeard, here. And it happened that another fellow up there had elbowed him out of place, knocked his crown all to one side, and blacked his eye a little, so to speak. He wanted to get back at him. He used to practice snap-shooting for an hour a day with his revolver. It was a wonderful sight to see him."

"Who had bumped his crown askew?" asked Grey.

"A fellow he called Rinky Dink." She laughed a little, looking before her at the image of the red-headed man. "Rinky Dink's a funny name, isn't it?" she said.

"It is," said Grey.

"Well, my redhead hated Rinky Dink."

"Because of the black eye?" asked Grey.

"No. Because this fellow Rinky Dink is a frigate bird. A pirate among the pirates. He robs the robbers. And Leonard Smith thought that that was pretty low."

"I suppose that it is," said Grey, "in a way. It's against the rules of the profession. This chap you speak of . . . it seems to me that I may have met him. He had a small mole under his right eye, didn't he?"

"That's the one! What was *his* name? Leonard Smith?"

Yes. That was Leonard Smith. Also, he was Missouri Slim, and Good-Time Harry, and Harry the Hop, and a lot of other names."

"He was good fun to talk to," said the girl. "And how he hated Rinky Dink. When he said good bye to me, he asked me to pray that he'd beat Rinky Dink. I've done it ever since. I've prayed every night."

"Hard luck," said Grey.

"Why?"

"Well, I was just thinking of the wasted time."

"Wasted?"

"He met Rinky Dink a few months ago," said Grey. "And he had a lot of bad luck."

"Horrible!" gasped the girl. "What happened?"

"It wasn't Smith's fault," said Grey. "He did his best. He had a couple of friends along with him, and he came in behind Rinky Dink, when Rinky Dink was sitting in at a game of poker. But it happened that the chap opposite to Rinky Dink was a good friend, and he kicked Rinky Dink under the table, so Rinky Dink did a rolling side dive for the floor and started shooting."

"What happened?" asked the girl.

"Oh, it was pretty much of a mess all around. But it was hard on Smith. He's only wearing one arm now, and that's his left."

"He came in behind, did he?" asked the girl.

"Yes," said Grey. "Smith was always a very careful sort of a fellow."

Chapter Twenty-One

She lifted the squirrels suddenly to the ground. They swarmed back at her, and two of them were running up her dress again as she stood up. They scolded her vigorously, and Graybeard actually got to her shoulder before she managed to lay hands on him and put him back on the ground. Then, in a little swirl of russet and gray, they ran about her feet, but at last darted off, each for its particular tree.

"Sorry for the pine nuts, but not a bit sorry to lose me," said the girl. Yet she laughed a little as she said it. "Are you going on to the house?" she asked.

He stood beside her. She was quite tall, and he regretted that he had not a few more inches. As it was, there was no question of looking comfortably down upon her. Her eyes, it seemed to the boy, were upon a level with his own, and he carefully kept himself to his full height.

"I'm not invited," said Grey. "I just came up the valley from *Padre* José's place. I thought I could have a look at things."

"Come on," she said. "Father's always glad to have a stranger or two around. He likes to sit down with pipes and beer and talk about things. He likes to gather news. He only gets outside about once in three years."

Grey was glad to go along, and, since the trail was reasonably wide, they could walk abreast most of the time.

He said: "Is this a good life? Do you like it up here?"

"Oh, you know," she answered. "It's all right. There are some mules and horses to ride. We have enough to eat, and plenty of firewood to keep us warm after the snows begin. It's all right for me while I'm still in school."

"You go to school, do you?" he asked.

"I mean," she said, "it's all right while I'm getting ready to break out."

"What do you mean by that?" he queried.

"What all young persons mean," she answered. "You've had your break. You've exploded. That's why there's a contented look in your eye, of course. I'll wager that you've done enough to write a book."

He turned upon her the most innocent eyes in the world. "I don't know why you should say that," he said.

She snapped her fingers. "Nobody could know about Smith as well as you do," she said, "unless he'd seen a good deal of the world. Just from talking to you, I'll wager that I could tell your nickname."

"I don't think you could," he said. "I've never been in this part of the world before."

She laughed again. "Do you think that he would have talked so much about you without even describing Rinky Dink's appearance," she demanded, "right down to the pink and white of his skin?"

Grey nodded. "All right," he said. "I should have thought of that."

"He really came up behind you?" she added.

"Yes."

"Then he deserved what he got," she said. "I'm sorry for him. He made a break in our life up here."

"And when you explode, as you put it," he said, "what will you do?"

"See things. See people and places, and take the luck that comes my way," she answered. She changed the subject. "You're down there with *Padre* José? What d'you think about him?"

"He's a fine old man," said the boy.

"Humph!" she declared. "He's not fine. He's been beaten. That's why he's so humble. I like a dog that fights when it's cornered. But *Padre* José's been beaten until he whines. He whines still. He wears a rough shirt. He makes a martyr out of himself. But all the same, I don't respect him very much. People ought to have tough skins and hard fists, I think. I have a hard fist," she added. And she clenched her hand and shook it at the world.

He smiled at her. "*Padre* José is as good as they come," he told her. "He does things for other people. He doesn't sit on a stone and pray for his soul."

"Bother *Padre* José," said the girl. "I can talk to him and about him every day. Tell me about yourself. What do you do in the world, Rinky Dink? Did Smith tell me some of the truth?"

"Well, what did he tell you?"

"Oh, he told me that you are what he called slick. He said that you could fade out through a six-foot stone wall or float in through a keyhole. He said that you could turn a glass of water into a six-gun aimed at a man's heart. He said a lot of complimentary things about you, Rinky Dink. Or should I call you Mister Rinky Dink?"

"Rinky Dink's enough for me," he said. "I'll tell you what I do. I just ramble around and take things easy."

"Is that all?"

"That's all."

"And do you make as much money as he said?"

"I make enough to live on most of the time," he said.

"Easy money, I suppose?"

"Well, it's easy sometimes." He frowned as he made a strong effort at visualization. "Sometimes," he said, "I have my bad spots. I've been sixty hours without water where it's pretty hot.

I've been nine days without food where it was pretty cold. Yes, I've had my stomach shrunk a good many times. I've had enough to give me bad dreams the rest of my life. So I can't call it easy money, I suppose, in the long run."

"It doesn't make you older," she observed.

"Because I only take care of myself," he answered. "That doesn't make a man old. It's when he's hitched up to a load to draw . . . that's when he ages pretty fast. A wife and kids and such things. But I travel light. Is that the house ahead there through the trees?"

"That's the house."

They came out close before it, and Grey paused for a moment. The face of it was seamed and wrinkled, like the face of a man. The heavy walls seemed all out of plumb, leaning a trifle to one side or to the other. There was a sense breathed from the place as from a man who is not very old, but tired of life. It seemed ready to sink to the ground.

"I'll hunt up Father for you," she said as they came into the patio. "You wait over in that room. I may have to spend ten minutes or so locating him. There are some books and things over in that room. Sit down and make yourself at home."

She left him there, and he, taking note of the patio, decided that he never had been in a place more down at the heel. There had once been a fountain in the center, its spray received into a broad bowl, big as a small swimming pool. But the fountain was dead now, and the stones were cracked across. What had once been the figure of a stag as the central piece was now broken by time, many winters of frost and springs of thawing, until it was like an image seen through a fog. Once there had been a garden along the edge of the patio, but the beds were filled with weeds and with dried stalks. Only over the walls a cloud of climbing vines was falling like green water frozen in mid-leap.

He went on through the open door of the room that had

been pointed out to him. The door was open, apparently, because the top hinge was broken, which made it difficult to pull the heavy door back and forth. From the furrow worn in the stones and the blunted lower corner of the door, it was plain that the door had not been lifted, as a rule, but simply dragged back and forth. How long had the door been hanging from one hinge? Months, perhaps—all through the preceding winter, one would have said.

Inside, the room was fitted up as a library, but there were not many books. He pulled a *Don Quixote* from a shelf. The front edge was ragged. Dust fell out from between the pages as he opened the volume, and half the print was gone. The binding, of a good, strong buckram, was discolored and warped. He put the book back. The room appeared a gloomy place to him—a prison, in a way; in fact, it seemed to be the reminder of better days.

On the floor lay a single big rug, heel-worn and moth-eaten. As Grey looked around, he decided that savages might as well have been residing in this place as white people who allowed it to go downhill so far. As for the books, he could have sworn that no one had touched them from one year's end to the other.

And this was the atmosphere in which the girl lived!

Then he thought of Missouri Slim wandering through the big, moldy rooms of the old house, drawling out to the girl's ear his viewpoint of life, his philosophy of rascality, his hard, callous wisdom. Of all the men he knew, Missouri was one of the least admirable. Grey felt he could understand why Missouri had troubled to send back money to the house. It was because he had his eye on the girl and still kept her in his mind. The two bullets that had left so little for the doctor to do in the removal of Missouri's right arm—they had also removed hope from his mind, no doubt.

Grey did not regret. Regrets, in fact, seldom came to trouble him by night, and never during the day.

There was an old atlas on the table filled with odd, early maps that bore figures of dragons writhing in the unexplored corners of the sea. It also showed storm winds impersonated by speeding devils with puffed cheeks and harassed ships staggering before the weight of the gale under reduced sail. He turned the pages of this slowly. Half of his mind was bent upon the book and half his attention was given to the drone of bees, wasps, and flies that sounded like far-off horns blowing in a weird harmony all together.

So, in his thoughts vaguely mingled all the strange forms and names and figures that had entered his quest—the marshal in the far-off city, the dying Forbes in Pittsburgh, the rascally rest of the family striving to thwart his efforts to find a worthy heir, the mysterious disappearance of John Ray, the distant sheriff, dead Jarvis, General O'Riley, Slade, *Padre* José, even Murcio, the innkeeper, and this Isabella Garcias, this adopted daughter of a dying house.

Said a polite voice in Spanish behind him: "One moment of your attention, *señor.*"

He turned his head, and through the barred window on the farther side of the room he saw the lean face of Cordoba squinting one eye down the sights of a large-caliber shotgun.

Chapter Twenty-Two

When it came to taking chances, there was hardly a thing in the world that Grey would not adventure. But there is always the exception that proves the rule, and in his case the exception was shotguns. He disliked them with a profound passion. They were not his weapons, for one thing. He did not go out to shoot birds, or to try at deer with buckshot. Birds or beasts, he preferred a rifle for long range work and a revolver at close hand.

Now he simply lifted his arms slowly above his head. "All right, Cordoba," he said. "You have me." At the same instant he was thinking of possible maneuvers—of hurling himself backward in his chair, for instance, pulling his revolver as he fell and shooting toward that window before he struck the floor.

"No tricks, *Señor* Grey," said a voice from the opposite direction.

He turned back. Another double-barreled shotgun was leveled toward him from the half-open door to the patio. Blinding white sun slanted into that court, so that the figure of the marksman was darkened almost to a solid black. He saw a man of middle age, solidly built, with black hair worn very long.

"I am your host, Garcias," said the newcomer. "I came hurrying so that I could pay my compliments at once. I have been waiting for you, *señor.* I was very glad when my daughter told me that you were here."

"What a little world it is," said Grey admiringly.

"A small world, but still large enough for a good many twists and turns," said Garcias, coming slowly into the room. "Keep a good aim, Cordoba. There, that's better, now that I'm out of line with your gun." He had worked his way down the wall, so his gun commanded Grey from a safer angle.

"Now, Mister Grey, just keep your arms raised. Turn toward the window and walk until your breast is against the barrels of the gun. No sudden jumps. No leaps, no throwings upon the floor. We watch you like a trained bird and expect you to do surprising things. The guns are loaded with double charges, heavy buckshot. They both scatter widely, even at short range. You could not dodge out of the field of one of them, to say nothing of two. A blind man could kill you, my friend, by pointing the gun in the direction of your voice, merely, and pulling one of the triggers. There you are. Rise very slowly. That's well. Now walk slowly, slowly toward the window. Very good, indeed. Ha, Cordoba! It was a very wise man who told us to use shotguns with him."

Cordoba's lean, sour face relaxed in a faint grin of satisfaction.

And Grey walked straight up until the double barrels of the shotgun were pressing against his breast.

"That will do nicely," said Garcias. "Keep the hands steadily up, as though you were reaching for something with both arms. I intend to search you. Be very still. I shorten my gun, take it under one arm. With the muzzles still touching you and my forefinger around both of the triggers . . . hair-triggers they are . . . I go through your pockets. All the while you stand very still. You listen, as it were." He laughed a little, softly, the breath coming out with a whistling sound on the neck of Grey.

In the meantime, with deliberate hands, the Mexican went through the clothes of Grey. He produced a considerable collection, although Grey was traveling light. For Garcias found a revolver under either armpit, another inside the band of the trousers, together with a heavy Bowie knife and a small, narrow-bladed dirk, like a stiletto, so keen that its own weight was almost enough to drive its needle point through a victim's heart.

"That's about all," said Garcias.

"I have irons for his hands," suggested Cordoba, outside the window.

"Irons for his hands?" said Garcias. "Irons for these delicate and subtle hands? Tut-tut, my lad. They think nothing of handcuffs. They slide out through them without difficulty. Even through ones made to order. All fits are too big for his subtlety, I tell you. But an end of rope would do well. Pass it through the bars. No, I have some cord with me, which will be better than rope. Watch him carefully, Cordoba. Mind you, this means something to your pocketbook."

"I watch him as a starving fox watches a stupid mountain grouse," said Cordoba. "But why did they warn us so much about him?"

"Because they were wise," said the other. "Because they leave nothing to chance. God bless forethoughted men like them. Now down with your hands, *amigo.* Down with them, slowly and steadily, bending the arms in behind your back. That's the very way. You are amiable and intelligent, *amigo.* I feel sorry for you. This will do very well. Now, Cordoba, I'm about to put my shotgun aside, and tie these famous hands on the middle of our friend's back. While I am working, if he so much as coughs or twists to the side, or speaks, give him both barrels. Living or dead, it's the same in our pockets."

"Do you need to caution me?" said Cordoba. "I would send him flying down to perdition with joy. By the grace of heaven, I shall be married on this money. The most beautiful girl in the world is waiting for me, *Señor* Garcias. Do you think that I could be careless, now?"

"Very good," said Garcias. He laid his shotgun aside.

Grey could hear the faint squeak of the rope as one end of it was tied, probably into a slip noose. He had been forbidden speech, but he risked it, although without stirring in his position before the muzzles of the shotgun. "Why do you save me?" he said, "if I'm worth as much dead as alive?"

"Because I don't want the girl to hear the shot," said Garcias frankly. "Women have nerves. Even Isabella has a nerve or two in her otherwise perfect constitution. They have scruples, too. And even she has one or more in her otherwise resolute nature. No, no, my dear young man, I haven't wanted to stain the floor of my house with you. Besides, my employer and rewarder wishes, if possible, that you may be kept alive until he comes to speak to you for a moment. He wants to talk with you, and then he wants to see you die."

"Very well," said young Grey.

Señor Garcias, behind his back, cursed the knot he had tied and apparently started to make a new one.

"And here's poor Cordoba," said Grey, to the lean-faced man before him.

"Poor Cordoba?" said the Mexican, grinning. "Well, if I pity myself today, may I never be lucky again."

"Well, well," said Grey. "Let it go. Though I can't help wondering how *Padre* José will make it right with you."

"Make what right?" asked Cordoba.

"You don't guess as yet?" said Grey with pity in his voice.

"Guess?" said Cordoba. "What should I guess about a man as clear as snow water?"

Grey sighed. "Well," he said, "there's the advantage of having a man with a reputation. And well the two of them knew it when they took you to *Padre* José."

"What two?" asked the bandit harshly.

"What two?" Grey smiled. "Why, the two who gulled you, of

course. Who else?"

"What two?" said Cordoba again, half lifting his glance from his gun to the face of the man he questioned.

The heart of Grey leaped violently. But he maintained the calmness of his smile. "The girl and Juan Gil, of course," said Grey carelessly. "What did they want except a day to throw you off your guard. It is too late for you to interfere now. They are safely at the church by this time."

"Sacred Mother!" gasped Cordoba, blanching. Then he freshened his grasp upon the gun. "You think you can take my eye from your breast, *señor,*" he said, "but in that hope you are a fool."

"Poor Cordoba," said Grey, "do you think that a man about to die would trouble with a wretch like you? I pity you, however. You were gulled so easily."

Cordoba began to pant. "It is all a lie," he said. "María loves me. She had been in a torment for fear she would be married off to that empty wit!"

Grey smiled again. "Come, now, Cordoba," he said. "In ways that don't touch women, you're a sensible fellow. Do you think that any girl would see much in a scarecrow like you, dressed up in false feathers? Great heavens, man, haven't you a mirror to look in or a pool to bend over?"

The slip noose was now fitted over his right wrist and drawn tight, while Garcias grunted softly with satisfaction. So hard did he draw the cord that it bit painfully through the flesh of Grey.

Cordoba, gray-green with emotion, tried twice to speak before he could manage the words. "That dog of a Juan Gil," he hissed, "he knows that I would cut out his heart."

"Poor Cordoba," said Grey. "Don't you know that two gendarmes are waiting for you now? Two straight-shooting fellows who will take perfectly good care that you don't come near to the newly married pair."

"You lie!" moaned Cordoba.

"Come. What is this talk? Attention, Cordoba!" said Garcias angrily.

"He's wincing from the truth like a dog from the whip," said Grey. "He's up here hunting for his girl, while she is listening to the church bells ringing. Tush, Cordoba, do you think Juan Gil would have taken the thing so calmly if it had not been a put-up job?"

Cordoba, his face convulsed, ventured one upward glance toward Lawrence Grey, as though to seek for some sort of silent confirmation there.

And Grey, that instant, whipped his left hand from behind his body and reached for the muzzle of the shotgun.

Chapter Twenty-Three

Who can say what makes the hand fast and the hand slow? It is some mental stoppage in the latter instance, some dam of thinking that prevents the free flow from the subconscious brain to the muscles.

So the Mexican, looking up to the face of Grey, although set and fixed for shooting at the first intimation of movement, although he saw in the eyes of the boy a glint of the coming danger, did not pull the triggers over which his right forefinger was hooked.

The least part of a second later he pulled them, to be sure, but by that time the thrust of Grey's hand had knocked the big double muzzle upward, and both chambers exploded so as to send a roar of shot and fumes just over the shoulder of his coat, scorching the fabric and shearing some of it away. The kick of the weapon, at the same time, almost knocked the gun out of the grasp of Cordoba and jerked him halfway around.

Grey, his left hand high above his head from the upstroke he had made, whirled on his heel as Garcias, with a wild screech of terror and surprise, grappled with him. So the boy twisted a little in the grasp and brought down the hard knuckles of his fist behind the ear of the man. As a slung shot falls, so fell the hand of Grey, and Garcias stumbled backward, his knees loosened and his body sagging, his hands thrust down to prevent his utter fall.

Cordoba, outside the window, realized the little trick of

language that had unnerved him and, cursing bitterly, threw away the shotgun and snatched at a revolver. When his grip was on its handle, he saw his enemy sweeping a pair of revolvers from the table.

That was enough for Cordoba. He was a very brave fellow, but he preferred a reasonable share of good luck to what was no better than an even chance against such a foeman. His brain had worked too sluggishly the instant before. It leaped to conclusions now as a deer leaps when the silent huntsman shoots into its grazing ground. He remembered, now, in a dazzling instant, some of the grave words that had been spoken in his hearing about this same man, and how it was better to take chances with a high explosive than with him.

So Cordoba leaped to the side. He sprang as though there were water and not hard earth beneath him. He toppled head over heels, but he fell well beyond the angle of young Grey's possible fire and, tumbling to his feet, staggered into full speed and made for his tethered mustang, behind the house of Garcias.

Garcias himself could not regain his balance. He staggered against the wall and on the recoil fell limply to his knees.

This Grey saw, and, instead of making a hostile move against the man, he stepped to the embrasure of the big window, reached through the bars, and, taking the shotgun by the muzzle, drew it inside the room. In a way, this secured him from attack in that direction. Even now he did not turn his attention at once to the dazed Garcias. Instead, although he kept a steady eye upon him, as a cat watches a mouse, he slipped to the table, picked up the rest of his weapons, and in an instant they had disappeared beneath his coat.

He saw Garcias blunder to his feet again, but still he did not draw a gun. He waited, and Garcias could understand the significance of the pause. It was simply an invitation to defend himself, to do more than defend himself, by making the first move to attack. But he who has been within the claws of a panther does not relish a new duel with the beast. Garcias merely stared and waited in his turn, as a man waits for lightning to drop out of the sky.

Footfalls raced across the patio now, and Isabella Garcias came rushing into the room. She glanced at the two men, wild-eyed, and then she cried out: "When I heard the gun, I had a wild thought, all at once, but nobody's hurt?" Her glance flashed from one to the other, and Grey, watching her and her foster father, felt a queer pinch of the heart, for the older man stood with a gray face to receive sentence.

Perhaps some thought of his own past came over Grey, then, and some dark memories of crimes in the other days and sins in this. But he said: "I've been playing the fool. We no sooner meet than we begin to talk about hunting . . . because your father came in with this gun . . . and I start telling him how I got seven ducks with one lucky shot one time . . . and there, you see?" He pointed to the ceiling and shook his head. "I'm sorry," he said to Garcias, "that such a thing had to happen."

Garcias gathered himself rapidly together, but he felt the coolness of his own face and the damp on his forehead, for he wiped it off. "It was a shock, Isabella," he said. "For an instant, with the roar of the gun in my ears, I felt as though something had struck me." He laid his hand over his heart and laughed shakily.

Isabella, looking keenly, critically at him, said: "You need a bracer. I'll run and get you a glass of cognac. You look like a ghost . . . you look ten years older." She ran from the room.

And it left Garcias alone with Grey.

He even made a gesture with one hand after the girl, as though to stop her, but he changed his mind in time. He stood before the boy with misery in his face. "Well, man?" he asked.

"I don't know," said Grey slowly. "You did the thing as

though you liked doing it. That's what sticks in my throat. You went after me as though I were a wild beast." Then he added: "This is your house, Garcias. I came here as a guest of your daughter, you might say."

Garcias blinked. He grew sicker in color than before. "Let me tell you the whole truth. You came here not as a man at all. You came here as fifty thousand dollars."

The boy whistled. "Fifty thousand dollars to you if you polished me off?"

"Fifty thousand. And two thousand to Cordoba. There's the whole story. I think I'd do it again . . . for fifty thousand dollars."

"Why?" asked Grey. "I thought you'd lived here quietly out of choice? I thought that you'd left the world?"

"I had," said Garcias. "I'd stay here forever. But what of her? You don't know her. Every bit of her soul yearns for the outside world. I would have cut your throat, man, and had no compunction. I would have felt as though the blood that poured out of you were dollars for Isabella." He looked hopelessly across the room at young Grey. Then, taking hold of the back of a chair, he lowered himself into it like a half-lifeless bulk. He put his face between his hands. He was shaking like a man struck with a violent chill. He gestured toward the door. "This rotten story . . . she'll see through it. She sees through everything. She knows that there's something wrong. That's why she went out, not to get the cognac, but because she wants to give us a chance to patch up something. She saw that I was done for. She wants to let us patch up our lie a little. Our hunting lie." He laughed again and his laughter was like a groan that racked him.

Then Grey dipped into his mind, sifted as it were, a dozen things that he could easily have spoken, some terse expression of disgust, some reference, perhaps, to another day in the life of this man when there had been a hunting accident. Instead, he said: "You know, Garcias, that all of us have certain days that we want to forget. Days when we're drunk, let's say, in one way or another . . . when we're dizzy, and out of our heads. We don't want our friends to remember 'em. We rub them out of our own memories. Well, I've had days like that, and this is one for you. Suppose you forget it. Pull yourself together. Say you had a shock. You felt it in your heart. That's all right. I'll keep a cool face. Do the same for yourself."

Garcias made a gesture of gratitude and misery. And then the girl came back into the room.

Grey watched her narrowly, but there seemed no hint of anything in her expression other than solicitude for her foster father.

She poured out a glass of cognac for him, and then insisted that he should lie down. He obeyed her willingly, obviously only anxious to get away from observation. She took him away, her arm hooked in his, walking with a gay step and laughing a little at his nerves. She called to Grey that she would be back in a moment, and she was as good as her word.

"Father's had a real shock," she said. "He's still trembling a good deal, and he's white around the mouth."

"Things that take one by surprise," said Grey, "they're pretty upsetting."

Suddenly she was looking straight into his face, with narrowed eyes. "How many thousands of times d'you think that Father has had guns go off practically in his ear?" she asked.

Grey shrugged his shoulders.

"Besides," she went on, "that shotgun was loaded with buckshot. And who would load with heavy shot around here, where nothing is ever aimed at except birds and mighty few of those?" She made a little gesture. "I saw where the shot ripped through the ceiling," she said. "They would have blown the life out of half a dozen men, as easily as not." Here she paused, still facing Grey. "Tell me." she commanded. "What actually happened in that library?"

"A gun went off," he said.

She laughed impatiently. "I know that things were patched up before I came in. But you were not holding that gun."

"How do you know that?" he asked her.

"You've handled too many guns," she said. "You wouldn't make such mistakes."

"Very well," said Grey. "That's all I have to say. A gun went off in the library. And no harm was done whatever."

He paused with her at the old patio entrance. She seemed to him to be somewhere between the moldering age of the place and an eternal freshness of youth.

"You might as well talk it out now," she said. "It will have to come out sooner or later, you know."

"I'm going home to ask *Padre* José," he said. "I've been pretty far away, and I'm going to ask his advice."

Chapter Twenty-Four

When he was a little distance off, he turned and found her still at the patio gate, looking thoughtfully after him. He waved his hat to her and went on into the woods. He felt as he had never felt before, that he wanted help, and he did exactly what he had told the girl he was going to do. He asked *Padre* José for advice.

When he got back to the stone hut—it seemed more of a tomb than a dwelling place—he found Slade stretched on the willow bed, and the boy demanded rather severely why he had left the place.

Slade merely grinned at him and said indistinctly, through his teeth: "Because I'm a fool, son. The thought of that creek haunted me. I went up the creek and tried that fishing line. It seemed to me that I'd die if I didn't get a hook into that water."

"Up the creek?" said Grey.

"Up a little branch of it," said Slade. "I found a spot where fish had to be. I could see the loom of 'em. But they wouldn't come near my bait."

Grey turned away rather thoughtfully, thinking how much a mere fishing trip had launched. At the door, his back half turned, he made his report: "They're going to make things hum for us here, Slade," he said. He told of his adventure in the Casa Garcias. He left out most of the girl's part. As for the squirrels, he said nothing at all about them.

When he had finished, Slade answered: "I see how it is. We've got to start on. If they're as close as that, they'll smoke you out of here in no time. This scratch of mine is nothing. I can walk as well as the next man."

"Slade," said the boy, "you got that hurt trying, with your empty hands, to tackle a fellow who had been trying to murder me. Do you think that I can let you go now, and turn that wound into a festering sore, with what results no man can say? No, we'll stay here and I'll keep them off for two more days."

He left the house to prevent argument, and in the garden behind the house he found *Padre* José patiently working away at the soil with a great hoe, whose blade was a foot across. The old man gasped a little with every stroke, although he kept patiently at his labor.

Grey took the hoe from him and began to strike the ground with it vigorously. But it was an awkward instrument and he made poor progress. It kept turning in his hands and striking on the corner. He began to sweat, and, seeing the shadow of *Padre* José still on the ground beside him, he looked up and found the white-haired old man smiling at him.

"That's enough," said *Padre* José. "Whatever you have to ask of me, you have paid enough already. Your hands, my son, should not be rubbed to a blister. They're not accustomed to such hard labor, or to grasping such rough wood."

Grey straightened with a chuckle. "It's true," he said. "I want to bribe you. I want to have your advice."

"There's nothing so cheap with an old man," answered *Padre* José, "as words. Here's a tree for shade, a pair of rocks for chairs, some good turf for a carpet, and a blue ceiling for our audience chamber. Now, then, my son, tell me what foolish thing you have done."

"I didn't say that I'd done a foolish thing," answered Grey. "I said that I wanted advice."

"No one wants advice," said the other, "unless he has done something he regrets."

"When Cordoba and Juan Gil," said the boy, "came up to you with María, I couldn't see what your answer was to be, unless you frightened Cordoba into keeping his hands off. But I think that you gave the right answer after all. Now see if you can answer me."

"Speak, then," said *Padre* José. He took out a corncob bowl, fitted a narrow stem into it, and, having packed in some tobacco, he began to smoke. The sweat of his labor was still rising on his forehead and running down into his snowy brows. He did not give all his attention to the boy, but looked, also, across the gorge and into the shadows among the trees.

Then Grey spoke: "I'm anchored here. I came to Mexico to find a man. To get him I had to secure a guide first. The guide is badly hurt fighting for me. While the guide is getting well and I stand by, the enemy tries to take my scalp."

"Leave your friend here in the hut with me," said *Padre* José, "and go on with your own work."

"I need him as a guide."

"Take another."

"I could get another, but not a man I could trust. *Señor* Slade has already risked his life for me, like a hero."

"*Señor* Slade," said the old shepherd, "has the air of a brave man. Still, you could find another guide to help you. It is better to do that than to let Slade be the bait that draws you into a trap and holds you there."

"I cannot leave him at once," said the boy.

"You could, I think," said *Padre* José. "There is something else that keeps you here."

"What?" asked the boy.

"What keeps young men?" asked *Padre* José, of himself. "Money, adventure, or pretty women. There is no money here. Of adventure you have already had too much. Therefore, it is a girl. Did you look a little too closely at María? No, she would not fill your eye. It is, therefore, Isabella Garcias."

He said it so calmly and quietly that the boy hardly realized what had been said. Then he quivered from head to foot.

"There is a demon in you," he said. "You could not have guessed that, *Padre* José."

"It was an easy guess. I saw you walking up the valley," said the shepherd. "I know that that trail leads to the Casa Garcias. You come home again walking in a trance. You walk out to help an old man with his hoeing. What could it be but Isabella Garcia?"

"Tell me," said the boy, no longer protesting. "Do you know her?"

"I have seen her many times," said *Padre* José. "I have seen her in illness and health, sadness and gladness, childhood and girlhood. But why do you ask if I know her? This blue sky over us, my son . . . who of us can say that he knows it, or the substance, or the space, or the height of it? Yet we see it every day. And it seems to me that every human soul in this world is as vast a thing, as strange a color . . . and, though we see a brother every day, how can we know him? Furthermore, how can a man know a woman? No, I cannot say that I know Isabella Garcias. But if you ask me if I have thoughts about her, then I answer . . . yes."

"Tell me your thoughts," said the boy.

"Would you carelessly ask a miser," said the old man, "for the key to his treasure?" He smiled as he gave the gentle rebuff.

Grey answered: "Well, I've seen her with her squirrels, in the first place. I suppose you know about them?"

"She probably saw you coming from a distance," said the shepherd. "There are places from which the trail can be seen to a great distance. And so she arranged a pleasant picture for you."

The boy flushed. "Now, that's unfair," said Grey. "Why

should she have been spying down the trail?"

"What else does she do, every day," said the shepherd, "except look down there toward the gate that leads to the outer world?"

"But why should she?" persisted Grey.

"Do you know what the Arab says of the mare when it walks out from the tent in the morning, raises its head, and looks into the eye of the horizon?"

"I don't know," said the boy.

"The Arab vows," said the shepherd, "that in the mind of the mare there is only this question . . . when will my master come over the rim of the world?"

"Hai!" exclaimed Grey angrily. "Do you think that of her?"

"Of course, I do," said the shepherd. "And it's not to her discredit. It's to her praise. Your weak wit shrinks from destiny, but your great spirit leans out and stretches both hands toward it. It is so with her. When she saw you walking up the trail, she asked herself if you might be destiny, after all? So you found her with the squirrels."

"I went with her to her father's house," said the boy. "What do you think of him?"

"I rarely think of him," said *Padre* José. "He is one of God's creatures, I suppose, but somehow I rarely think of him."

Grey smiled. "He had a trap laid ready for me. Cordoba, María's friend, helped him spring it. They had me cornered, too, as badly as I've ever been, but, by a stroke of luck, I managed to get away. A gun went off in the course of things. No one was hurt, but Cordoba ran away. Then the girl came hurrying in to see what had really happened, and. . . ." He paused.

"You said there had been an accident?" suggested the old man.

Grey exclaimed with utter amazement: "There is a demon in you!"

The shepherd shook his head. "I have been young, also," he

said. "Also, I have been in love."

Grey sighed. "Now tell me what I am to do?" he said.

The shepherd sighed. "Good advice would never be followed. Safe and sane advice would be for you to leave Slade with me and hurry out of this valley. If you must have Slade, have him meet you at another place when he is healed. But why should one give safe and sane advice to a fire-eater? The fire-eater must have the fire, or die of spiritual starvation. Therefore, I say, stay here. Meet the dangers. Love them. Accept them. Dance with them when they come. Make furious love to Isabella Garcias. Dream of her. Adore her. Afterward, let things happen as fate rules they must happen. That is my advice to you."

Grey looked at him with great eyes. "You speak," he said, "as if you were already living inside my mind. You speak out of my own heart, *señor.*"

The shepherd waved his hand. It was brown and callous, but the fingers were, nevertheless, shapely and slender. "There is a sort of universality in old age," he said. "Tell me now, my son, what man it is that you hunt for?"

"A dead man, it may be," said the boy. "A man named Juan Ray, who was once very rich and lived in San Vicente."

"Juan Ray?" said the shepherd. "Well, I have heard of him, too, though it takes a great noise to be heard from San Vicente to this place. But that was many years ago. For fifteen years, I have seldom heard men speak of Juan Ray."

"He's dead, I suppose," said the boy.

"Dead, perhaps," said the shepherd. "For that matter, I sometimes think that we all die not once, but many times. Who is today what he was ten years before? But this Juan Ray is surely dead. When he lived, there was a great deal of talk about him, even up here in the distant mountains."

"He may be dead," said Grey, "but, if he's dead, why should people offer fifty thousand dollars for my death?"

"Fifty thousand? Fifty thousand dollars?" cried the shepherd. "That is a great sum! Why should they offer so much?"

"For fear that I may find this same man, do you see? They're afraid that I may be able to find Juan Ray. If I did, a great deal of money would come to him."

The shepherd shook his head. "I try to understand these things," he said. "But, after all, it is a little difficult. If you find Juan Ray, a great deal of money comes to him, and some other people are trying to keep you from reaching him for that reason. It seems a strange story, my friend. Is it a great sum of money, then?"

"Six millions," said the boy dreamily. "That's all. You can turn it into *pesos,* if you want to. Six million dollars for *Señor* Juan Ray, if I can find him."

The shepherd made a soft, singing sound. "That would be as much as he threw away, perhaps? Yes, and much more. Poor Juan Ray. If he could know, he would turn in his grave, would he not? He would turn and try to rise, and his ghost would come hunting for you and the money." He paused before adding: "And with a great deal of money, also, they hired you to undertake this dangerous trail, my son?"

"Oh," said the boy, "you know how it is with a fellow. You've said it before. I had to have something to do. And then a friend of mine asked me to do this." He sighed and smiled at the same time, thinking of the battered and weary face of the marshal in that far northern city. But, after all, the marshal could be called a friend. He added: "I get expenses, and a little plus. I don't know how much."

"And the game of it?" The shepherd smiled.

"Yes, the game of it," said the boy.

"And now a hurt friend on your hands and enemies around you, with a lovely girl to go mad about in addition . . . treachery and danger breathing out of the ground. What advice can I give to you, my son? Only this, to rejoice in every priceless moment of your life, for now you are living, and all the rest of the men in the world are dead."

Chapter Twenty-Five

The hoeing was abandoned for that day, and the old shepherd took Grey through the woods to a berry patch where the fruit was half a blooming red and half a ripe, bursting purple-black. They picked a quantity, until the mosquitoes began to gather in clouds and drove them back.

All the gorge was filled with twilight as they returned to the hut, but in the sky above them was the rioting rose and gold of the sun that, beyond the mountains, had not yet set.

When they came clear of the woods, old *Padre* José paused. "Now," he said, in a meditative voice, "the San Vicente River is almost the color of blood between its green banks, the people are gathering under the cypresses, and the youngsters are rowing their boats in the lagoon, among the big pads of the water lilies."

"You know San Vicente pretty well," said the boy.

"Ah, yes," said the *padre*. "San Vicente is the star in our human sky in this part of the world. Besides, it is beautiful for its own sake."

"Sometimes you wish you were back in it, I suppose?" said Grey. "But, no, I can see that you wouldn't be happy there. It's a pretty place, but there's as much dust and dirt and wrangling and fighting and scoundrelism there as in any other town of the size, I suppose."

"Why not? And what of that?" said the calm old man. "This human soul of ours and this human life must be finger-marked with a dusty existence, my son. If there were no scoundrels, there would be fewer honest men, and if there were no cowards, there would be fewer heroes. We all are bad enough, and close enough to the dumb beasts. Our virtues, you know, need a very dark night before they shine like stars." He walked on again.

So they came down the slope, through the rocks to the house. Doll, the bay mare, who wandered loose while the mules were tied, came up behind her master and followed him, nipping alternately at his hands as they swung out behind him.

"How did you teach her to love you?" asked the shepherd.

"Well," said the boy, "first, I made her learn lessons, then I loved her for learning them. I gave her the whip and a hard rein . . . afterward I trusted her. Horses like to be trusted. They get fat, with trust, even if the other half of their diet is thistles."

"We can learn from the horses," said the shepherd. "For my part, I have to have my tortillas and cheese. Every day I have to have them."

The boy laughed at this, and they went on together with their eyes meeting, every few steps, and smiling on one another. Grey felt that he had found a friend who would endure forever. Through that friendship, his mind lightened. It seemed to him that the world was a brighter and a simpler place.

When they came to the door of the hut, they were surprised to see the leather flap that closed the entrance torn down and lying on the ground outside. The interior was as dark as the mouth of an inkhorn. It was old *Padre* José who, with a faint exclamation, ran inside. He was already striking a light when Lawrence Grey entered and found the place empty.

Slade was gone, and there were signs of the struggle he must have made when he was swept off. The mattress was gone from the bed and the willow slats themselves were torn and broken, as though he had put his grip on them in the hope of saving himself. Finally, on the jamb of the door, they saw a large smear of blood. As though his hand, first wounded on the slats, had fallen here again in an effort to tear himself away from danger.

Grey, staring about him, felt his wrath rising. Shame got hold of him, also. He said: "*Padre* José, if I had been here, this would not have happened. I go off with you and pick berries, like a fool, and my friend is taken while I'm away. What sort of a friend am I? What sort of a man?"

"A young man," said *Padre* José. "That is all. We should only blame ourselves for faults that are not so closely a part of our natures."

Grey dropped down on a stool and stared at the floor. "They can't be trailed in this light," he commented. "One thing staggers me. Why should they have taken him away? If they wanted to remove Slade, a bullet through the head would have turned the trick for them just as well as the trouble of taking him off."

"Perhaps," said *Padre* José, "they wanted to extract from him what he knows about you. And they wanted the proper place and the means for torture. They could not tell when you would come back. And they would not want to have you interrupting them, my son."

This suggestion threw Grey into a spasm of anxious misery. He said: "If they've touched him, if they've harmed him, if I don't have their blood for it. Where could they have taken him?"

"The world is a large place," said *Padre* José.

"Garcias helped them before," said the boy. "Perhaps Garcias has helped them again. They may very well have taken him up there."

"I don't think so," answered *Padre* José. "You know that shame, after all, is a strong passion even in a bad man. You have shamed him. His foster daughter before this has suspected some of the truth concerning what happened in her father's house. I don't think that Garcias would plot against you again, or even lend his house to the criminals. Yet, it is very hard to tell. Fifty thousand dollars for your head. Why, that is enough to buy a thousand deaths among poor mountaineers." He shook his head and added: "That rascal, Cordoba, I doubt if even he would still work against you. He's a sensible fellow. He might risk one murder to make his little fortune. But I don't think that he would risk two. He'll take his bad luck today. Still, in his house and that of Garcias is our best place for looking."

"*Our* place?" echoed the boy. "Do you think, *Padre* José, that I'll let you ride with me tonight?"

The old man smiled at him. "Do you think, my son," he said, "that I have lived such a short time that I still have many hopes before me of the years to come? Besides, is not *Señor* Slade my guest? Was he not stolen from my house?"

To him the matter was as clear and as simple as could be. It admitted of no argument, and the boy, after one look at the iron calmness of that old face, said no more.

He simply went out and saddled the two mules.

Chapter Twenty-Six

It was such a night as one often sees in the mountains. The moon, thinner than a reaper's hook, gave enough light to show the clouds, but hardly dimmed the stars, and these, in droves and drifts that seemed moving on wings, showed in the gaps of clear sky. The two riders came slowly toward the Casa Garcias, for they had taken not the easier valley trail, but a far more obscure one that hugged the face of the opposite cliff. They came to the house upon the farther side, laboring up a narrow defile, with the building aloft, held up into the sky with a strong arm of natural rock. This was the southerly face of the Casa Garcias. It was so imposing as the dim cloud shadows blew over it, and as the starlight and the moonshine gleamed on it and were gone, that both *Padre* José and the boy reined in their mules with one accord.

"He loves the girl," said the old man. "There, you see, is the balcony that he built for her at a time when every *peso* he spent was like a portion of his own blood. A man like that is not all bad. I remember when he planned the thing. He used to come here with me and talk about the cost of the building."

It was a good-size balcony, corbelled out from the wall on thick stone beams. There was a slanting roof above it that sloped and gathered to a point, and four slender pillars held up the roof. Between the pillars, there was a network of stone tracery, a delicate and graceful pattern such as one finds in the church windows of the late Gothic style.

"No," said the boy. "I suppose that he's not all bad. But in my part of the world, a guest is a guest and a host is a host, with certain duties to perform."

Padre José chose to take no notice of this last remark. He said: "See what a blind thing love for a child is. There is a station to which a bird could hardly fly . . . yet, instead of giving Isabella a free view of the mountains from her balcony, and instead of letting the wind and the sun come freely to her, he's fenced it away with that scrollwork of stone."

Young Grey looked critically at the wall that arose, without embrasure, sheer up beneath the balcony of Isabella. "Now, *Padre* José," he said, "tell me the truth. What do you think that we can do together, now that we've come to the house of Garcias?"

"If there is danger to you here," said the *padre,* "then I shall be a protection to you, of course. For I don't think that even these people who are hunting you, my son, would strike at you if I were nearby."

"*Padre* José," said the boy, "they would strike at me if there were twenty like you."

The old man reached out his hand and laid it on the shoulder of Grey. "I am about to tell you something," he said. "Will you try to believe it?"

"Of course I will," said Grey.

"It is this," resumed *Padre* José. "If twenty of them came on you and I were beside you, I could take every particle of danger from your head."

"With a word?" asked young Grey lightly.

"With four words," said *Padre* José.

"Padre," said the boy, "I've never met a man like you. I've never met one that I respect so much. But as for trusting you or any other man when I know that there's a fifty-thousand-dollar price on my head, I can't do it. That's all there is to the thing. I

can't do it."

Padre José did not argue. He simply said: "What do you propose doing then?"

"I'm going to search this house in my own way," said Grey. "An hour from now, I'll try to meet you in the wood nearest to the patio. Is that agreeable?"

"Certainly," said the other.

"And what will you do?"

"I don't know. I may not enter the house, or else I may call upon Fernando Garcias."

"If you go inside," said the boy, "I beg one promise from you."

"You would give no promise to me," said *Padre* José mildly. "But what is it that you want?"

"Your promise that you'll remember, when you get inside, that you're with people who are as likely as not to forget that you are an old man."

"I promise," said *Padre* José. "Do you leave me now?"

"I leave you," said the boy. "If I don't meet you again, I want to tell you that you've put more ideas in my head in a day than any other man ever has done in ten years."

"My son," said *Padre* José, "let me tell you in my turn that, since I have talked with you, for the first time in years I have had a desire to be young again. Good bye for a short time, I hope. If it is good bye forever, bless you, my son, and may you die in a brave and worthy way."

Young Grey watched the *padre* riding up the slope, and he could not help a slight sinking of the heart. Never before had he heard death referred to in such a casual and cheerful manner. He had known desperadoes without fear, but they could not speak in this manner of the end of things.

Padre José disappeared, and the boy felt suddenly lonely. For the wall was great, and it seemed to represent power, a solid force against which he was a fool to contend. He was half of a mind to follow the old man and hastily trust to the promise that he had made, that, with four words, he could turn all danger from his head. But he altered his mind at once. He was no believer in miracles.

He took the mule back into a nest of high shrubs that closed above it like the darkness of seawater. Then he went again to the wall of the house, beneath the balcony. From a distance, it looked a solid slab, but close at hand, as he had expected from the age of the masonry, he could see a thousand slightly shadowed crevices, where the mortar had been chipped away by the innumerable small chisels of time. Here and there stones projected a little; again there were veritable holes where a portion of a stone had fallen out.

Even so, it was a tremendous task that he had before him. He contemplated it for some minutes, but at last he had mapped in his mind what seemed a possible way to the top, as nearly as he could judge by the number and the size of the shadows. Then he took off his shoes and his coat, and threw them back into the brush near the mule. Finally he began to climb.

It was not nearly so difficult as he had imagined. The most solid portion of the wall was that at the base where, perhaps, it had been a little less exposed to wind and weather. As he mounted, he found more convenient crevices in which to take finger- and toeholds. Still, it was a hard climb. The weight and bulk of two revolvers hindered him, and he wished heartily that he had taken only one.

Halfway to the balcony, he found a deep indentation. The whole outer half of a big stone had fallen away, and there was room for both his feet. So there he rested. When his arms no longer ached, he resumed the climb, and presently the balcony was just above his head.

To swarm over the projecting edge of it would have been no

difficulty for a cat, and it was no hindrance to Grey. He climbed up the corner and, taking a grip on the pillar nearest to him, with his feet on the balcony's edge, he was himself again.

The darkness within the stone latticework was alive. The life there was the movement of the thousand little branches of climbing vines that, apparently, grew out of pots within the rail of the balcony. The gentle breeze stirred them, rattled them softly together one moment, and the next set them all whispering.

Now he was at his post, what was he to do, and what was he to say? He must speak with the girl, if she were in her room. But it was not very late, and she might not yet have gone to bed. So he hesitated for a moment, and then he began to whistle the tune of a serenade that was at that time popular in Mexico. It was somewhat appropriate, at least, and to take it out of its complicated, jingling rhymes, it went in translation something like this:

You are the spendthrift, I am the miser.
You throw away the better half of life;
I only use the day to wait for night.
Wake up, my dear, and stretch and yawn a while.
The wind is here with me; the flowers are breathing.
"The mischief take you, slug-a-bed," say they.
And so do I.
The sun is out, and there's a better chance
To see the sky.

So whistled young Grey, as he clung to the balcony's edge. When he had finished whistling the song, he waited for a long moment. He could hear a sigh within the room beyond the balcony, but he knew that it was only the wind.

So he began to sing the song, and he finished it through to the end, giving the latter words a good deal of force. When he had ended, he heard no response. There was only the continued, secret whisper of the wind.

He grew impatient. He cleared his throat once or twice. He thought of repeating the song, in fact. Instead, he tried his hand at a few imitations of birds. He felt that they came very successfully from his lips. When he had ended them, he waited again.

But there was nothing inside the room he could see except the same thick darkness; there was nothing that he could hear except the rattling of the leaves, for a moment, and then their busy, scandalized whispering.

She was not yet in her room, it appeared. He could have sworn at the thought that he must descend again. But now a voice immediately before him said: "Do you think, Rinky Dink, that larks would be whistling at midnight?"

Chapter Twenty-Seven

He almost lost his grasp on the pillar, his start was so great. "Hello, there, *señorita,*" he said unromantically.

"Hello, there, *señor,*" said she gaily.

"Here I've gone and risked my neck," said Grey, "to climb a ladder with no rungs in it, and all I get at the top is a lot of criticism of my whistling. Why shouldn't I do a lark?"

"You left out half the notes," she said. "And the ones you put in were mostly out of key. Besides, as I said before, would a lark be singing at this time of night, loudly enough to wake the whole house?"

"You're critical," said Grey, "and that's a bad fault. When did you come out on the balcony?"

"I've been here all the time," she said.

"All the time since I came up?"

"Yes. I've been sitting out here all the time behind the vines."

"And let me wait all that time?" he said.

"You might have waited longer," she said. "But I couldn't quite stand the lark business. That's why I spoke." She added: "I thought you were a robber, when you came up the side of the balcony."

"And you didn't say a word?" said Grey.

"I have a gun with me," she said. "I'm not an expert with it, but I could hit a mark that's in touching distance. What brought you here, Rinky Dink?"

"You did," he said. "I couldn't keep away."

"Are you going to be romantic?" she asked.

"No. I'm a truth teller," he assured her. "What did you think of the song?"

"I've heard it before," she said. "By the way, you'd best climb down from there. Sometimes the wind comes with a sudden gust and it might knock you whirling like a dead leaf. It's a long way to the ground."

"Go on and be romantic, Isabella," he said. "Nobody else ever took the trouble to climb up to this balcony, I'll lay my money."

"Crowds have," she said. "I've done it myself."

"You? Yourself? With a ladder, maybe."

"The same ladder you climbed," she declared. "Look here, Rinky Dink . . . my father is about due to come in and say good night to me. You'd better get down."

"I'll stay here," said Lawrence Grey. "He won't be apt to see me here."

"You're as clear as day from the inside of the room," she answered. "Anyone could see you at a glance, against the stars."

"Well," he said, "a man has to take his chances. I've come too far for this talk to be cut off now like a long-distance telephone call. You ought to be a little more romantic, Isabella."

"You know what I think?" she said. "You're up here on business. What's the business, Rinky Dink?"

"No business at all," he said.

"Come, now, you've seen me today for the first time, and the only thing that you know is that I have a sense of humor, Rinky Dink. You can't depend on much else."

"You've laughed at me enough already," he told her. "And now it's time for you to be deadly serious."

"Why?" she asked.

"Because I'm begging for help," he said.

Suddenly he saw her for the first time, the pale glimmer of

her face close to the stone tracery. A bar of shadow crossed her, and made her face grotesque, at first. Afterward, he could half see and imagine her beauty again.

"I will be serious, then," she told him gravely. "What is it?"

"I want you to give me the plan of this house," he answered.

"You'll have to tell me why," replied the girl.

"Because I want to search it, room by room," he said.

She was silent for a long moment. Then she responded: "Was that why you came here today? To search as far as you could?"

"I came here today for a different reason," he said frankly. "I came because I'd heard a lot about you. I wanted to see you, Isabella."

"Was that all?"

"On my honor."

Suddenly she broke out: "Why don't you tell me the truth? Why don't you admit that there was some odd game in your mind when you came up here today? What it could be, I can't guess. There's nothing worthwhile in this place."

The shock of this kept him silent for a moment.

"I don't steal from the poor," he answered at last.

"You're like Robin Hood, then, I dare say?" she asked him. "You take from the rich and you give to the poor?"

"I've done that, too, in my time," he replied. "I take from the thugs, though, and I spend most of it on myself. But in the first place, I told you the truth. I came to see you. And you swear that I came to rob the house. Why should I want to rob your house, Isabella? I never heard of you or your father before today."

"Am I to believe that?" she asked him sharply.

"You ought to believe that," he assured her.

And her astonishing reply was: "Well, I shall, then. I find it pretty easy to believe you. Though you have strange things happening around you . . . guns going off in your hands and such things."

He merely said: "I want the plan of the house. Will you give it to me? And will you let me in?"

"The whole world would call me a fool, Rinky Dink," she said.

"Listen to me," he argued. "Your friend, Leonard Smith, hated me. He thought he had reason to hate me, because one of his best friends was started on the long road by me. But when he was telling you about me, even Smith, he didn't accuse me of being a liar, did he?"

"No," she said thoughtfully. "He didn't. He said almost everything else, but not that."

"And I give you my word that I would not touch anything in the house," he said. "I want to look through it. That's all. I could jimmy a window. I could go prowling. But my time may be short. A man may be dying now, Isabella?"

"Dying," she breathed.

"A man who already has come within an inch of death for me," he said. "I've had friends before, but never one like that. A fellow I've known for hardly two days. But he was ready to die fighting for my sake."

He thought she had not heard, or that she was debating what he had said. But presently there was a slight grating noise, and a section of the balcony tracery opened wide.

She stood before it, saying: "You may come in here."

"Not through your room," he protested. "If you'll let me in by a side way . . . and tell me the lay of the land. . . ."

"And a man dying, perhaps, for your sake? Hurry," she commanded.

He hesitated no longer, but stood inside the balcony with the leaves of the climbing vines touching coldly against his face. He was breathing hard. It seemed the strangest moment in his strange life.

She said to him: "I may be half out of my mind. I can't believe what I find myself doing. But I think that today you won a right to my trust. Let me ask you one thing. What makes you think that your friend may be here? Did he come here?"

"No. But he may have been taken here. He was overmastered in *Padre* José's hut, and taken off while I was strolling about like a careless fool."

She did not question him further. She merely said: "On this floor there are seven bedrooms. They are all large rooms. This is the smallest of them all. There is a hall running past them, overlooking the patio. The rooms themselves look out on the gorge, here, and then front close to the cliff the landslide fell from. Is that clear?"

"That's all clear. Seven large rooms, and no small ones?"

"No."

"Where are the stairs?"

"At the farther end of the hall, after you leave my door. They lead down with a big sweep, and they go up with a narrow twist a little farther on."

"What do they go up to?"

"The top floor. That's where the servants live. There are only two, now, and some of the rooms are falling to ruin. The roof has broken in several places. There are only four or five of those servants' rooms habitable."

"And two of them occupied?"

"Yes."

"Very good. Go on. What's on the ground floor?"

"The ground floor is very like this one in arrangement, except that the hall is the size of the two largest of the bedrooms."

"What's in the hall?"

"Nothing except the tatters of some old tapestries and whatnots. They're generally flapping in the draft. The ground floor rooms are all wider than these, because they don't open on a hall, but directly out onto the patio. It's a clumsy arrangement."

"Do the rooms connect?"

"Two of them. The dining room and the pantry. That's all. Otherwise, you have to go in from the patio."

"Is there a cellar?"

"Yes. The house is as deep underground as it's tall above the ground."

"Why is that?"

"Well, there's a small cellar just underground. That's where the wood and the food and such things are stored. Under that, there's another level of cellar, much, much bigger. It's larger than the floor space of the house. My great-grandfather was a collector of wines. He used to ship them up from San Vicente on muleback. All his life he worked laying down a cellar. He got young wines from Burgundy and from the Medoc. He got Stein wine and Rhine wines. Some of them didn't stand the traveling, young as they were. But others lasted. And he kept digging and digging, making the cellars greater. He dug three times as much as he needed to. It was a hobby with him. He finished the cellar of the second floor, and then he dug out a third floor, underneath. That's how the house happens to have three. . . ."

She stopped in midsentence. Then Grey heard the soft opening of a door.

Chapter Twenty-Eight

With the opening of the door, no light came into the room. Presently a low voice said: "Isabella?"

"Yes, Father," she answered.

A heavy step entered the room. Grey saw the pale gleam of her hand as she raised it in a signal for silence and caution. Then she left the balcony.

"Who are you talking to . . . here in the dark?" asked Fernando Garcias.

"Who was I talking to?" repeated the girl. "To a very great man, indeed."

"Light a lamp!" commanded Garcias furiously. "I'll have a look at the very great man."

"You'll have to have a fine eye," said the girl. "He's been dead a few hundred years."

"What silly nonsense is this, Isabella?" asked her foster father. "Tell me at once. I heard you speaking English."

"My eyes were tired of reading," she said. "I was quoting, as far as my bad memory would last me, and that wasn't very far."

No one spoke for an instant. "Light a lamp!" commanded Garcias sharply.

"Are you going to look for Mister Shakespeare?" she asked.

"Light the lamp, and have no more talk," said Garcias.

That moment, as he heard the scratch of the match, Grey parted the leaves at the corner of the balcony and stepped back in the vines as far as he could. He drew a revolver from beneath his coat and held it at arm's length behind his leg.

He was in the worst quandary he had ever known. If Garcias found him, there would surely be a gun play. If he killed Garcias in the girl's room, what would be her reputation thereafter? Sick with trouble, Grey waited. He saw the broad, dull beam of the lamplight sway slowly across the balcony, as Garcias moved from side to side of the bedroom, apparently searching. His foster daughter made cold suggestions.

"You haven't looked under the bed," she said. "There's the wardrobe, too. A dozen men could be hiding in there. And what of the balcony, Father?"

"You won't shake me," he said. "The bees have a way of finding the flowers. I'll trust you, Isabella, just as far as any woman deserves to be trusted . . . which is, not at all. I love you . . . but I trust you not a single inch." He closed doors, of the wardrobe, perhaps. "Now for the balcony," he said, and straightway the lamplight came wavering to the door and suddenly shone with a dazzling brilliance straight into the eyes of the hidden youth.

Garcias, coming forth, carried the lamp in one hand and a revolver in the other. He walked straight up to Grey and then turned his back upon him.

Surely he had seen. Yet, no. There he was opening the deep window of the balcony and leaning out a little. He turned and went slowly back. "I have to believe you, Isabella," he said. "It is a bitter pain to have to watch you and suspect you. But still, for a time, you must talk more to dead men than to living. But I tell you this . . . the day is not far off when I'll have money together sufficient to take you out of this old, crumbling barn. We'll go together to some happier place. You will have proper clothes to wear, instead of rags. I will set you in fine gold, Isabella, as a jewel ought to be set. Then you can speak to such men as you ought to know. You will move among gentlemen and ladies. No other wish is left to me. That will round out my wretched life, my dear."

He heard the girl say: "How can you make money grow out of the rocks, Father? I would rather marry a goatherd, or never marry at all, than to be trimmed up with dishonest feathers, you know."

He answered her sharply: "Never question fortune. She's a blind woman and a fool. Take what she gives you, if she comes near enough. Snatch the gold out of her hand, if you have to. That's all. Remember it, Isabella. There's one more thing for me to tell you tonight."

"To say my prayers, I suppose," she suggested dryly.

"To keep close to your room," he said. "Isabella, whatever happens, don't leave your room. I am going to make the thing impossible. I'm going to lock the door from the outside. There are other people in the house."

"What sort of people are they?" she asked.

"That's a question that can be answered another time," he told her. "At present, the fact's enough for you."

"If I have to be locked into my room, I can imagine what kind of men they are," replied the girl.

He broke out into an impatient exclamation. "Isabella," he said, "what is now going forward, you cannot understand! It is a thing of a vast importance. I can only tell you this . . . that I am working with the most brilliant man it has ever been my happiness to know. He has the greatest power, the greatest wisdom. If I had known him twenty years ago, I should now have been rich for twenty years. Nothing is impossible to him. He opens doors of steel and fades through walls of solid stone to achieve his purposes. The wills of others are as nothing to him."

"You know, Father," said the girl, "I've heard of another man who does exactly the same things . . . opens doors of steel and fades through walls of solid stone, so to speak. I mean Rinky Dink, you know."

"You're speaking of a mere boy, and I'm speaking of a man, Isabella," said Garcias. "Remember. It may be that strange things may happen in the house tonight. Isabella, close your ears. Think no thoughts. Ask no questions. Good night."

He left the room at once, and then Grey heard the double turning of the key in the lock.

Isabella came back to him on the balcony, and beckoned him into the room. She was rosy with excitement, and there was a sparkle of anger in her eyes. She said: "How under the sky did you manage to keep away from his eyes? I almost fainted when he went out onto the balcony."

"He walked straight up to me," he told her, "and then turned his back on me. I was pressed back among the vines. I suppose that the leaves made a screen . . . and he wasn't expecting anyone to be hidden in such a shallow place."

She nodded, with a sigh of relief, and then she said: "I couldn't keep him from locking the door. You'll have to climb down again, Rinky Dink. Heaven alone knows how you can do that. It's hard enough to climb up, let alone climbing down."

"It's not decided, yet," he said. "Let me have a talk to the lock of that door. I may be able to change its mind." He went to it and dropped upon one knee, and the girl came up beside him.

"You can't do anything," she urged. "The key's in on the other side."

He had taken into his hand a slender, flat piece of steel, and this he inserted into the keyhole. "It's hard," he murmured to her, "but there's a certain amount of play in an old lock, and a good deal in this one," he added.

She stood close beside him, pressing to the wall so that she could have a better view of his face.

His eyes were closed, his forehead was wrinkled, his lips were tense. He had the look of a poet composing, and a musician who interprets with all his soul.

The small sliver of steel moved softly, slowly inside the lock. Once she heard the slightest of grating noises, then no more.

"I've lost my touch," he said, snatching the steel from the keyhole with a sudden vehemence. "I've lost my touch completely." He stood up and began to walk rapidly back and forth through the room. He paid no attention to her. His brow was contorted with angry impatience. "These blunderbuss locks," he said through his teeth, "they're like a team of oxen compared with horses. But. . . ."

Suddenly he was on his knees again, working rapidly, intently as before. After a moment, she saw that not his fingers only, but his entire hand was turning slowly, cautiously. There was the lightest of clicks. And the door sagged a fraction of an inch ajar.

"There it is," said Grey, rising to his feet again, and he smiled, suddenly aware of her again.

"Now what are you going to do?" she asked.

"What do you think?" he asked.

"You're going down into the house, though you must have heard him say that there are other men here."

"I heard him," said the boy. "But I have to go down."

"Where?"

"To the wine cellars, but not exactly for wine," he said.

She stepped between him and the door. "Rinky Dink," she said, "I know more about my father now than I even dared to guess yesterday. But I can't turn loose a pest on him, as you're likely to be."

He merely smiled and shook his head at her. "Whatever comes out of this," he said, "there'll be no harm for your father. You heard him say it . . . he has other men in the house. I think he has one that I want. I mean nothing but that. I want the man who's been taken from me. I may be wrong, but I've an idea that he may be here."

She drew away from the door, slowly. "Rinky Dink," she said, "I'll never see you again."

"You're no prophet," he answered. "You will see me. Depend on it. Good night, Isabella."

"It's nearly midnight," she said. "Good morning may come in just a few minutes."

"You mean that you might leave your room and come down?" he demanded anxiously.

"Why not?" she replied, lifting her head.

"I'll give you a good reason," said the boy, and, stepping through the door, he closed it, and double-locked it behind him.

Chapter Twenty-Nine

He heard the lock softly shaken behind him. He heard the murmur of her voice calling after him in angry and yet guarded tones. Grey smiled a little. She was better than any he had known before; she was apart from all other women. When he thought of her courage in even contemplating a descent into that house of danger, it chilled his blood and fired his mind at the same instant. For him every shadow was a peril.

He slipped down the hall. His manner was careless, he walked erect, his head was high. No one, seeing him, would have been attracted by anything unusual about him; no one would have seen in him any of the attributes of the hunting cat. It would have required a second thought to note the soundlessness of his step.

When he reached the head of the stairs, he heard a pattering of swift footfalls ascending. In an instant, he was lying prone on the floor against the wall, in the dimmest place.

Two men mounted to the second level of the house. They were booted and spurred, but the spurs did not jingle. He saw that each of them had tied rags about the boots to keep the metal work silent.

"Suppose that she should break out?" said one in Spanish.

The other laughed softly, replying: "If she breaks out, she'll very quickly think that she's not in her father's house." And they went on, their murmuring voices soon beyond the range of Grey's hearing.

He got quickly to his feet again. It was plain that Garcias, not quite sure about his daughter, even when a double-bolted door secured her, was placing a guard over the hall. Ten seconds later he would have walked out of that same door into the arms and the guns of this pair.

He went down the stairs with the greater precaution, because it was very plain, now, that when Garcias said his house contained men this night he had not exaggerated.

He passed from the stairway through the open door into the patio. A smoky lantern burned by the entrance gate. There was no other visible light, at first. The window of the library was dark, and so was the hall next to it. But the dining room contained a flicker of illumination on the windowpanes. To that window he went.

It was hard neither to see nor to hear. For there was a corner cracked out of a lower pane. Through this he saw three men talking earnestly together. One of them was Garcias. The other was a tall and burly fellow who wore a long cloak and a plumed hat, like a gallant of the 17th Century. The third was small, wizened, his face being almost covered, except for eyes and nose like a hawk's, with a dense, short-cropped growth of hair. He seemed chiefly a listener, and a silent dissenter to everything that he heard.

"Luck runs in and out easily with every man," Garcias was saying.

"Luck has run out, mostly, with you," said the man of the cloak.

"Well," replied Garcias, "you haven't tried your hand with him yet."

"I shall when my turn comes," said the big fellow. And he laughed a little. It was not sheer boastfulness. He had the square, broad, blunt chin of a fighter, and it seemed clear that he looked forward to trouble as others look forward to a banquet.

"Your turn may come," said Garcias darkly. "There may be space and time for all our turns to come, before the work is ended."

"And so I say," said the big man, "that we're fools to wait. We should go and tackle the lad where he's to be found. We know that. We're sitting up here like buzzards on a perch, waiting for a horse to come and fall dead under it. Every man that follows our tactics is sure to starve. For my part, I say action is the easiest."

They were talking of young Grey, it appeared. The boy pinched his lips. All of these men here for him? One would have said that the evil one had told them he would come.

He was half of a mind to turn on his heel, that moment, and leave the house, get back to the mule, and ride for his life. But he could not go. When it was a matter of life and death in that dim hallway, Slade had not hesitated to venture his life for a friend of one day's knowing. And Grey blushed for his own fickleness of mind.

The little man with the black beard was saying: "Do you know better than he?" And he pointed significantly away.

It chanced that he pointed straight toward the cracked window, and therefore toward Grey outside it. All three followed the direction of the gesture, and then, as though it showed them something of importance, Garcias said: "No, he's bound to be right. He's never wrong."

"He's never wrong," admitted the big man in a grudging tone. "Only this isn't the way that I like to go about a business."

"Keep your own ways for your own business," said the little man sharply.

The man of the cloak did not answer this remark. He merely

said: "What about the dampness down there in that accursed cellar?"

"It won't rust him," said Garcias.

"But the air's bad. The lantern's burned blue down there."

"And what's that for us to worry about?" said Garcias.

"The first cellar would have been just as well," said the man of the cloak. "The second one, certainly, would do. But the third? I'd rather go into a dungeon that hadn't been opened for a hundred years."

"That one has a tough skin," said the man of the beard. "Don't worry about him."

"You'll find the guard sick of his business, though," declared the big man.

"You've talked enough to make me sick of you," said the smallest man.

Grey waited to hear no more. Someone was kept in the third cellar, someone whose skin was thick, held in the bad air of the old cavity. And it might be Slade.

It seemed to the boy that he was following a clue smaller than a spider's thread. But still it led him on from bit to bit of a web too complicated for him to understand.

The entrance to the cellars, fool that he was, he had not asked from the girl. However, it was probably in the kitchen or the pantry. So back to the kitchen he went, and found inside of it the two servants of Garcias.

The man sat in a corner grinding coffee, not in a machine, but in a mortar under a stone pestle. He wore a broad hat on his head. His outer shirt was off. He was dressed in an undershirt of a blue flannel or some cheaper, heavy cloth, and around his neck was a bandanna loosely knotted. His arms were bare, and the purple silhouette of a ship was sailing up his forearm. An anchor, a flag, and a girl's face appeared upon the other arm.

The woman worked before the stove, tending to the pots and pans.

"*Frijoles* were made," she was saying, "to keep some fat on the ribs of poor Mexico."

Her husband grunted.

"Well, without them, where would the poor people be? What do they eat twice a day in this very same house, I ask you."

"Tell me it's raining," growled her spouse, "when I'm too deaf to hear the drops falling."

"Oh, you're a wise man," said the woman. "You can tell me, also, what all these men have come to the house for?"

"Well, I'll tell you what's as good as a proverb," he said.

"Tell me, then."

"When more than two men meet at night, it's for wine, or women, or both."

"I could eat those coffee beans sooner than you will grind them with that pestle," said the cook.

"Eat them, then," he said. "I don't care, I'm sure."

"One of these days," she cautioned him, "these airs of yours will turn us out of our home."

"Our home is more fit for bats than for men," he answered. "I've been ready to go a good many years."

"Go where?" she asked. "Are we young enough to make new masters love us?"

"I'm tired of masters," he said.

"You talk like a fool," she said. "Every man has a master, and every woman, too."

"Aye," he said, "but the woman's master is not always the man."

"Why should it be? Here . . . finish the coffee, will you?" she said. "Did you say they'd gone down to the third cellar?"

"Yes."

"I've always suspected that something worth money was

buried down there," she said.

"Something worth money is likely to be buried down there this same night," he said.

"Hai?" she gasped. "What? What's likely to be buried down there?"

"A man," answered her husband, and grinned contentedly at the ease with which he had entrapped her.

She shook a dripping, wooden spoon at him: "Lazy stupid," she hissed.

"Call me a fool," he said. "For birds of a feather, as the saying goes. . . . Hey, shut the door or the wind will blow the lamp out!"

"I did shut it," she said, "and now. . . ."

"There it goes!" cried the husband.

At that moment the door flung open, and a great gust of wind, entering, knocked the flame of the lamp up its chimney and put it out.

The husband got to the door in time to push it shut. The woman relighted the lamp.

"Did you see or hear anything in the dark?" she breathed cautiously.

"No, I'm not an owl," he said.

"Something crossed the floor. I could swear that I saw it going toward the pantry door," said the cook.

"Follow it then," he answered with an idle yawn. "It may be your fortune."

Chapter Thirty

Inside the swinging door that led to the pantry, Lawrence Grey listened to the last remark without a smile. As the door swung back and forth from the forceful cuff of the wind, he saw by gleams and glimmers of light the other doors of the pantry.

He tried one. It opened upon the wreckage of the old dining room. By the night light that came through the great windows he could see the long table, the files of chairs along the walls, and the dull glint of highlights on the armor above.

In a flash he thought of the old days, when that armor was not allowed to rust; when the ancient guns, with their bell-shaped mouths, had been used to blow down whole ranks of screaming, charging Indians in their quilted armor and their frail, feathered helmets. He closed the door with a frown.

The room was totally dark now, but he felt his way along the wall to a second knob that he had seen. The moment he opened it, a smell of mustiness and stale air came up to his face. He asked for no further proof that he had found what he wanted, but stepped inside, closed the door, and began to feel his way forward.

A flight of steps began at once. He looked downward, not to find the way, but the sooner and more perfectly to accustom his eyes to the darkness. He counted the steps with a precise care. There were eighteen. At the bottom they opened onto a wider passage, which turned and descended a second flight. There were twelve more steps in descent, and he judged that he was not on the first level of the basement.

Then a door slammed above and behind him. He heard footfalls coming, and started running to find some doorway in which he could hide, or some turning of the passage.

It maddened him to find nothing. The passage ran straight as a die before him, and then, catching his foot, he pitched forward heavily and rapped his head against the side wall. He got to his hands and knees, swaying from side to side, half stunned. When he regained his feet, he was still staggering a little, and at the same time two men rounded a corner behind him and came straight forward, carrying a lantern.

"Halt, there!" called someone in Spanish.

"Your hands up!" said the other. And he saw the shine of the weapons they carried.

He might draw and manage to drop them both, but he was caught in a labyrinth. The sound of the firing would be heard. They would simply bottle him up in the underground damps of the house. And that would be the end of Lawrence Grey.

Instead of throwing up his hands, he turned about, stood wavering a little, braced himself with one hand against the wall, and thumbed his nose at the pair.

"Who is that?" he heard one of them ask of the other.

"I don't know. I never saw him. He's drunk," said the second.

"He's drunk," agreed the first. "A fine thing to have a drunk on our hands on a night like this."

The lantern bearer had put down his light, the better to manage his weapons. Now he picked it up again, and the pair came on. Grey, turning, resumed a course that he purposely made more uneven than needed.

The two came rapidly up behind him. Twice and again he was on the verge of wheeling, drawing his revolvers as he turned. But each time he controlled himself. They came up with him. And one was that same big fellow of the long and spreading cloak, the figure from another century.

"What are you?" he asked sharply of the young man.

Grey turned quickly, but with an uneven lurch. "I'm Innocente Oñate Cambrino y Sanvaldo," he said. "And who are you? And what are you?"

The man with the cloak sneered openly at him. "I am not drunk," he said.

"The red wine is the trouble," said Grey thickly. "It's filled with fire, and with poison, too."

"There must be a thief in it," said the smaller of the pair. "For it seems to have stolen your wits."

"My wits?" said Grey. "*Señor,* I am Innocente Oñate Cam- . . . ."

"Oh, I know all of that by this time," said the man of the cloak. "It's a long song, but one hearing of it is enough for me. What are you doing here, Cambrino?"

"He sent for me," said Grey. "Therefore, of course, I came."

"Who sent for you?" said the smaller man of the beard. And he looked with his bright little eyes straight into the face of the boy.

Grey assumed a cunning, stupid leer. "You ask me for his name, do you? And what is yours, my friend?" he asked. "And why do you ask me for his name?"

"He's one of us," said the man of the cloak. "The drunken young fool," he added, half under his breath, but loud enough for Grey to hear.

"I'm not at all so sure," said the man of the beard. "I don't smell any liquor about him." He moved forward.

Grey, recoiling, reached for his belt and pulled out a knife. "I'll slice your nose for you, *señor,*" he said. "Don't come lurching on me! We have a right to a little room, we men of the family of Cambrino y Sanvaldo."

"Let him be," said the big man. "There's the curse of

Mexico . . . the young bloods, the fools, the weak wits, the empty heads. There's nothing to be gained by talking with him."

"I'm not so sure," said the smaller and older man, still shaking his head and staring at Grey with his little, over bright eyes.

"Why not?" asked his companion. "You can see and hear for yourself."

"Would Felipe," said the other, lowering his voice until it was hardly above a whisper, "employ such a fool as this lad seems to be?"

"He may have taken him sober and never have seen him drunk."

"I don't like the look of this," said the man of the beard.

But he of the cloak suddenly hooked an arm through that of the smaller companion and, taking the situation by force, as it were, fairly dragged him past Grey and down the corridor of the cellar, merely saying: "Let's get out of this soon. The damp will start rheumatism all through my body before long. A vile, damp piece of business, and I hope that it's soon finished."

So they went on, and Grey, leaning against the wall, and smiling faintly, murmured to himself: "Big body, little brain . . . little body, great wit." He took the swaying lantern as his guide and followed it carefully, keeping to a secure distance.

It was good for him that he had a light to follow, or he promised himself that he would have tripped and fallen again a hundred times, so uneven was the floor in places, particularly where the naked rock was badly worn and rutted, or had been finished off carelessly in the first place.

It seemed to him that they went through twenty passages, up and down almost as many flights of steps, small and long, and everywhere the old wine cells opened to the right and to the left with the innumerable niches where the bottles had been laid. A mad lot these Garciases must always have been. Who but a madman would have laid down such a cellar of wine, here in the wild heart of the mountains? Again, who but the Garciases would have had head, stomach, and followers enough to have emptied that same cellar and drained it dry.

All had been careless waste, apparently. He could see, here and there in corners, the glimpse of old, dusty bottles, little heaps of them, barely distinguishable. No doubt they had been overlooked until they passed their prime, and then the spoiled wine, only its fragrance remaining and all its body gone, had been allowed to lie there and deteriorate further.

Here and there he passed doors built deep into the walls of the corridors, and at one of these he saw his leaders pause. They seemed to fit a key into the lock, and then the door opened wide and the two walked inside.

Young Grey, left in utter darkness, shut his eyes again to regain the sharpness of his vision. Then he opened them, and moved slowly ahead. There were two doors ahead of him, he had seen, and the second was that through which the pair had disappeared. He reached the first door, passed it, and, coming to the second, he watched for a moment the stiletto point of light that shone glistening through the keyhole.

He could hear a dim stir of voices inside. When he applied his eye to the keyhole, he saw nothing within. When he leaned over and listened, he could hear the man of the cloak maintaining his argument.

"A poor young fool, drunk as a lord, and staggering in the hall! What could Felipe have wanted with a scoundrel like that? Well, we'll have to sweep him out of the way."

Grey recognized the voice of the man of the beard answering: "Rodrigo, take a man with you and go back there on the top level and find the fool swimming in the black of the passages and get him out. Tell the old woman to give him a drink of hot coffee. That may bring him partly to his wits again."

Grey stepped back, gritting his teeth. Wherever he moved in

this house of many curses, he seemed to flounder from one peril into another. He thought of retreating as he had come. But no. Rodrigo and his companion would be walking that way. So he moved hastily a few strides farther down the hall, and, coming to another entrance, he flattened himself against that door just as the other opened and two men came out. They were dressed as *vaqueros,* and each was armed to the teeth.

Chapter Thirty-One

Behind them the air of the room was reeking with the fumes of cigarettes and billowed in a mist about them. Their finery glittered through it, for they were a pair of gaily dressed fellows.

One of them wore a crimson sash about his waist: "*Señor* Perez," he said.

"Yes?" answered the voice of the man with the cloak.

"I went in to him half an hour ago and removed the gag."

"What did he say?" called Perez.

"That the man would come for him in spite of all the demons."

"Well," called the voice of Perez, "we are not all the demons, but a good part of them."

To this remark there was a response of many people laughing heartily.

"I told him," said the man with the red sash, "that other would have to be half earthworm and half ferret to come to him. But *Señor* Slade has a strong belief, nevertheless."

A strong belief in what, thought the boy. A belief that he, Grey, would come to the rescue, no matter through what difficulties, and so great was that belief that, rashly, he had dared to express his confidence.

"This time his belief will do him no good," said Perez from within. "Go on, Rodrigo. Go hunt for the young drunkard. Watch his hands, for he seems one ready to use a knife."

"If he draws one, I shall break his wrist for him first," said

Rodrigo, "and afterward his head. Come, *compañero!*" So he closed the door, but opened it at once to say in parting: "You had best look to the gag. I put it on him again and drew it rather tight. He may be half choked by this time." So saying, he closed the door and went off down the corridor.

Grey slipped back past the room in which the many were gathered, and now he heard, inside, the sound of a door opening. Then the needle of light appeared from the door of that chamber in which poor Slade, it appeared, was imprisoned.

He heard Perez saying: "Now, man, fill your lungs with air. It's filthy air, at best, but take a few deep breaths of it."

"I have enough as it is," answered the indubitable voice of Slade.

And the heart of the boy leaped. For he felt as the prospector feels who had tapped ten thousand rocks and squinted at ten thousand films of color, when at last the true vein opens, broad and rich, before his eyes and he sees a huge fortune swimming before his imagination, with a mansion arising among broad, green acres all his own, servants waiting for his word, and the company of the wise and the wealthy surrounding him.

So much it meant to Grey when he heard the voice of Slade and knew that a single door parted him from the man who had ventured his life for the life of a stranger whose acquaintance was only one day old. He thought back with a warm glow to General O'Riley, that jovial Mexican-Irishman who was able, instantly, to put his hand upon a man of this mettle.

In the meantime, he heard the odd dialogue continuing.

Perez was saying: "If he were ten times the man you say he is, he never could come to you. You're hopeless and helpless here, and bound to choke like a miserable rat."

Slade replied tersely: "Do you know me, Perez?"

"No one knows you, *señor,*" said the other with an odd intonation of respect in his voice. "I know a little of you, however, as you already understand."

"Have I been in many countries, Perez?"

"You have, *señor*," said Perez with an even more marked accent of respect.

"And have I had an opportunity to know a good many men of courage and possibilities?"

"There is no doubt of that," admitted Perez.

"I have made the most of my opportunities," said Slade. "I've seen them in a great many countries, across a great many seas. But I have never seen one like this boy. He is half quicksilver and half wildcat. He is a ray of light, Perez. And he will come where you least expect him. You have a thought, now, that you are holding me securely?"

"It seems most certainly so to me," said Perez.

"And you have armed men all through the house?"

"Yes."

"You have the corridors watched and men walking in them on guard?"

"Yes, that has all been done, of course," said Perez.

He seemed perfectly willing to name all his measures of precaution to his prisoner. One might have said offhand that there was an air of frankness, almost of friendship between them. It flowed, of course, from the absolute certainty of Perez that he was the master of the situation.

Perez added: "Finally there are present four well-armed men sitting in the next room. Their ears are keen enough. And the partition between the two rooms is thin."

"I wonder," said the prisoner, "that you don't keep men sitting here in this room beside me?"

"There's no need," said Perez. "Besides, the air is especially foul here, and the floor is slippery with damp. I feel, for my part, as though I already had prison fever entering my bones."

"Now listen to me," said the prisoner.

"I listen, *señor,*" said Perez with that same queer air of deference in his tone.

"In spite of all your precautions, in spite of all that you have done, the lad will be here before the morning. When he comes, you will have to burn gunpowder if you wish to keep me from him."

"Very well," said Perez. "I have men who won't flinch from that."

"Be sure of them . . . be sure of yourself," said Slade. "I am warning you for the last time. You think that I am securely yours, but I could almost laugh."

"Very well," said Perez. "I won't argue. But if you were wise, I think that you would give up this misery and surrender this. . . ."

"Surrender? Give up?" cried Slade. "Man, don't I know as well as you can possibly know what hangs on this night and the boy's search? Now get away from me and leave me alone. I cling to what I have said. I fight it out on these grounds. That's the end."

"The end, then," said Perez. There was a moment's pause.

The boy could hear Perez muttering and cursing at something—the cords, perhaps, with which he reclosed the mouth of Slade.

A vast pity swelled in the heart of Grey. He could not see, looking back, what he had done to justify this man's enormous faith in him, this faith that he would pierce mountains to come to his aid. It touched him; it stirred his pride. He told himself, in that moment, that if he had a thousand lives, he would lay them all down in behalf of such a hero as that calm and strong man within the room.

The course of the thing was clear enough. They had captured Slade and striven to make him talk of the plans of the boy for the tracing of Juan Ray. When he refused to talk, perhaps they had tortured him and he had laughed at their torments and promised them that a rescuer was even then on the way to save him. No wonder that they had been imposed upon, that they had spoken to their captive with an air of respect, and that they actually delayed the full pressure of their tortures in order to use Slade as a bait with which to capture the other.

Grey waited beyond the door until he heard another slammed rather heavily within. Perez, no doubt, had returned to the other room.

The light that had glinted out at the keyhole was now extinguished. Then he began to work. At the very first touch of the thin steel he read the mind of that lock and understood its most hidden workings. In another moment he felt the sliding bolt inside it giving slowly before the pressure of the cams.

The door sagged backward beneath his hands. Softly he let it come, for there was a slight current of air from the inside pressing it wide. He allowed it to stand ajar, and so, entering, he felt his way with cautious feet and with extended hands.

It was as Perez had said. The floor was slippery and wet. The tips of his fingers, reaching downward, touched greasy-faced mold. In the near distance he could hear the monotonously regular dripping of water that sounded like the ticking of a clock that had run down and was about to stop forever. So life, it well might be, was running down and about to stop for him and for that hero who was hidden in the room behind its thick blanket of darkness.

It was a long moment before he found what he wanted.

They had stretched on the floor, it seemed, a damp, thin pallet of straw. A foul smell of decay issued from it. And upon that pallet he felt the warm body of a man lying. He felt the knee. He leaned beside the face of Slade.

"Slade," he whispered. "It is I . . . Grey. One moment and I'll have you free." He fumbled at the cords that held the gag. No matter with what respect Perez had spoken to the captive, still he had not hesitated to bind the gag with the most cruel force upon the face of the prisoner. How he could breathe was a wonder. It took a few seconds to loosen those cords, however. He withdrew the gag. And it seemed true that the captive had been almost stifled, for his first breath was a faint groan. It chilled the blood of the boy. He pulled out the knife that he carried with his left hand and sliced the ropes that bound Slade's hands. He swept it lower and cut the cords that tied his feet together.

Then, as he had feared, the door to the next chamber opened, and a broad rush of light entered the room of the prisoner. Grey now crouched, with a revolver ready in his hand, leveled upon the form that appeared there.

Chapter Thirty-Two

Grey heard the voice of Perez from the next room speaking impatiently and asking: "What's that?"

"I thought that I heard a groan in here," said the man who appeared at the door. He was half turned back to meet the voice of Perez.

"You thought you heard Satan," said Perez. "Close the door and keep out the moldy smell of that room. I'll be glad when this night ends."

The man hastily closed the door.

Grey fell to work massaging the places where the cords had bound the ankles of the captive together. Then he rubbed the wrists briskly. He could hear Slade panting.

"Are you better, Slade?" he murmured. "Can you stand up now? Will you try?"

"Yes," said Slade.

"Softly," said the boy. "They're listening hard, and they have ears like the ears of foxes." He fumbled, found the armpits of Slade, and raised him to his feet.

Slade swayed as he took the weight of his body upon his own feet. "I knew that you'd come," he gasped. "I knew. As well put up walls of crystal to keep out the light as to put walls of stone to keep you out."

"No talking," whispered the boy. "You can't control your voice. You don't know how loudly you're speaking. Steady, Slade. You're not yourself."

"I will be," said Slade.

Again his voice seemed to the boy to toll like a bell, so great was its volume. He hurried Slade across the floor. With one hand he helped the man forward. With the other hand he fumbled before him, making swift strokes ahead to the left and right. Once he slipped on the wet floor and almost fell. But at last he found the door, passed through it, and, turning to the left, they started up the hall of the cellar.

Only then, with what seemed nine-tenths of his work accomplished, Grey realized how great was the task that still lay before him. True, Slade would probably soon become steadier on his feet as the act of walking made the blood circulate. But even if he were in the condition of a first-class fighting man, there would still be much to conquer before they were clear of the house of Garcias.

He thought of *Padre* José. What was the poor old man doing now, and what was he accomplishing with his foolish task? These were his thoughts for the first half dozen steps, and then Slade unaccountably reeled and fell heavily forward.

The fall was alarming enough, but with it came a loud cry of surprise or pain from the crippled man. Red rushed across the eyes of the boy. It was the end. That cry was sure to give the alarm.

He was not surprised when a door behind them was cast open and a pale glimmer of light passed up and down the corridor. A man leaped out and Grey fired. He shot low and saw his target fall to the floor with a screech of pain. Then he turned as several other forms checked their first outward rush upon the threshold of the room, fearing the bullets that might fly down the narrow limits of the hallway. The stricken man writhed about and drew himself back toward the safety inside with his hands like some amphibious creature.

Grey spared him. He was no destroyer for the sheer joy of

destruction. What he wanted now was to get forward toward safety. So he turned again, and, turning, he saw the face of Slade, almost completely masked with bandages, but with his eyes flaming, as it seemed to the boy.

"Give me a gun," said Slade.

"Go on . . . go on . . . ," answered Grey. For his part, he ran backward. Half a dozen shots were fired blindly by hands that reached out from the edge of the door and then pulled the trigger at random in the hope of reaching a target.

He tried another shot himself, planning it so as to make a ricochet along the wall. If the bullet drove splinters of stone before it, all the better chance of striking some wrist exposed for another shot. So he fired, and was instantly answered by a loud yell of pain and rage. A gun fell clanging to the floor, and from the door the half-dimmed voice of the wounded man poured forth a stream of imprecations.

That would keep those heroes cooped up for a few seconds at the least. And now the boy took Slade beneath the arm and started hurrying him down the corridor.

He heard Slade panting: "Go on and save yourself. You've given me my start, and that's all I can ask. Go on by yourself."

"I'm with you," said Grey, his voice quivering, "till the finish. I'm here beside you till the finish. Here's the gun you want. It shoots straight. It has six shots in it. Keep the last one for yourself in case these wretches should get their hands on you once more."

Slade made a gesture of assent.

Behind them came a fresh burst of bullets. But they were around two turns from the chamber now. Only the echo was terrible, as it took up the noise of the explosions and multiplied them with a thousand reverberations until it seemed that the roof would tumble in upon their heads.

So they pushed ahead into the thick blackness of the passageway, and Slade, with every moment, seemed to be surer and surer upon his feet. He was now running. He seemed even more at home than the boy in the darkness. Then, ahead of them, they saw a glimmer, and afterward a bright gleam of light.

"They're coming back," said Grey. "The two that have gone out looking for me, likely. The noise that we make in running is covered up by the roar of the guns back there. Are the fools going to shoot at nothing forever?"

He caught the arm of Slade and slowed him to a stop. "Here's a corner," he said. "As they come around it, hit for the head of the nearest man with your gun barrel."

"I'll send a bullet through his ribs!" said Slade savagely. "The fools!"

"Dead men will do us no good," said Grey. "But a living man might steer us through this infernal labyrinth. How far are they hearing this roar of guns now?"

"Not far," said Slade. "Not even on the cellar level above us. Solid stone swallows sound."

Long before Grey expected it, straight around the corner swerved the light, a lantern swinging in a man's hand. He went down that instant from the weight of Grey's blow. And he saw the gleam of Slade's revolver brought down with a force sufficient to crush the skull of an ox. However, the sudden rush of the men had apparently made him miss his direction completely. It was the head of Grey that the gun missed by a fraction of an inch. Then, leaping to the side, Grey jabbed the muzzle of his revolver into the stomach of the second of the two men. It was Rodrigo. He recognized the man by the broad, crimson sash that was bound so jauntily about his hips.

The other guard lay flat upon the floor. It would be some moments before he rose, if ever, so heavily the barrel of the gun had rapped across his skull.

"Pick up the light, man," urged Grey to Slade, who stood as though paralyzed by these events. "Pick it up. Give it to this fellow. That's better."

At the same time he was fanning Rodrigo, and upon the floor of the passage he dropped the two guns and the knife he took from the man.

"Now, Rodrigo . . . ," he began.

"All the sweet saints," breathed Rodrigo. He was staring neither at the revolver that threatened him nor at the man who held it, but sidewise, toward the bandaged head of Slade.

"Yes," said Grey, "he's free again, and there'll be many a dead man before he's taken again. Now, Rodrigo, you've a long and happy life ahead of you if you get us out of Casa Garcias. But if you can't steer us to freedom, I'll break your spine in two with a bullet from this gun before I turn it on the others. Do you hear?"

"I hear," moaned Rodrigo. "I hear, *señor.* Mother of heaven." His moaning continued.

"Get your wits together," cautioned the boy. "Straight on, now, and go fast, but go sure. How many other men are there now in the lowest cellar?"

"No more, *señor.* I've just been through it."

"And in the level above?"

"At the farther end. . . ."

"And can't you go up the nearer way?"

"Yes. There is a broken stairs . . . we could try it."

"Go on," said Grey. "And you after him, Slade. I'll be the last. You have a gun. Shoot him through the small of the back if he tries to dodge away. No, never mind that. You carry the lantern and I'll tend to the shooting. Go on, boys. We're two-thirds of the way to the clean, open air again."

So they started on, running in this fashion, in single file, with the lantern dancing in Slade's hand. Twisting through the winding galleries, they came to a door through which they passed into a small room. Here they found the broken stairs of which the Mexican had spoken. Half of the steps were missing, but the stairway was easily climbable. Up they went, therefore, and, turning briefly around the landing place in the second level, they went on up by a less battered continuation of the same stairs toward the first cellar floor.

They had come to the second winding of this, and all noise from beneath had died out completely, when they saw a strong flare of light and heard voices immediately above them. At the head of their means of exit there was a room of some sort, and in that room there were lights and men posted to guard the way.

Chapter Thirty-Three

The three halted upon the stairs. Above them they could hear a loud voice saying: "Look, Garcias . . . a man's luck cannot last forever. It is not made to wear like shoes of iron, but one day it gives out. That is the way with you. Your luck has given out tonight. Why should you groan and tear your hair? You have lost a horse and saddle and some clothes. Well, you never paid cash for them."

"I paid more! I paid blood!" cried the voice of the man who was apparently Garcias.

"You've gained the blood back again," said the apparent winner. "Look at him, Diego, and tell me if he hasn't gained back his blood?"

"Oh, he's fat as a pig," decided a third voice, "but there's not much blood in fat."

"You laugh?" said Garcias. "Two times and three times a curse on all of you. I have lost the ring that Alicia gave me after I returned safely from Monterey, where the guns so nearly got me. *Hai!* And I have lost her ring, also, at the cards. Give me back the ring, Diego. Be a man . . . be a friend . . . and give me back the ring."

Diego spoke in a calm but ugly tone. "I'll see you a dead toad, first. Because it's mostly like a toad that you look."

Rodrigo leaned on the stairs toward Slade and Grey. *"Señores . . . amigos,"* he said. "You see what we have done? We have come up a blind alley. There is no passing here. We must turn back."

But as he spoke, it seemed that a door opened down below and a burst of shouting voices, very dim with distance and with intervening walls, came with a tremor to their ears.

"You hear that?" said the boy. "We go on. There's no turning back. Straight on, Rodrigo. Slade, jab your gun into the small of his back. Put out the lantern. We don't need to hold a light for others to shoot us by."

The lantern was accordingly extinguished.

Above them Grey heard the voice of Garcias saying bitterly: "You think that because I am working for him tonight, and cannot use my hands for myself, I shall forget, Diego?"

"You forget? Yes, you'll pretend to forget," said Diego. "I know you, Garcias. All fat men are cowards. Fat keeps the body warm and the soul cold."

"I'll see how hot your own blood is in the middle of your cursed heart before noon tomorrow," said Garcias.

"Good," said Diego. "We have a witness here, that if I see you by noon of tomorrow, I'll pull your fat nose for you and give you a few cuts with my whip across your fat face. That's the way to treat a dog. You and your pockmarked Alicia."

Garcias groaned. "Demons!" he said in a passion of rage. "Must I sit here and listen? No, no! Now! Now is the time, brave Diego, for your whip and your nose pulling."

"Why, you dog," said Diego as calmly as before, "you know if we raised a hand in our own business tonight he would have us flogged to death tomorrow. You can bluster tonight, but tomorrow will give you a sun to see by and you'll find your way to a safer path, I warrant."

"Up, up," Grey was whispering. "They're half blind with their own talk now. Straight up, Rodrigo, if you want to live. Straight up, Slade, and we'll run through them before they know that we're near. No shooting. We'll trust to our heels."

At the same time, as it appeared, another door opened down below, and they heard the dull, ominous roar of many voices much nearer now than before. This uproar was plainly audible in the room above them, and, as they stole ahead, they heard the wrangling end and the voice of Garcias saying: "What is that? What is that thing I hear?"

"The wind," said the third man.

"The wind? It's those demons raised by that fiend of a *gringo* of whom they have told us. He is here, and he is fighting with our men. We must get down there and help them."

It was Diego, a big, raw-boned, powerful man, who now suddenly appeared in the doorway immediately in front of Rodrigo. He carried a short shotgun in his hands, whereas Rodrigo was unarmed, of course. But the latter's fear of the shotgun was far outbalanced by the pressure of the gun on the small of his back, it appeared. He swayed forward as Diego stepped into the opening, and with all his force he smote the big man in the stomach.

Surprise probably hurt unlucky Diego more than the fist. He doubled up, however, and fell backward, the shotgun hurtling out of his hands. And over his body the three ran.

Grey, coming last of the three, saw in the corner of a small room half littered with old boxes and barrels, a small man with the face of a fox, bending over a cask and gripping the edges of it as though he wished to lift it and hurl it. But Grey knew the staring eyes and the white face. The man was frozen to stone with astonishment and with fear.

Close to him was a fellow of a different caliber, that same Garcias who had been so gibed at because of his fat and his lack of blood; he who had been losing, as it appeared, in the game the three had been playing with the cards that were still strewn over the top of the cask.

For Garcias now was whipping out a long-barreled revolver

and bringing it calmly down to a level for a shot. He was not a fancy gunman, not one of the snap shots. He apparently believed in deliberation. And Grey feared such a fighter more than a dozen of the more flashy sort. But he himself was one of those oddities who can combine speed and accuracy. His Colt was already in his hand. He took a cross-shot at fat Garcias, aiming, as always, low. He tried to strike below the hips. He had no will to harm this valiant fat man seriously.

And he saw Garcias sway and stagger, then bring his revolver down and fire.

It was poor Rodrigo who swayed sidewise like a tree chopped through by the axes of the woodsmen. He threw out his arms and fell on his face. He was dead, or nearly dead, thought young Grey to himself, and he gave Garcias the compliment of a second bullet that brought him down out of sight behind the cask.

That much was done. That other hurdle had been cleared.

Before them opened the narrow mouth of a doorway that yawned upon a stairway beyond.

Grey scooped the lantern from the top of the cask, and hurried on behind Slade.

But he found Slade like a man bewildered, standing still, his revolver poised in his hand, a desperate look glinting like sparks from his eyes. He seemed to be staring at Grey himself, like a man about to shoot.

The boy caught his hand at the wrist. "On, on, Slade!" he gasped. "Get up the stairs. We have two parts of a chance!"

Slade, as though recalled to himself, turned and fled up the steps, with the boy behind him.

They reached a higher floor, on the same level with the kitchen cellar, through which Grey already had passed, and here he was able to guide, calling to Slade, as the latter ran ahead of him, the various turns that ought to be made.

They got to the last steps. They mounted to the pantry. They cast the door wide.

How many minutes before had Grey gone down through that same doorway? Hours, centuries? Only scant minutes, but here he was returning, and the prize he sought was before him.

Always before. He caught Slade by a heavily muscled shoulder and steered him as a man steers a boat through crowded waters. And they blundered together into the smoky light of the kitchen where the manservant was busily whittling at a stick, as a sailor would have been apt to do. And the woman was still bending over the reek of the pans that littered the stove.

The man saw them first, naturally. "Ha," he said, and shifted the heavy knife he was using into the palm of his hand, ready, with Mexican adroitness, to hurl the weapon. Then he saw the two naked guns, the set faces of the men, and changed his mind at once.

They were through the kitchen by the time the woman had turned from her stove. Taking the back door of the room, they stumbled over some boxes in the rear yard, and so came out beyond a fence of young saplings, tall and thin, like fence posts, and not at all like a hedge.

In this manner they stood, at last, under the tall, looming, black wall of the house. Above them was spread the wide book of the stars, written in the print that men most love to dream over, although they never may read its words. A keen, fresh wind blew up the gorge to them and stirred and rattled the leaves. But still, like a miracle, all of the house beneath them was still. Not a sound, not a whisper came from the tumult that must be raging up from the bowels of the house.

What would happen? Who was the *he* of whom all of those hardy fellows stood in such awe, from whom they took their orders, whose disapprobation they seemed ready to die rather than to merit? These thoughts came at once to the boy.

But at the same time, holding Slade close under the armpit, he was steering him forward to the spot where the mule had been left.

He took the revolver, snatching it from his hand. "You'll travel lighter and faster," he breathed at the ear of Slade. "And speed is what you need now. Speed, speed, speed. Run, Slade, run. These wretches will be ranging for us soon."

At that moment, to tag his words, a wild uproar broke from the house. And then a score of shots in rapid succession. What could they have found, or thought that they had found, to fire at?

But Slade and the boy were already in the thicket, and there they fairly stumbled over the mule, lying peacefully asleep.

Chapter Thirty-Four

When she was left in her room alone by the departure of Grey, Isabella Garcias swept a shawl around her shoulders, since the night was turning chilly, and sat down on a couch in the dimmest end of her apartment. She was brooding bitterly on the very name she bore, and telling herself, of all things in the world, she would the most readily part with the name of Garcias.

She had grown up in the old house and learned at first to have a certain affection for the place. She had loved Garcias himself, also, in the beginning, as a child will naturally turn to a real or foster father. But then she learned the gruesome story of Fernando and his brother—how the brother had been brought home dead after that hunting "accident"—and after that she could not tell whether Fernando Garcias really loved her as a daughter, or whether her adoption into his family had been an act of penance to make his peace with heaven for the greatest of all sins.

Perhaps it had been this in the beginning, and a true affection had followed. Even of that affection she could not be sure.

Like any beautiful girl, she knew something of her looks. And she felt, sometimes, that the interest of Garcias in her was that of a man who has a jewel with which he wishes to dazzle foreign eyes. When he spoke of the future, it was always in terms of her appearance in great cities, in brilliant assemblies. It was not her happiness that appeared to concern him so much as the quantity of light that she might shed and that he might shine in. He spoke of her marrying millions; she had no doubt that he expected to share in them.

He was, in short, in every way a man of many contradictions. She told herself that she was very fond of him, and she was grateful for what he had done for her. But she could not say that she either loved or respected him. It was that impossibility of pouring out her heart to him that had made her a little cold and hard and sharp in her manner to other people. There was one exception, that odd shepherd, *Padre* José.

She had known the *padre* for years, intimately, as only a child may know an old man. He had seemed to her, at first, the incarnation of all wisdom. He seemed to her, still, far more than a mere shepherd and freak. The spell that he had cast over the simplest of the mountaineers, he had cast over her, also. To him she talked as though he had been both mother and father.

Now, as she sat in her room, the big house of Garcias seemed to Isabella a vast dungeon. The last interview with her foster father had not been long, but it had been enough to strike her with horror. The house was filled with men, he had said. She was not to leave her room. Indeed, she now heard the deep murmur of two men speaking quietly together just outside her door. They had been posted to make sure that she remained inside!

When she realized this, an angry frenzy came over the girl. She jumped up from the couch and began to walk hastily up and down the room. *Where is Rinky Dink? Why are men in the house?*

Then her mind concentrated on the remembered picture of the boy kneeling at the door, working at it with the sliver of steel. Had he been here, perhaps even the presence of the two men in the hall would not have deterred him. Noiselessly he would have turned the bolt. And then, jerking the door open, perhaps he would have sprung out and taken the two guards by utter surprise. They would have been helpless before his lightning speed of hand and accuracy of eye, as though a leopard had leaped at them in the midst of a jungle.

But Grey had already gone, and now, beyond a doubt, he was probing the mystery to its heart, one man against many. She struck spitefully at the sweep of her dress. If she were a man, she told herself, she would have found a means of coming at the business, too.

The more she waited, the more feverishly the thing took hold upon her, until at length she was leaning over the edge of the balcony and looking toward the ground below. She had told young Grey the truth; one time she had made that perilous ascent, even though her heart more than once had been choking her. But the descent would be doubly dangerous.

Then she remembered a lariat with which she often had practiced on foot and on horseback when, as a youngster, she had envied the accomplishments of the *vaqueros*. It was not full length. It was hardly more than thirty feet. But the supple rawhide was still quite strong, no doubt.

When the idea came to her, she instantly had it in process of execution. She brought out the long coil, tied an end of it to the strongest pillar of the balcony, and at once she went over the side.

She had not gone down three arm's lengths before she realized that, like a headlong fool, she had not taken care to measure the distance to the ground and see how close the rope reached to it. Furthermore, her strength was not sufficient to climb up the rope again. As for the wall, the rope hung out more than a yard from it, and she could not reach its crevices.

She was suspended in mid-air, and a scream came up to her lips and made them tremble. But she checked it and then resumed the descent. The weight of her body pulling against the tender palms of her hands forced them into painful wrinkles that meant blisters, she knew. But she went on down steadily.

She gripped at the rope with her knees. It was too narrow for her to gain much hold in this manner. Then she came to the end of the rope and found that her feet still swung above the ground. How far could it be? Would she dare to let go of the rope?

She turned her head and looked, but in the darkness, and with the dizziness that had come over her, she could see nothing but a seemingly limitless well of black.

It was useless to scream out for help now. Calmly she told herself that, even if by a lucky chance her voice were instantly heard inside the house, nevertheless she could not maintain her hold on the rope until help came to her and a ladder was brought. And there was the deep night for the servants to stumble about in, doing everything wrong.

She closed her eyes. Then, as she faced death, she told herself that she had done nothing, she had been nothing. She had lived as a plant lives, and there was no fruition to her life. To the sum of existence she had neither added nor subtracted, and therefore her death mattered nothing.

Some tears of self-pity came into her eyes. "I'm a sentimental fool," she said aloud for only her own ear to hear. Then she threw back her head. If only the fall would be long and the death mercifully sudden.

She relaxed her hold and jerked down into space—some six inches. Her knees buckled; she fell flat, and, lying there, looking at the glorious brightness of the stars that she had never expected to see again, she began to laugh feebly. There, as she hung at arm's length from the rope end, she had been practically standing on the ground.

She got up. The fear, having gone from her, she felt no paralyzing reaction, but instead this new, wild laughter was still bubbling in her, and a warm feeling of strength spread through her body.

She had not thought out any plan as she sat in her room. Her one desire had been to escape from the room simply, and now that she was outside the house she did not know what to do.

So she began idly to circle the outer limit of the walls. When she came opposite to the entrance to the patio, she made a wide detour to the verge of the brush. Coming back on the farther side, she went down the row of the windows, doubly black in that they were on the northern side of the house. Not even the horizon stars cast their images into the panes of the glass.

She came, in this manner, to that same hall in which young Grey not so very long before had seen Perez and the man of the beard talking, but it was a different pair that she saw within now.

It was her foster father and old *Padre* José.

Chapter Thirty-Five

She was amazed to see *Padre* José. The old man was the last of all human beings with whom she was prepared to connect this night, which was fairly reeking with crime. The set jaw and the gleaming eye of Fernando Garcias were in tune with all that she half expected to meet. The calm face of *Padre* José seemed utterly incongruous.

The shepherd was now filling his pipe out of a red, cloth sack. He lighted it. Midway in this operation, Garcias broke out: "Any night but tonight, *Padre,* I would be happy to see you here. I know that you are a great friend to Isabella. But tonight I have important things to occupy me."

The shepherd, holding the match poised, had allowed it to burn to his fingertips as he listened. Now he dropped the burned match and took out another, for the pipe had not ignited. He removed the pipe from between his teeth.

"I understand the nature of your business tonight, *Señor* Garcias," he said.

Garcias was so struck that he remained agape. The shepherd scratched the second match and quietly went about the thorough lighting of the tobacco, moving the match in a circle about the edge of the pipe bowl. By the time he had finished, his head was dressed in clouds of white, which gave him a look of mysterious dignity.

Garcias leaned toward his guest. "Now, then, *Padre* José," he said, assuming a tone of lightness that it was clear was not natural, "you have a very keen, good wit, but I don't think that you can have looked into the heart of my business tonight."

"We all feel," said *Padre* José in his gentle way, "that there are veils that fall over us, as if from heaven, shutting us off from the view of other men. Ordinary, common men, we call them to ourselves. For each one of us possesses a unique radiance, from his own point of view. Well, *señor,* I sympathize with your attitude. But still, you may be wrong. Perhaps I have peeked through the mist into your most secret thoughts."

He smiled as he spoke.

"Perhaps, perhaps," said Garcias, impatiently looking over his shoulder toward the door—a very broad hint to his guest. "But now, *Padre* José, suppose that you tell me what's in my mind at this very moment?"

"Murder," said the shepherd without emphasis.

Yet the word lifted Garcias half from his chair. He fell back again limply. "Murder?" he echoed. "You don't often make jests, *Padre* José."

"Murder is in your mind," repeated the old man. "That is why I came here tonight."

Garcias forced a ghastly laugh. "Murder?" he said again. "Then tell me who it is that I wish to murder."

"The young American who has stayed with me with his hurt friend," said the *padre*.

Garcias bit his lip. He was turning gray, as a man does when all his body is immersed in icy water. "I am going to kill the young American?" said Garcias, nodding, beginning to sneer. "And why should I wish to kill the boy? I have seen him."

"So he told me," said the shepherd.

"He told you, did he? And the little jest we played on him?"

"He told me of the little jest, too," said the shepherd. "This has been a lucky day for you, *señor.* You already have been closer to death than the thickness of a spider's thread. And still you are sitting here and able to speak." Not the slightest passion had crept into his voice.

"You tell me that I wish to commit murder," said Garcias, "and you tell me that the man I am intending to murder is the young American. But you haven't told me what makes you so sure."

"Because," said *Padre* José, "you stole away the other American from my hut so that the boy would follow you back here."

"So? So?" said Garcias, his face more frozen than ever. "*Padre* José, you are a fellow of a great imagination." Then he added: "Since you know these things so well, as it seems, tell me then my motive in wishing to destroy a young man I have never seen until this day."

"Your motive?" said the shepherd. "Oh, your motive comes from outside. You were asked to do the thing, and promised a great deal of money for the doing of it. You are to murder him, so that he may not find Juan Ray."

"May not find Juan Ray?" cried the other. "May not find a dead man? What nonsense are you talking, *Padre* José?"

"Not dead, though he has been missing," said the shepherd.

"Ah?" said Garcias. "If you know so very much, *Padre,* no doubt you are sure that the man is alive?"

"Yes, I am sure," said the shepherd.

Garcias actually writhed in his chair with excitement. "You have even seen his face, I dare say?" said Garcias.

"Yes. Every week or so I see him."

"You know even where he lives?" cried Garcias.

"Why should I not?" said the shepherd. "I know his house fully as well as I know my own."

"By heaven," muttered Garcias. Then he asked: "You wish me to believe what you say, *Padre?*"

"Oh, I think you will believe me," said the shepherd. "Because the truth is that you cannot think I would lie to you, now that I've come so close to the end of my days."

"Padre," said Garcias, "if you know so much as this, I still cannot think that you would come and tell it to me if you also believe that I have in mind the purpose that you attribute to me."

"And why not?" asked the shepherd.

"No one but a madman would speak as you have spoken," said Garcias, "if what you believe of me is true."

"If you could see your own face, my son," said the shepherd, "you would understand how clearly guilt is written on it. Heaven forgive you for it as freely as I might forgive you."

Garcias groaned aloud in excitement, in shame, and in anger. "Make this clear to me," he said. "What earthly thing would you gain by coming in this manner?"

"I gain the life of the boy," said the old man.

"What is that to you?" asked Garcias sharply.

"I have known him one day and I love him," said the old man.

"You love a thief, then, and a man-killer," said Garcias spitefully.

"I love a brave man and a truth teller," answered the shepherd.

"Tell me, after all, how what you say is of service to him?"

"Why not? Suppose that you trap him and destroy him with your hired men, still you have accomplished nothing. For if he does not come back to my hut in the morning, then I shall send word of the truth to Juan Ray."

"What truth will you tell him?"

"That a rich man is fighting away death until he can hear of Juan Ray, and, if Ray is living, he will be made the heir to six millions."

Garcias leaned back in his chair, stunned. As he sat there, a fire gathered gradually in his eyes. "If we suppose that everything you say is true," he said, "then you are a rash fellow."

"In coming here?"

"Yes."

"No, not a rash man. Because you believe me, and you will not kill the boy for nothing. No matter how your trap is set, you know that it will cost your people some of their best blood to deal with him. You will be glad to let him go when you understand that I, after all, am the only person in the world who knows where Juan Ray is to be found."

"And if *you* are brushed out of the way, *Padre* José," said Garcias, "then there would remain not a single soul who could find Ray. That is clear."

"I am in no danger," said the shepherd. "You are not a man of many scruples, *Señor* Garcias, but still, even your hand would be held by a small thread from destroying me. Partly on account of Isabella, and partly on account, let me be vain and say it, of myself."

"And if I have other men?" questioned Garcias, who seemed fascinated almost evilly by the course of the argument.

"They are almost without exception the men of the mountains. And the men of the mountains have a certain respect for me, and even a certain fear. They would be more apt to help me if I asked them for help, than to serve you, in spite of the money you offer to them. Think a moment, and you will see that this is true. However, if God takes me, he takes me, and this is an end of everything on the earth for me. I should not be very sorry. I have traveled so much of the way that I think I know what the rest of the road is like."

"You are a brave man and a good man," said Garcias. "I admire you. I respect you. But, as you have said, there is one man above me in all this. I must ask him what to do. I won't say that all of your guesses have been wrong. Wait here. I shall return soon."

"Thank you. There is no hurry," said the *padre.*

Garcias left the room.

The girl, listening with all her might, thought that she heard the key turned in the lock.

Apparently old *Padre* José heard the same thing, for he instantly left his chair, crossed to the door, and tried the knob of it. It turned in his hand, but the door did not budge. *Padre* José, turning slowly from the door, clasped one hand upon his breast, frowning at the floor. Perhaps he felt, then, the pinch and the pang of separation from this life. But it was over in an instant.

The girl, frozen with terror and horror as she was, now felt a sudden rushing of tears that stung her eyes when she saw *Padre* José lift his head suddenly and smile straight before him.

He faced the window, so that the smile seemed to be one of encouragement and recognition for the girl who was crouched outside it, but she knew that his thoughts were fixed far, far beyond her. She gathered her strength and nerved her knees to the work. Only by degrees she was able to bear her own weight. Then strength came back to her with a rush, and she was running with all her might around the side of the house. When she came to the entrance to the patio, she was amazed to find that it was unguarded. But she breathed a prayer of gratitude for that deliverance. Then, walking stealthily down the side of the patio, she came to the door of the hall.

She could not believe that she saw the key in the lock. By so small an omission her guilty foster father might be saved from the crowning crime of all. She turned it. Once and again the bolt moved back, and then she thrust the door wide.

She found *Padre* José seated in the chair, calmly smoking his pipe, and he turned his head only gradually toward her.

She, clinging to the side of the door, weak with relief and joy, cried feebly to him: "Come, *Padre!* The way is clear, as you see.

Come quickly, quickly, I say."

He leaned forward to rise, and she glanced swiftly over her shoulder to make sure that there was still no one in sight. When she looked back at the *padre* again, he had not left his place.

"*Padre* José!" she cried in a sudden terror. "Are you coming?"

"No, my child," he said.

Chapter Thirty-Six

She could not believe what she heard. She cried at him, more loudly still: "*Padre* José! Do you hear me? The door is open!"

He waved his hand to her and shook his head as in resignation. "Go away quickly, my dear," he said to her, "or you will be seen here. As for me, I have made up my mind, and it is not so easy to do that. Nothing matters to me now."

"*Padre* José!" she cried. "You are quite mad. He will have you murdered."

"Oh, Isabella," said the shepherd, "murder or illness or old age or honorable battle, they all bring one to the same end. But it is different with you."

She sprang inside and closed the door behind her.

This got him out of his chair. "Isabella!" he exclaimed.

"I am staying here, if you do," she said. "I'll be a witness."

"Child, child," said the shepherd. "You are only his daughter in name, and not in blood. You cannot tell what he would do in such a case."

"I'm not his daughter in name or blood after tonight," she answered. "The detestable. But I stay here as long as you stay. I'll go when you go."

He went hastily to her and took her hand. "Do you mean this?" he said.

"Yes, I mean it," she answered.

"Now, heaven teach me what to do," said the good old man, actually lifting his eyes in this quandary. "I must stay here for the boy. And yet I should go to take you, Isabella, if you really are leaving this house."

"Forever and ever," she answered passionately. "And every minute that you wait here is dangerous to you. And besides. . . ."

Now, swelling louder from the bottom and the rear of the house, they heard a noise of many voices shouting, then the booming of guns firing rapidly.

"Whatever has happened, it's finished now!" cried the girl.

"The poor lad!" cried the shepherd. "And no soul to help him! It is he. It could be no other person. Let me go, Isabella!" He tried to run toward the noise, but, when he had gone as far as the door, she clung desperately to him.

"If they've killed him," said the girl, "do you want to kill his work after him? You know Juan Ray."

"Curse the name of him!" said the shepherd fiercely. "Except for him there would be none of this crime and this wretchedness. But you are right. If he is gone, then I must save myself to do the thing that he has left undone. If I had told him before . . . if only I had told him before." So, half groaning, he turned at last with the girl, and with her hurried out of the patio.

Behind them the uproar now increased to a great volume. And a voice that yelped above the rest came to their ears.

"That is my father," said the girl. "No, he is only Fernando Garcias now to me. He is mad with rage. He has failed, and I swear that the young American is living. Living and free, or there would not be this uproar. He is shouting like a man frantic. Hear him . . . it is like the yelling of a dog."

"This way," said the shepherd. "If this is true, then heaven has been good to me. This way . . . there is a mule left yonder in the woods."

They hurried on. Presently, as they reached the trees, they saw just before them the shadowy silhouette of a mounted man. The girl, with a gasp, caught at the arm of her companion and strove to draw him back, but he merely murmured to her: "Whoever it is, it is likely to be a man who knows me." He called aloud: "Who is there?"

"Someone who has been waiting for you, *Padre* José," answered a voice. "You're a little late, partner. What's all the fireworks yonder at the Casa Garcias?"

"It is he," said the shepherd. "He is here again. It is the boy."

Isabella said nothing at all, but her hand shook upon the arm of her companion.

They hurried on.

"Who's with you?" asked the voice of Grey again.

"Isabella Garcias," said the shepherd. "Or Isabella of some other name tonight, for she's thrown away the last one. Who is that beside you on the other mule?"

"It is *Señor* Slade," said the boy.

"You have done the thing you wanted to do," said the shepherd. "This is a night of miracles."

"Wait here with them," said Grey. "There's a whole nest of horses back in the woods where the thugs staked them out. We'll take what we want and give the others a run before us. Garcias and his pets may not follow us so fast then."

They did not wait. They pushed on behind him, and they found in a small clearing at least a dozen saddled mules and horses. On a mule they mounted the girl and put the shepherd on another. The reins of the others were cut rapidly, and, as brush crackled under the feet of the men who were rapidly approaching, they started the herd before them and swept down into the trail to the lower valley.

Shouts and curses followed them. Even a few random bullets went crackling through the branches not far from their heads. But they got safely into the trail and rode away.

The thin moon, riding higher in the sky, gave them a very indifferent light, but their mounts were used to mountain trails, and they went forward at a good rate.

Slade led the way, his shoulders bulking, broad and heavy, before the rest, the girl followed, the *padre* behind her, and last of all rode young Grey, with a song continually bubbling softly on his lips.

Joy filled him like wine. He could not be still in the saddle, but was fidgeting and twisting from side to side all the while.

So they came down the rocky steps into the lower gorge, and now all four rode abreast. It was the girl who brought on the next turn of talk, for she said: "Ask *Padre* José, Rinky Dink, what news he could have given to you long ago?"

"What news, *Padre?*" asked the boy.

"News that would have ended your trail, Rinky Dink," urged the girl. "For he knows where Juan Ray lives."

"He knows?" broke out Slade with a hard, high ring in his voice.

"You have a right to be angry," said the shepherd. "I should have told you as soon as I knew what was keeping the pair of you in the mountains, where there was so much danger for you both. Failing to do so, I nearly brought ruin to you both. I intended to tell you, also. But you must remember that it was not an easy thing for me to say. For fifteen years Juan Ray has lived true to a promise to himself that he would never tell the world again his name. Fifteen years of truth to such a course of life is not an easy thing to violate."

"Of course not," said the boy. "But tell me now, *Padre* José. All that I want to do is to find the man. If he's near, I'll start now on the trail of him. Give me half a hint of the way to ride and I'll start now. Eh, Slade?"

"Start now?" said Slade, the same ring in his voice. "Yes. Even if we had to ride over ice and fly down cliffs. What is it, *Padre* José?"

"A thing you will find hard to believe," said the old man.

"Hard to believe?" said Slade. "After tonight there's nothing in the world that's hard to believe. I have seen a dozen armed men behind locked doors fail to keep out one youngster who had made up his mind to enter. After that, *Padre* José, what is there in the world that would be hard to believe?"

"Stuff," said Grey modestly but happily.

"It's truth," said Isabella. "It was a glorious and a wonderful thing. You haven't told us a syllable of how you did it."

"I'll tell you the whole story," said the boy. "I started walking, and I had good luck beside me all the way. Besides, that's ended, but Juan Ray isn't. *Padre* José, suppose that you tell us now where the trail to Juan Ray lies."

"Come, come," said the shepherd. "You are all fire and eagerness. Do you know the story of the boy and the wishing gate?"

"Oh, confound stories," said Grey impetuously. "Tell me where I can find the way to Juan Ray?"

"You want to cut me short," said the old man. "But I won't have you clip the wings of my story, because it's a reasonably long one, and strange enough to be worth the telling, I think."

Chapter Thirty-Seven

Grey groaned with impatience, but the shepherd, like one who loves a good story, cleared his throat and imperturbably began: "We go back to the last days of Juan Ray in San Vicente. All of you know a good deal about him? Yes, for I've heard you all speak of him many times. He was the sort of a fellow who catches the eye, not that there was very much to him, but even a fool can turn himself into a light if he soaks his clothes in oil and then touches a match to himself.

"That was the way with Juan Ray. He had made a good deal of money. He had made so much of it that he thought he had enough to last forever. He got tired of taking gold out of the ground, you might say, and he decided that he would, during the rest of his life, spend the coin he had piled up.

"So he settled down in San Vicente, because it was pretty and pleasant, and he already knew it well. Besides, he wanted to be the center of attention, you see, and therefore he chose a comparatively small place. He was like Cæsar in this, if one may compare small men to great ones.

"When he came to San Vicente, he had so much money that he felt he could buy the whole city, if he chose, and keep it or throw it away. Perhaps, for that reason, he conceived a great affection for it and for the people in it.

"You know those people in San Vicente are cheerful, good-natured, and nearly all of them are pleasant to talk to. When they saw what sort of a fellow had come among them, they very quickly gave one another the wink, as the saying is. They agreed with each other about him. They humored him, and he was happy. Why, the happiness of that man, if you could have seen him in those days, was a shining thing that could be seen at a distance. He was a great fool. All that he knew was what his eyes saw and what his ears heard.

"If he went into a theater, there was an outbreak of hand-clapping. When he went down the street, men and boys took off their hats to him. Why not? It is an easy thing to salute a fool or a madman. Such people are humored, like children. If he was riding by the river, people stood up on benches and looked, clapped their hands and laughed. He thought that they were laughing in sheer pleasure at the sight of him. He did not guess that there was any mockery in them.

"In a short time, he loved all the people of San Vicente even more, in his heart, than they seemed to love him in their manner. It followed, since he was rich, that the beggars of San Vicente began to come to one door only. Well, that was a good thing, too. He liked it. He used to set up a big round table in his garden, and around that table the mendicants gathered. Sometimes there were thirty or forty men and women out there. In the field behind his garden, he set up some tents. Those beggars lived in a sort of Gypsy camp. They had plenty to eat, red wine or *pulque* to drink, and, in addition, tobacco was distributed among them. That's enough to make a Mexican happy, and they were very happy. Nothing pleased Juan Ray more than this Gypsy camp.

"When he looked out of his window in the morning, he saw the tops of the tents shining, and he felt as if all of those lives were in the hollow of his hand. At night, he used to go out there and sit among them. At first they were constrained. But after a while they accepted him, and they would sing their songs and tell their stories of wandering, misfortunes, wild adventures, folk tales, legends, yarns of thieving and all sorts of mischief. For most of the poor wanderers on the face of this earth, it appears, are cast out because they are not worthy of being kept within the bounds of society.

"Juan Ray loved those evenings among his Gypsies, but he did not have as much time with them as he could have wished. He could not, every evening, go out to hear their songs and see their dances, some of them a thousand years old. Instead, he had to give the greater part of his time to the work of chatting with the gentlemen of San Vicente and to dancing and gossiping with the ladies.

"You know that Mexican families guard their women with a hand of iron. They shut out strangers, particularly foreigners. But with Juan Ray it was a different matter. It was easy for the heads of the families to see that Ray was not a philanderer. All doors opened to him as if by magic. The old women, the young married girls, and the children were always flocking about him. Once he dined under the cypresses with the pretty young wife of the *alcalde*. And yet not one thread of gossip was woven into San Vicente's dark garment of scandal.

"You will say that this was very strange. But it was not. For Juan Ray was the fountainhead from whom blessings flowed. If a man fell into bad circumstances, he would casually tell Ray how he had to call back his two sons from school, and Ray was sure to give the additional money that was needed. If someone made a bad investment, a word to Juan Ray would very likely bring him the sum of his loss.

"Of course, with such a fool as Ray about, people soon began to make up stories of their imaginary losses. No one could have enough money, no one except Ray himself. How many hundreds of times the sly rascals must have sat about in their gossiping circles and exchanged tales of how they had 'done' the American fool. At any rate, the years ran merrily along for Ray. And every year it seemed to him that he had worked his way deeper into the hearts of the people of San Vicente.

"One day, he heard a pair of youngsters talking loudly, and one of them swore by the beard of *Señor* Ray . . . by the double beard of the *señor.* That filled the cup of Ray. Poor idiot. Poor, childish idiot. He felt that he was almost deified in the eyes of the townsmen. After that, he turned on the tap of his fortune and let it run, and filled the very gutters with it, so to speak. But a running faucet will drain the biggest tank in time. One day, Ray got a note from his bank. Only then did he actually awake to the facts.

"He had a few thousand *pesos* left and that was all. Nevertheless, he merely looked at the letter and shrugged his shoulders. It was true that he had not invested his money in banks or in farms or in stocks. He had done better. He had given it to honest and honorable people. So he simply went to a great friend of his, a man who dined with him every Saturday, and he said to him that he now needed a part of the two hundred thousand *pesos* which, from time to time, he had lent the fellow.

"He was greeted with absolute silence. When he looked at his friend, he saw that the face of the man was pinched and distorted with fear and with greed. He said that, at the moment, he was without ready cash, but that he would soon raise the money. He then asked if Juan Ray would come three days later, at three in the afternoon.

"Juan Ray came three days later, having spent his last penny, meanwhile. When he came to the door of his friend, he was told, coldly enough, that the man was not at home. The servants did not know where he was or when he would return. The situation was now clear to Ray. He said good bye to the two hundred thousand *pesos* that he had given without asking for interest, note, or security.

"He went to another friend . . . it was the same. Suddenly a number of people left San Vicente. They were all friends of Juan Ray. They were all people who owed him quantities of money. He understood at last. It was not that he had loaned money to one rascal, but that the whole list of his friends had turned against him.

"One evening, as he sat in his room with both his hands hard-gripped on the table before him, a note was brought to him. It was from General O'Riley. The general had never received a penny from Ray, but he declared that he considered the American a public benefactor. He said many other pleasant things and begged Juan Ray to use his checkbook as his own, having heard, as he said, of his misfortunes. With that note, he sent a little sheaf of checks that were not filled out except for the big, sprawling signature of the general.

"When Ray saw this note and looked at the contents, something crumbled in his brain, as though his wits were dissolving in a flame. He threw the note and the checks into the fire. He ran down to the stable and saddled his best horse and he rode out into the open.

"He rode through the streets of San Vicente and cursed them as he galloped. He rode under the cypresses by the river and cursed them there, also. He galloped on. He crossed the bridge. He saw a road before him. He hardly knew where it went. He only knew that there was an open way before him, with green, naked fields on either side and no men . . . no men. For that he was grateful.

"He rode far into the night. He rode until the horse reeled beneath him and fell down. It was dead. He looked at its glazed eyes and at the white foam around its mouth, and he felt no pity. He walked on, and still he only knew that he was walking away from San Vicente and the face of man. That was his only goal, do you see?

"He got into the mountains at dawn, and there half a dozen

vagrant ruffians met him, stripped him of everything, threw him some of their rags, and went off. He put on the clothes, and he laughed. For he felt, suddenly, the stripping away of a great burden.

"Do you understand how it was with him? After his life of wealth, struggle, and happiness, then heart-burning pain in the end, he was as he had been at the beginning of life . . . naked and helpless, except for his two hands.

"He stood on a high place and looked back, saw the sun redden, saw the green plain of San Vicente, the white of the town, and the river running like gold through the plain. It appeared as only a little thing. He could have held that distant town in the hollow of his hand. And so he laughed again, and the last bitterness was washed out of his heart.

"I want you to understand. He had been spending his time, his money, to make San Vicente a thing that he could hold as his own, through the love that the people had for him. But now, as he left the town far behind him, he saw that it was worth nothing. It was the beginning of understanding, for him. He said to himself . . . 'Juan Ray has lived and Juan Ray is dead. I shall forget him as quickly as the world does.' He stopped at the house of a charcoal burner and got a razor and shaved off his beard. Then he went on and came through a pass into a narrow valley, and he found a sick old shepherd sitting on a rock, with his head hanging, like the head of an old horse that stands in a corral and waits for death.

"So Juan Ray began to work for the old man, and that same winter, death carried the shepherd away, and Juan Ray, with a new name, inherited the flock, and kept on living among the mountains, as you see him to this day."

When he had finished, a wild, sharp cry burst from the throat of Slade. "You are Juan Ray!" he cried. "You, you! Oh, eternal fool that I am! And already I had half guessed." He broke off with a click of his teeth.

But young Grey had reached out and grasped both the hands of the shepherd. "You see what's happened, *Padre* José?" he said. "The thing you thought that you'd thrown away has come back to you, and now you're to be richer than ever."

Chapter Thirty-Eight

In this brief narration of the tragedy within a life, it seemed to Grey that he had beheld a thing greater than the great mountains around him.

He heard the old man saying: "Have I told you the whole story for nothing, my son? Do you think that I wish to be John Ray of San Vicente, or New York, or Rome again? No, no! Money can buy me nothing, now. Nothing remains that I value except the peace that I find here inside the arms of the mountains. These simple people, they truly love me, and they need me. They come to me as if I were a father, a judge, and a priest. Could all the millions that Forbes leaves to me accomplish so much? No, that money would gather around me liars and sycophants again."

"True," Slade said suddenly and with force.

"Listen to me," said the boy. "Do you think that your life will be safe? We know the truth about you. Slade . . . I don't know how . . . already had guessed it. Garcias and the other scoundrels may guess it, also. You will not live long, if you stay here."

"As for my life," said the old man, "it was a gift for which I did not ask. It will be taken away from me as such gifts are always taken. Do you wish me to run away like a frightened dog? No, no, my son. I remain here."

"*Padre* José! *Padre* José!" cried Isabella. "Don't you see . . . you're just as blind and stubborn now, in a different way, as you were in San Vicente?"

"Well," he said, "perhaps I am. We see only by what light is within us, and that is only a feeble glimmer to shine down a very great road, my dear."

"You've looked at it," said the boy, "from one side only. If you look at it from another, you'll see something that's worth seeing. You'll see that poor fellow Forbes, yonder in a sick bed, fighting away death for four years, setting his teeth, living on milk and water, praying and waiting for news of you, *Padre* José. Now, are those four years to be thrown away like a bad penny?"

"Ah, ah . . . ," said the old man. "That's a thing, too. I should have thought of that. Poor Forbes on his sick bed, and four years of waiting . . . four years of pain and expectancy. Why, I can remember eating my heart out because a train was half an hour late." He added: "You see, my children, what a fickle and changeable old man I am? I shall do as you say. Not to take the money he wants to give me, but to see him and thank him, perhaps to give him something that will make the end of his days pleasant. That's why I shall go to see Forbes. Aye. But I shrink when I think of the distance. Besides, what's to become of my sheep?"

"True," said the girl. "There are the sheep." But she laughed as she spoke.

They had come, now, within sight of the round-topped hut of *Padre* José, and they were surprised to see a light gleaming from the open doorway.

But the *padre* said: "That is simply one of my people. Someone has come for me, and will sit there by my lantern until I come back. That often happens. They will miss me, I think, when I have gone on the long journey."

He said it with a simple happiness, and Grey, looking back, thought of the picture of the man with the divided beard, galloping fiercely under the cypresses.

This was not he. This was a new man, in a new existence, with another soul.

A shadow appeared on the trail before them. It took on the form of a man, who cried out: "*Padre* José! *Padre* José? Are you there?"

"Here I am, my son," said the *padre*. He waved to the others to halt their horses, and rode forward by himself, merely saying: "This is one of my people in some great trouble." For there had been a ring of pain in the voice that had called out.

As the *padre* rode forward, the others could see the shadowy form running to meet him, casting out his arms before him, like one who hurried to welcome safety.

They heard his voice, which strove to be repressed, but whose emotion broke out strongly: "It is I, *Padre*. It is the wretched Cordoba!"

"Why should you be wretched?" asked *Padre* José. "When I saw you last, you were planning to marry pretty María, weren't you?"

"Padre," said the miserable man, and they saw him drop to his knees in the dust and lay hold on the stirrup of the rider. "*Padre,* this day I fired upon a man, and only heaven turned the bullets aside. Then I saw that it was a miracle, and I went home and held my head in my hands, and tried to think, but I could only say to myself that *Padre* José would tell me the truth."

"Now, I'll tell you what I think is the truth," said the *padre*. "Perhaps it was a miracle. Perhaps it was not. But it is a thing for which you should do penance."

"Aye, ten years of penance," said the man. "I see his face, still. He was your guest, *Padre* José, and heaven will never be kind to me again."

"Son," said the old man, "you speak like a fool. Would heaven have turned the bullets if it had not had a future use for you?"

There was a groan from Cordoba. "Here I vow to the kind

San Cristóbal. . . ."

"You'd better save your vows for another day," said the *padre*. "You ought to hear your penance, first."

"Good *Padre* José," said the brigand, "speak to me, and tell me. If ten years of my life. . . ."

"No," said the *padre*, "but a month or two might do very well."

"*Padre* José, command me. I am miserable as a worm at your feet."

"You've shot at men before, Cordoba," said Ray. "You must have indigestion to feel this little affair so much."

"His face was like the face of one who saw through my soul," said Cordoba. "He smiled, while I pressed the muzzles of the gun against his heart. Still my soul freezes when I think of it. He smiled. And he told me some wonderful lies. When I got back to María, I took her ten times in my arms, and still I could not believe that she was there."

"And the penance, my son?"

"Ah, yes, make the penance bitter and long."

"Well, it will be bitter for you. You know nothing of sheep, do you?"

"No. Nothing, *Padre*."

"This is your penance, then. I am going away on a journey. It may be two months, three before I return. While I am gone, you, Cordoba, will tend to my flock."

"Sacred heavens," said Cordoba.

"With care, night and day," said the *padre*.

"It shall be done," said Cordoba. "I know nothing of sheep, the silly fools. I ask ten thousand forgivenesses, *Padre* José."

"You can ask advice," said the other calmly. "You can ask María."

"True," said the man. "The good girl knows sheep as though they were her brothers and sisters. I shall ask my dear María.

She will tell me."

"There is Pedro Negro, too. He keeps his flock very well. Although he doesn't like to tell his secrets, if sickness should come into the flock, he'll tell you what to do, for my sake."

"I once held him up," reflected Cordoba, "and I got from him a good hunting knife, except that the blade was a little worn, and a big skin of wine, and seven *pesos* fifty. But I was wearing a mask and it was the dark of the moon. He cursed me terribly when I held the gun into the pit of his stomach, but, although he talked loudly, his actions were like those of his sheep. Yes, I can ask Pedro."

"Now go home and sleep, if you can," said the *padre,* "and tell María to pray for your soul, because it has spots that need to be washed away."

"Ah, that poor María," said the bandit. "She already prays so long and so hard for me that her knees are covered with calloused places, she says. She prays so much for me, that I am beginning to pray a little for myself. I pray to be better."

"Then you are better already, my son," said *Padre* José. "But take all things slowly, and believe that you are better when you find yourself doing good for others. I'll tell you this, my child. Ten thousand prayers do not do as much for you as ten good acts, and the reason is that good actions may become a habit, and by habit we are ruled, all of us, good and bad. And when your actions are good, then your immortal soul is saved, Cordoba."

"I write your words, *Padre,*" said the bandit, "in the center of my heart. As for the respected sheep of my father, when may I have the honor of coming to take care of the fools? I beg ten thousand forgivenesses again."

"Come in the gray of the morning," said *Padre* José.

"And that's not very far away.

"Good bye, my friend. Go home. See María, if you can, and

ask her advice. All will still be well with you, my son. I felt it long ago. I feel it now. When I come home, I promise you one thing."

"Ah, *Padre,* and what is that you promise?"

"That you will have found new ways of cursing and very strange oaths, but you won't be calling the sheep fools."

"I listen and shall remember," said the devout bandit.

"*Adiós,* Cordoba."

"*Adiós,* my father, my saint," said the bandit. "María, also, loves you."

He departed, and the rest of the company rode up. Slade somewhat hanging to the rear, his head down, as the boy noticed, like that of a man lost in the deepest thought.

"There is still another in my cabin," said *Padre* José. "Ah, my friends, what shall I do without my people, even on a short journey . . . to say nothing of my poor sheep, in the hands of a brigand."

He laughed a little, as they rode on toward the hut.

Chapter Thirty-Nine

As they came up to the house, no one stepped out from it. They had dismounted, and Slade held the horses while the girl and Grey went in with the old man. There they found a tall, long-nosed, freckled-faced man of forty, who rose up to greet them. He wore a flannel shirt, four inches too big for his scrawny throat, and a coat that hung upon him in folds.

He looked at the shepherd, and then he turned to Grey. "Why, Rinky Dink," he said. "Dog-gone your socks, but I'm mighty glad to rest my eyes on you. I've come a long way to parley with you, son."

Grey shook the big, bony hand of the man. "What brought you here, Jim?" he asked. He explained to *Padre* José: "This is Jim Parson. Jim is an old friend of mine. We punched each other on the nose and got up friends. You know what that means."

"But you got up the soonest," said Jim Parson, "and I got up the most friends. Boy, but I'm glad to see you now, you will-o'-the-wisp, you burn-by-night. I've rode myself sore to get to you."

"What is it?" asked Grey.

"Why," said Jim, "I've traveled all the way down from the border, son, and I come from Neilan. You know which one."

"Does Neilan want a report?" asked the boy.

"He wants to send you a warning, that's all. He's got a new word. Do these people parley English, son?"

"As well as you do, Jim."

Jim Parson drew the boy to one side. But his voice, harsh and hoarse as it was, was louder than he meant to make it. "The marshal has a new tip, Rinky Dink," he said.

"About what?"

"About the game that you're riding on. And he got the name of a man that may put the kibosh on you."

"And where did he get that from?"

"Why," said Parson, "he got it from Broom, that's just turned up, after being given up for dead."

"Ah, I'm glad of that," said Grey. "But Broom is a tough one, and he would take a lot of killing."

"He got almost enough to do his job for him," said Parson. "That's what he got. But he lived through it and come to El Paso a pretty skinny shadow of the Broom that we used to know. Cast iron, we used to call him."

"That's right," said the boy. "What about him? You look a little sick, Jim."

"Sick is what I am," said Parson. "I tell you what I seen. I seen Broom setting in a chair, among friends, talk about things that made him bust out crying."

"I don't believe it," said Grey, compressing his lips.

"Nor would I, if another man told me," answered Parson. "But I tell you what I seen, and the shame was so clean gone out of him that he never even cared about his tears. But he sat there and blubbered like he was two years old. Oh, he was hurt bad, was Broom. He was hurt to the quick, man."

"I hate to hear it," said Grey. "What happened to him, poor chap?"

"What happened to him? That's what I'm here to tell you, and who done it."

"But how did you find me, old son?"

"I found your trail. It was a hard job. I hit a fellow called

O'Riley that gave me a steer in San Vicente. And out of that, I made out something. I did a lot of talking in bad Spanish now and then, and so I got here at last."

"Poor Broom," said the boy. "I would have bet on him against a thousand."

"Aye, but he met one man in ten thousand, and it was him that put Broom down."

"One man?"

"Aye."

"Mexican?"

"American."

"What was his name?"

"His name was . . . ," began Parson.

Then a revolver shot boomed in their ears, and poor Parson spun like a top and fell his ungainly length to the floor, both arms flung out wide.

Grey let him fall. Instead of catching that lumbering weight, he conjured two revolvers into his hands and, whirling toward the door, he faced—Slade!

"Slade!" he gasped. "Slade! In the name of the eternal powers!"

"In the name of Satan," said Slade calmly.

"This is a thing that you'll have to answer for," said Grey.

"To whom?" asked Slade as calmly as before.

"To me. I'm a friend of his and an older friend than I am of yours. I've owed you something, Slade. But I've owed as much to Parson. What's got into you, man? What's wrong with you?"

"I said that I'd get them, one by one," said Slade, in the same manner as before. "I swore that I'd get them, if I had to live a thousand years to do it. And here's the first one. This is one of the demons that I found in the house of Garcias."

"You?" exclaimed the boy. "You found him there?" He gaped at Slade.

"He's the one," said Slade, "who wanted to polish me off here and not wait to get you. Then the other had the bright thought of using me as a bait to catch you, and Parson agreed. Why, it was Parson that swore the best place to put me, as a bait, was in the third cellar, because he said that the deeper they put me, the harder you'd try to find me. Parson is the one, lad. And thank heaven I've paid him off."

"Jim Parson," said Grey, blenching. "Old Jim. Why, we've been hand in glove. We've bunked together. I can't believe it of him."

"It's a hard thing," said Slade. "But money rots the soul of a man."

Padre José, with the girl, was kneeling at the side of the fallen man. "Yes," he said as he looked up. "Money rots the soul of the world."

"He's not dead," breathed Isabella. "Thank heavens for that."

"Not dead?" exclaimed Slade, with a ringing lift to his voice. "Not dead? With a bullet through the middle of his brain?"

"It glanced!" exclaimed Isabella. "There! See the frightful furrow that it made down the side of his skull. He's living, and I can feel his heartbeat. Don't you, *Padre?*"

The *padre* was pressing his ear to the breast of the fallen man.

Said Grey: "It's a bad business, Slade. I've had enemies. I've had men that I hated and had hunted, even, but I gave them their chance when it came to the final showdown. I don't shoot men when they're not looking, Slade."

"You've lived only a short time down here, Rinky Dink," Slade said in his even way. "But let me see. You say that he's not dead, yet?"

There was something about that last word that made Grey watchful, and started his flesh crawling. He saw Slade step across the hut to where Parson lay, and, with a sudden movement, Slade brought a revolver into his hand. It would have been far too late, had not the boy been on the alert. As it was, he was barely able to leap and catch the hand that held the gun.

He found himself contesting with an iron arm, but a little trick that he had learned from an old Japanese in California helped him, and he made the gun fall out of the numbed fingers of Slade.

He growled at the man: "Slade, you've gone mad! You're losing your wits. What's inside of you?" He found himself facing eyes that glared at him with a straight, fiery regard. If the boy could have believed what he saw, he would have said that there was hate in the glance that the other gave him.

Then, without heed for the gun that lay on the floor of the hut, Slade turned on his heel and left the place.

Grey, his brain spinning, went to the door of the house, and he was further amazed to see Slade spring upon the back of a mule and kick it into a gallop down the road.

Slade was gone, but where?

"Nerves," said Grey to himself. "He's had more than he could digest at the house of Garcias. Poor Slade. He's had a good deal. It's touched his brain a little, and no wonder." For he could remember, then, the smell of mold in the cellar of the house of Garcias, the slippery floor, and the horrible, monotonous sound of the dripping water. Yes, Slade had been through enough to turn the mind of even such a man as he. Yet, the pity of it. For Grey had begun to look upon him as a matchless hero, a man with nerves of steel.

He turned back, as Parson groaned on the floor, then gasped and finally sat upright. He presented a strange appearance, with blood trickling down over his face in three separate streams. He clapped a hand to his head and said: "That's the way with 'em. The body's the proper place, but they will try for the head. Who was it, Rinky Dink? Who did it? And what did you do to him?"

Grey could not answer. It seemed impossible for him to face his old friend and say that he had done nothing to apprehend the would-be assassin. Then a thought struck him like a thunderclap. It made him stagger. It was a thing not to be believed, but it forced him down upon his knees beside the wounded man. He caught Parson by the shoulders and shook him a little, regardless of his wound.

"Tell me, Jim," he said, "the fellow who broke the heart of Broom, who was it?"

"Him?" said Jim Parson, rather dreamily. "Yes, I remember now. That's what Neilan wanted me to tell you. Him that smashed Broom. Him that's killed others that traveled your trail . . . a fellow by name of Slade."

Chapter Forty

Upon the ear of the boy, the name fell like the stroke of a bell. He heard the confused exclamations of the girl and old *Padre* José like the babbling of running water in the distance. He began to recall the words and the actions of his guide. Now that the blow had fallen, all seemed clear enough. It was Slade's own ingenious mind that had devised the plan for luring him to the house of Garcias. Slade, in the first place, when the boy left the house that day, must have wandered up the valley and given warning to Garcias and the brigand to make the first attack upon Grey, which so nearly had succeeded. Then Slade it was who made of himself a living bait to trap Grey. The part seemed so utterly detestable that the boy could hardly believe it at first. And this from a man who had risked his life for him.

Yet he could remember, now, that at the inn, on that other night, the door had been mysteriously opened, as if from the inside, and Slade had made no motion to assist him until the attack on him definitely had failed, and the man in the hall had been put to rout. Was it not Slade who had suggested the lighting of the lamp, thereby having his companion hold the very light by which he was to be shot? Only the accidental failure of the first match had saved Grey, even as early in the game as that.

Yet Grey groaned when he thought of the trust he had placed in this man. It had seemed to him that Slade stood out among other men as the crowning peak stands out above the range.

Then that rush down the hall in pursuit of the scoundrel who had lain in wait was the merest sham, for all the while Slade knew, bare-handed as he was, he was in no danger from the brigand. The accident of the fall upon the steps was what had sealed, completed, and made the performance perfect.

Again, the boy could remember in the house of Garcias, that night, how Perez had talked to the captive. No wonder he had been troubled about the gag, the cords, and the plan. For it was the master of them all who was lying there bound up on his own order.

Sweat rose upon the face of Grey. How completely Slade had seen through him, in planning that last, contemptible coup.

There were other evidences of Slade's purpose there in the house of Garcias, such as his fall in the hall and the blow he struck with the revolver that barely missed the skull of Grey, and the moment when he had turned upon him at the top of the passage—and each time murder had been in the heart of Slade.

Yet, it seemed strange that he had not given the alarm at other times; for instance, when Grey had just cut the cords and the door from the guard room had opened upon them. True, it had been the groan of Slade that caused the door to be opened, but one syllable, after it was wide, would have caused the armed men to rush in.

Perhaps, no matter what a villain, something in him was stirring in response to the situation. He had told them with his own tongue that, in spite of dangers, Grey would get to him. Perhaps a grim pride in the accuracy of his prediction may have kept him silent at that crucial moment. Besides, he must surely have been convinced that the game was still in the hollow of his hand, even when they were stealing up the corridors, with Rodrigo to guide them.

Yet, when Grey looked up from his reflections, having

completed in his mind the train of evidence that proved that Jim Parson had spoken honest words, his face was sad.

The girl saw it. She was helping old *Padre* José to bandage the wounded head of Parson, but she had time for one smile of sympathy and understanding.

"He's not worth your sorrow, Rinky Dink," she said.

She could say that, and it was true. And yet, when an ideal and an affection with it have vanished as a bubble vanishes, the mind and the heart for a moment cannot be adjusted. That which seemed to be still exists.

Grey went outside and stood under the stars of the sky, trying to think.

Slade and Garcias and all their hired men grew dimmer in his thoughts now. He was thinking of John Ray and that dying man, Forbes, and of the need of bringing them together. He was thinking of that man with the battered face, yonder in the northern city, Marshal Neilan, who, at his desk, had planned all this.

In honesty there is strength, and well do the honest men know it, but the thieves and the scoundrels know it better still. Otherwise, how could Neilan have done so much? He was not as intelligent, as supple and subtle of mind as Slade. He could not have conceived the deep schemes of the latter. Nevertheless, he was multiplied in his strength by the power of right.

Never before had the thing appeared to Grey so manifest. His heart warmed. He only hoped, when Marshal Neilan knew what his emissary had accomplished, he would approve all that he had done so far. But the work was only half done.

It was true that he had blocked the attempts of the others. He had found John Ray, which none of the others had done. And now he had the second half of the task to perform, to escort John Ray north to the land of law more strictly enforced, to usher him, perhaps, to the bedside of Forbes.

That made a full half of the unfinished task that still lay before him. And Slade, Slade's money and men were all against him.

But the right was with him, and he felt, somehow, that he could lean upon that abstraction more than upon any of the party with him. What a party it was. An old man, a young girl, a badly wounded man, and himself. Not a person to help him, but three separate weights upon his powers.

"Now, then, Rinky Dink," said the voice of *Padre* José from the doorway, "what do you think the best thing to do?"

"San Vicente," said the boy. "That place first, where General O'Riley will surely help us all he can . . . and his all is a good deal. With his help, then north as fast as we can ride . . . or else down to the sea and take a ship."

"There's a sad trouble with O'Riley," said the *padre*. "It is that he cannot help telling all that he knows. In his house there are always servants who are ready to pick up the news and spread it. He has no more real privacy than a horse in an open pasture. He would give his heart on a golden platter, if a friend asked him for it. But General O'Riley's gift would probably be dropped by the servant that brought it to you."

The boy was silent. He could not help feeling the truth of these remarks.

"For another thing," said the *padre*, "the moment that you get inside of San Vicente, even if you only stay a few hours, you are sure to be marked, and the life of every one of us is in danger."

"The lonelier we can stay," put in Jim Parson, "until we hit the sight of the Río Grande, I reckon the better it will be for all of us."

"Much the better," said the *padre*.

"Whatever you decide, I'm ready to do," said Grey.

"I know these mountains," said the *padre*. "I could guide you through them blindfolded. We have livestock to carry us. I know the way. It seems to me, the best thing is to break through the mountains and head straight across the northern desert for the Río Grande. It means a long ride and a hard ride. But I would lay my money that the last thing your friend Slade suspects is that we'll go north, instead of turning east toward San Vicente. Mind you, it's the San Vicente road that he'll have his hirelings watching now. If we can gain a quarter of a day's march on him by starting now, perhaps we'll beat him to the finish."

"Where is the girl to be left?" asked Jim Parson. He said not a word of the pain of his hurt. He was making and lighting a cigarette as calmly as though the bandage were not now strongly gripping his torn scalp.

"Where is the girl to be left?" repeated Grey.

Both of them faced *Padre* José.

She, at this, threw up her head.

"The girl does not need to be dropped. You can ride on, and she'll take care of herself."

"Would you go with us?" asked old *Padre* José, turning to her.

"No," she said. "I wouldn't go with you. I wouldn't weight you down."

Grey, from the shadow by the door, looked darkly out at her. A highlight gleamed on the hair of her bare head as she looked straight back at him.

"If she stays here," said the *padre,* "Garcias will have her again. He knows his rights as a . . . father. And now that the mask is dropped and she's seen him as he is and he knows that he has been seen, you'll lead a sweet life, my dear. It won't be long till he's married you off, whether you will or not, to a fat fortune, *frijoles,* grease, and all."

"I can take care of myself," said Isabella.

"Listen to me," said the *padre*. "She can shoot much straighter than I. She can ride much better and much longer, and she's lighter in the saddle. She must go with us."

"We'd be fools to do such a thing," suggested Parson.

"Fools or not, that's what we must do," said Grey.

"I'll go my own way," insisted Isabella. "I won't be a dead weight."

"Tush," said the boy.

She looked at him half angrily. "I'll not be bullied," she said.

"Come, come," said Grey. "It's time that we took you in hand. *Padre* José, you finish talking to her. We'll get the horses ready for the march."

Chapter Forty-One

They crossed the mountains. There was no mishap until they were in sight of the wide stretching plains to the north, where the broad sands shimmered and the rocks gleamed far away like mirrors. Then, as they dipped down a narrow trail, Jim Parson's horse slipped on a rolling stone and, the next minute, was pitching head over heels into the thin vacuity of the gorge on their right.

They thought that Jim was gone with his horse. They could hardly screw up their courage to look over the side, and there, far in the bottom, they saw the unfortunate brute sprawled in a strange position, with its forelegs thrown out before it, as though it were attempting to rise. But the body of Parson was not in sight and presently they saw him clinging to some shrubbery twenty feet below them.

They let down a rawhide lariat and pulled him up. He had a few scratches but no other hurt, and explained that the lurch of the horse as it stumbled on the rock had thrown him half out of the saddle, and the first flip of the poor animal as it turned in the air had cast him out from his place.

They rejoiced to have him back. And they had, as an extra mount, Doll, the mare. Grey shifted to her. Now that the mountains were ending, her speed of foot was far better than the endurance and the sure step of the mules. Grey made Jim Parson take his saddle, for, like a veritable Indian, Grey rode as well with stirrups as without them. And so they struck out onto the desert.

They were ten days to the north, now, and there had been no sign of the enemy on all that march. Confidence grew in them. They made their fires fearlessly at night and in the morning, regardless of how far the smoke column might be seen, or the bright eye of the fire through the darkness to watchful eyes.

All through that march, the girl held up bravely and steadily. She made no complaints. She refused no hazards. When she dismounted at a halt, she was the readiest hand to collect forage or cut down brush for the fire. She could be the last to turn into her blankets and the first to rise in the pink of the dawn.

The others made a sorry spectacle, after the first week. Grease will spill and dust will collect in the spots. The sweat of horses and humans commingling with its own salty deposits will cake the clothes with gray. So the men looked a vagabond trio, after a time. Mostly they were unshaven. They smoked much, ate hugely, talked little. All day long they looked at Isabella as though she were the music and the dance of running water. For she, mysteriously, kept herself fresh in spite of the torrid marches. If they passed a brook, she fell back behind the march, and before very long she was galloping up with them again, after a plunge. And she persisted in patient laundering, for which the men had neither time nor energy to spare. Her crimson-and-yellow neckerchief looked each morning as though it had been ironed the night before or else knotted for the first time on this day. Yet they were thankful, not so much for the pleasant sight of her as for her still pleasanter voice and ways. And what should call for thanks, if not a bright eye and a smile in time of trouble?

For three days, Jim Parson, who bitterly opposed the inclusion of her in the party, looked at her sourly. On the fourth he went to her and said in the hearing of them all: "I been a fool, and a great fool. Look here, Isabella. You're a better man than I am, a better hand around a camp, you ride more slicker, and you got more sense."

At the end of a week, Jim Parson said: "Where's the man you're ridin' to meet, Isabella?"

The day-long familiarity of the marches was so great that each knew each other as members of a family by this time, and the girl did not blush.

"Somewhere out yonder," she said, and waved to the skyline.

"I tell you what," said the tall man, "you send him to me for a reference, will you?"

Out of the mountains, four days through the sands they rode, and the work was harder than ever before. But still there was no token of an enemy at hand.

The heat had increased every moment, after leaving the high lands, and, since there was now a full moon shining in the night, they started their marches not long before sunset and pressed on through the cooler hours. It was much better for the riders; it was even better for the livestock, although they did not graze as well during the heat of the day as they had formerly done in the evenings and the early mornings.

Their guide was no longer old *Padre* José. They had long ago passed north of the domain that he knew by heart, and, crossing a no man's land of which none of them had much knowledge, they now reached a region over which Grey had ranged many and many a time.

So he guided them at last into a narrow pass that cut through a low-lying range of rocks. It might be said that this march was the beginning of the final stage of the journey. Beyond those hills of stone, they would soon have the long, brown sweep of the Río Grande before them.

Their fears had subsided. All that weighed them down was the thought of the labor of the march, and that labor was well-nigh ended.

The night was utterly still as they entered the pass, and from the rocks of its narrowing walls and from the sands under their feet the heat was still pouring forth. The place was an oven that had not yet cooled. All of them were continually mopping their brows to keep the sweat from running down into their eyes. Only Isabella Garcias seemed cool and at ease. They had nicknamed her the salamander, because heat seemed to make so little difference to her. Now, as they rode along in a scattered single file, she was singing, from time to time, and whistling like a boy.

Grey rode behind her. And now old *Padre* José urged his mule up beside the mare. "Rinky Dink," said *Padre* José—for that was the name by which they all called him now—"for five miles you've seen neither the sand, nor the rocks, nor the moon in the sky. You've looked at nothing but the girl."

"*Padre* José," said the boy, "for fifty years and fifty thousand miles, I could ride along and look at nothing else."

"Have you told her that?" asked the *padre*.

The boy looked sharply askance at the other. "Tell her that?" he said. "She knows it. She knows the way I feel. There's no need of talking. And she knows, besides, what I am. She knows that I'm a loafer and a drifter and an idler. Those are the weakest things that you can call me, in fact. No, no, *Padre* José. The less I talk to her the better."

"Well," said the old man, "if you don't talk to her, I shall talk for you."

"Hold on," said the boy. "You wouldn't do that. You don't mean that, *Padre?*"

"Why," said the other, "I'm fond of the girl, am I not, my lad?"

"Of course, you are."

"And suppose that a person I'm fond of has a gold mine on

his farm and doesn't know anything about it . . . well, what sort of a friend would I be, Rinky Dink, if I said not a word?"

Before Grey could answer, the sand splashed before his horse, as water splashes when a stone is shied into it. They reined in their horses. Jim Parson and the girl, in the lead, looked suddenly back to them. At the same time, from the black rock wall of the ravine to their right came a sound as though two hammer faces had been struck together.

The four, in silence, stared at one another. No words were needed. They had underrated Slade, after all, and now he was at them.

"Back, back!" called Grey. "Turn back and . . . !" As he spoke, he whirled the mare about.

Instantly the sands splashed to the right, to the left, and ahead of them. Deceived by the clearness of the moonlight, the marksmen on the walls of the ravine must have fired point-blank. But they would soon make the necessary allowance for distance, and then their fire would tell.

From the right wall and from the left, they heard the guns and the echoes calling.

Jim Parson sang out: "They've got the place lined for us! We've gone and shoved our heads into a trap, Rinky Dink. Make for the rocks straight ahead. That's better than this." He interrupted his last words to swear and duck his head, as the waspish singing of a bullet flew past his face.

There was no doubt about the wisdom of his advice. They quickly spurred their mounts for the rocks that jutted up in a black, jagged group not so very far away from them. The girl, being in the lead and a light rider, gained on the rest, but the white furrows were leaping in the sands about her as the marksmen increased their fire from either side of the ravine.

Then Isabella's mustang, Pinky, stooped, put its nose into the soft sand, and turned head over heels. Isabella herself lay in a crumpled heap just ahead, a dark spot on the white of the sands.

Every man of them would have given his life for her, but it was the good sense of Grey's mare that brought him first to her. He leaned from the horse as she strove to sit up, and, drawing her up before him on the horse, he rode on into the shelter of their little fort.

She was their first concern, but she dismissed their worries instantly, leaping down from the horse to the ground. To be sure, she staggered a little, but, with one hand leaning against a jagged stone, she recovered herself and managed to speak a word to Grey.

"Poor Pinky," she said, speaking of the mustang. "And poor all of us, for I think that Pinky is only one jump ahead of us on the long trail."

Chapter Forty-Two

It was the first discouraged word that she had spoken, but there was reason for her discouragement now. The rocks, which had seemed so safe a retreat for a little distance, exposed them to the fire of the enemy. On every hand there were gaps among the big stones, and through these the marksmen on the ravine walls were firing blindly, hoping to strike a target.

So, first, they made the horses lie down; next, they sheltered themselves at the bases of the biggest rocks. Then, in the hot stillness, broken only by the clang of the rifles and the splashing of lead against the outer walls, they had time to consider.

They might live through one day, without water, the sun beating straight down upon their heads. But the livestock would perhaps go crazy or die before that day was ended. After that? They could pray in vain for a cloudy night in this place, in any season of the year. And without clouds, this moon beat upon the valley like a silver sun, pouring down steady, endless fountains.

Hope was as dim and as distant for them as ever it had been for Grey on that night of nights, when he wandered through the damp, vast cellars of the house of Garcias. It was more distant, even, for there he had had the advantage of darkness to aid him and cover him, and twisting passages through which he could dodge as a fugitive.

But here, all was light. All things that threw a shadow were mercilessly visible from the rimrocks of the ravine. Beside the dead mustang lay a small image of darkness. Though the body itself, even at a short distance from the rocks of their refuge, was almost invisible, still the shadow stood out plainly.

Grey stretched himself. His feet, instead of slipping easily through the softness of the sand, struck into the resistance of Jim Parson's slicker that lay there, the old gray slicker, turned by the moon into the very color of the sand. He picked it up and looked hopelessly out through a rift between the two rocks opposite him. It came very near being the last move of young Grey, for a rifle bullet clipped a lock from his forehead. Another man would have cowered back into shelter; Grey merely crouched like a cat, ready to spring. Some shrink from a blow, others leap at the striker.

Suddenly his mind was perfectly clear. He saw their future as though it were mapped by his own hand. Either this night something must be done to save them, while still they possessed their full strength, or else they were totally and miserably lost.

"Hello," said Jim Parson. "There's a fellow riding out across the sand toward us. He's waving something as he comes."

"A flag of truce, eh?" said *Padre* José. "Let him come up."

The rider came within ten yards before he halted. His face was in black shadow, but the voice that came from him was that of Garcias.

"Isabella?" he called.

She stood up among the rocks. "I am here," she said.

"Ah, child," said Garcias. "I am thankful to see you again. I have begged heaven on my knees, and it has been permitted me to come for you. The others are lost men, but men they are, and they will let you come out to me."

"Aye, Isabella," said *Padre* José. "Go out to him. Better Garcias than what is coming to the rest of us."

She turned her head, deliberately looked at *Padre* José, and then quickly turned back to her foster father. "Father," she said, addressing Garcias, "for all the kindness you've shown me, I'll pray for you and wish you well all the days of my life. But to go back to you, I'd rather go back to red perdition."

"You speak, child," he said, "because of that one night. You can never know under what compulsion I was placed, or how I struggled against it. The truth is that I was not my own master. All that I did was only for the hope of pushing your own fortunes forward. There was nothing for myself."

"Do you think," she answered, "that murder would have helped me? Not the first murder, either! Oh, Fernando Garcias," she added with an outbreak of emotion, and a sort of childish wail in her voice, "I loved you as though we were the same blood. But that night I threw away the name you gave me."

"Ah, good girl," said Jim Parson, through his teeth.

"Isabella . . . ," began her foster father again.

"Listen to me, you hound," said Jim Parson. "The girl's spoken the truth. It's a better thing for her to take her bad chance with us than a worse chance with you. Turn your horse around, or I'll knock out your teeth with a half-inch slug of lead. I've got you covered now."

That ended abruptly the mission of Garcias. They saw him ride off, striking his hand against his face. They heard his groaning voice. And then the pitch of it rising to curses that died out at length.

There was a murmur as the people among the rocks began to confer again. *Padre* José was outraged by the manner in which Jim Parson had cut off the girl's chances. She herself was firm that her old life was ended and that she would rather die than go back to it. Jim Parson vowed that if she were his dearest sister—one, he said, who was the champion hominy-maker and cook of the world—he would rather shoot her through the head than allow her to return to such a man.

"What do you say, Rinky Dink?" asked *Padre* José, turning

about from the talk.

But Grey was not there!

They looked at one another in amazement. "He's gone!" cried Isabella. "He's gone to try some wild, crazy, hopeless thing. I should have watched him. I meant to. I knew beforehand that he would try. Rinky Dink! Rinky Dink!"

There was no answer. Anxiously they scanned the sands from all sides of the rocks. He had disappeared. The silver-gray of the desert had swallowed him up, and all they could see, of a living or a dead body near the rocks, was the body of the horse, with the steep black shadow beside it.

A long hour and more passed, and then, at the rim of the valley, where a small gorge opened from it and a trickle of water ran down, to be soaked up in the sands of the larger cañon, something seemed to rise out of the desert and take on the shape of a man.

That was Grey, and what he rose from was not the sands themselves, but the old slicker of Jim Parson, gray and battered, filled with ten million wrinkles, and taking on the color of the sand, beneath the bright moon. Under it he had crawled on hands and knees, slowly, slowly, like a turtle.

Once, a bullet struck the sand just before him. He had lain flat, and waited for the second shot to break his back, but no second shot came. Someone had thought he saw something move across the sands, no doubt, and had changed his mind afterward.

So Grey came to the verge of the rocks, and then, among them, safe from observation, he stood up with a fire in his eyes that was no reflection of the moonlight. He had fought fair, even against thieves and liars and traitors, but now he would fight for the sake of the girl who was yonder, crouching among the rocks. And heaven help the man who came in his way.

He rounded the corner of the rocks and saw the smaller gorge before him, the southern half in blackest shadow, and the northern wall gleaming with light. He could see the small glimmer of the water in the little cañon, also, and small trees blooming like dark flowers beside the narrow creek. Two men walked among the rocks, close to him, and he made himself small as they passed by him.

The voice of one was Garcias, and the voice of the other was Slade. Garcias led a horse; Slade, however, was without one, and walked with a jaunty step, swinging a stick.

The boy heard Slade saying: "Make the round. Tell every man that his pay is doubled the minute the job is done, and a good bonus, besides. As for the girl, Garcias, women don't matter really. They're appurtenances and properties of a man's life, not a vital part of it. She has to go with the others. It must be a clean sweep. I tell you, the boy has turned her head. She's seen him playing the part of a hero and a demigod. She can't help but be in love with him, and after his death, you couldn't keep her from blabbing."

Garcias attempted to reply, but the other stopped him with a curt gesture. "No good in talk, Garcias," he said. "You see for yourself. Or you will see, later, that I'm entirely right, and that the thing has to be this way. You've wasted some time raising that girl. Well, that wastage of time will be made up to you in hard cash. What can you ask more than that? Nothing, I think." He waved his hand again. The air of the man was jovial, bursting with confidence. And Garcias slowly mounted into the saddle, as Slade added: "Tell every man that the time when he must keep his eyes open, especially, is about the time of dawn, when there's just enough daylight to make the moon dim. That's the hour when they may try to make a rush. If the rush is made, let them train every shot on the boy. For once he's down, the others are nothing . . . dust in the fingers, that's all. Garcias, the game is won, the greatest game I've ever played. The cards are in our hands. We only need to use common sense and keep our eyes open to push the thing through to the end."

Garcias, without an answer, his head bowed a little, rode away. Slade, looking after him, threw back his head and laughed silently, as the wolf laughs when it sees the calf stray within the reach of its teeth. So Slade laughed, and then, turning a little, he sauntered up the side of the twisting water, swinging his stick, like one who has almost finished a big task, and now gives himself a little relaxation. Behind him, dim and thin from the rimrock about the larger gorge, he could hear the rifles cracking at regular intervals.

And now Grey rose up from the rocks and stepped out after Slade. He walked in time with him, but with a slightly longer step that quickly closed the distance between them. He was very close when he called out: "Slade!"

Slade did not turn. He stopped short, frozen in the midst of a step, and Grey saw the man shudder from head to foot. He seemed to grow taller as he stood there, riveted to the ground.

"Slade," said Grey, "I'm going to kill you. I've fought before. But I've never fought for the sake of killing. You're different. You're not human. You've put a price on so many men, that you've a price on yourself. Still, I won't do as you tried to do with me. I won't take you from behind and murder you. I'll give you a fighting half chance. You can turn and fill your hand as you turn. Because the moment you're around, you're as good as dead. And as you die, Slade, I want you to know that your scheme has dissolved in smoke. It's disappeared. It dies with you, because the rest of the rats will run when they smell your dead flesh down the wind. And if. . . ."

He was watching, as he spoke, and it was well that he was, for Slade chose that moment to whirl, snatching out a gun as he did so.

It seemed to Grey, for his own part, he never in his life had drawn a gun with such deliberation, and never aimed so calmly and with such a cold surety. Yet, his bullet was in the brain of Slade before the latter had pulled on the trigger.

Chapter Forty-Three

He left Slade lying on the edge of the creek, with his face upturned, smiling toward the starry sky, his eyes open and as brilliant as they had been in life. His right hand lay in the water as though, with his final gesture, he strove to wash it clean of sin.

"Slade!" called a voice. "I say, Slade!" A tall Mexican came hurrying with great strides.

Grey drew back among the rocks.

"Slade!" yelled the man again. "Who fired up here and . . . ?" He saw the dead man then. He came close with his hands stretched out before him, as though he were thrusting away the thing that his eyes saw. When he came up to it, he whipped suddenly about and ran with a skulking stride back in the direction from which he had come.

The moon was on his face, and Grey never had seen such incredulous horror as he saw there. There was the fitting tribute to Slade—that the ruffians he had employed could not believe in his destruction and were utterly unnerved by it when it came.

From the mouth of the smaller ravine, hoof beats began. Grey followed to the corner where the two valleys met, and he saw the fugitive streaking across the distant sands toward the south as though wings pursued him.

Those others on the rock might see, and some of them might come to inquire, and find there the dead body, and learn that the destroyer of the great Slade was still at large.

So it happened. Exactly as he had imagined, exactly as he had told Slade himself, the death of the leader dissolved all the work that he had done, and the last and surest of his traps faded into smoke and was lost in the pink of the morning mist.

By that time Grey walked out into the valley with the slicker of Jim Parson thrown over one shoulder. He watched, as he stepped along, the gleaming rimrock that bordered the ravine. But there was no shot fired at him, and no form stirred along the crest. They were gone. The very last of them was gone.

So he walked up to the little natural fort, smoking a cigarette, and waved to them. Big Jim Parson, with a wild whoop, started to run out to him, and then flung up his hands and jumped back behind the rocks.

"It's all right, everyone," Grey announced, drawing close. "We're as free as the air. There's nothing but miles between us and the Río Grande now."

They did not swarm about him with outcries and questions. They came out slowly, like animals from a den, and with hollow, weary eyes they looked at him. Only the girl, last of all to come, held back close to the rocks. Her face was reddened and swollen as if with weeping. She looked at him as at a ghost, and not a true man.

"Rinky Dink, man," said Jim Parson, at last, "will you tell us what happened?"

"Why, they simply blew away like dust," said Grey. "Slade died during the night. And the rest of them took to their heels."

"I ain't a man that loves questions," said Jim Parson, ". . . neither puttin' nor takin' 'em . . . but how did you fade yourself into thin air last night? And how did you get at Slade in his crowd?"

"You know, Jim," said the boy, "I just had a streak of luck." He could not put his tongue to the words. To explain it would be too simple. But in his own heart he felt that there was a mystery in the thing and that from the time he received Marshal Neilan's commission, he had been acting under a guidance that he did not understand.

So it was that, in the story of Lawrence Grey, or Rinky Dink, there grew up the legend, the ghostly tale that was rumored and whispered from town to town, and from camp to lonely camp. Three sane people attested to the fact of it. But who could offer an explanation? To this day, some of the old-timers will sit with pencil and paper, drawing the diagram of the valley, and offering their explanations of how Grey crossed the sands. But no one hits upon the simple truth. No one ever connected the death of Slade with the odd fact that a certain slicker, under the moon, appeared the very color of the sand.

They saddled their horses and mules in haste. All offered their mounts to the girl, but she declared that she had earned the right to walk as well as the best of them. At last, Grey fixed a baleful stare upon the other two. It was old *Padre* José who accepted the hint and, pulling Parson by the arm, made him ride on. Grey watched them go, and, when they were a little distance away, he spoke to the girl as she started after them.

"Isabella," he said, "I'm a mighty tired man. But if it comes to a showdown, I'm going to put you into the saddle."

She turned about at him, staring. "Rinky Dink," she said, "if I thought you were really foolish enough to lay a hand. . . ."

"Stuff," he said, and, with a laugh of confidence, he strode up to her. Now his first step was long and sure, his second slipped a little, as it were, in the sand, and his third was very short, indeed. At last he stood still. He wanted to keep his eyes on her, but he found the task a hard one. His glance was slipping away. "Suppose that I give it up," he said, "and simply beg you to take the mare, and let me walk along beside you. We'll change places, after a while. But you know, Isabella, I feel like walking alongside and looking up, like one of those squirrels."

That was how Isabella came to take the saddle on the bay mare. Somehow they did not seem able to overtake the other two riders very easily, although surely the mare could outstep the mules in this going.

Padre José and Jim Parson took turns in glancing back covertly, and each time one of them looked, the other asked: "Well?"

And he who had looked would answer: "Nothing . . . yet."

At last Jim Parson, as he glanced behind, suddenly reined in his horse. "It's all right, *Padre* José," he said. "You can turn around and look now. The whole world can look, and they won't give a darn. Now, there's a pair of high-grade folks. But look at 'em makin' a show of themselves. Look, now, will you. They're walkin' along, hand in hand, like any fools. And dog-gone me if they ain't forgot all about having a horse."

"Yes," *Padre* José agreed, with a sigh. "But the horse has been taught to follow."

"What d'you mean by that . . . behind that, I should say?" asked Parson.

"Nothing except what time will tell," said *Padre* José. "But maybe Rinky Dink won't continue to win all his battles to the end of his days."

Some six weeks after this, Marshal Neilan came wearily home to his house. The day had been a long one, and the marshal was more tired than usual. As he passed through his front gate and a shadow detached itself from the hedge, he turned like a cat, and a gun jumped into his hand.

"It's all right, Marshal," said the voice of Grey.

"Rinky Dink, confound you," the marshal said with a breath of relief, "when will you get over your ways of a hunting cat? Why do you have to wait for me in the dusk, when you've a right to prance down the main streets in the middle of the day?

Are you still afraid?"

"You know, Marshal," said the boy, "habit's a pretty powerful thing."

"Aye," said the marshal, "it is. The eating habit, for instance. Come in and have supper with me."

"Thanks," said the boy, "but the fact is that she expects me . . . Isabella, I mean to say."

"Oh, let her wait and expect," said the marshal.

"Let her wait?" Grey murmured. "No, sir, I know better than that."

"Well," said the marshal, "here's another letter from John Ray. He's coming West again. He's bound for Mexico. He only wants to stop off for the wedding."

"Is Forbes dead at last?" asked the boy.

"Dead? There's the trick of it. It did Forbes a lot of good to see Ray. It did him so much good that in a week he was sitting up. In another week, he started walking. And he's put on ten pounds and says he'll live forever. It wasn't heart trouble. It was a fool doctor's fool medicine. Digitalis, or something, when no digitalis was wanted. And so it looks, son, as though you've had all your work for nothing, except for putting Forbes back onto his feet."

"Speaking of work," said Grey, who did not seem to heed the rest of the marshal's speech, "it seems that Isabella thinks that I ought to have some sort of a job. D'you think that you could find me one?"

"D'you know cattle?" asked the marshal.

"No."

"D'you know sheep?"

"No."

"Can you run a farm?"

"Dog-gone, Marshal," said Grey, "what are you talking about?"

"I'm talking about work," said Neilan. "What sort of work can you do? You don't seem to be much good."

"I know it." Grey sighed. "That's the way it seems to me, too."

"You could do my work," said Neilan, "for next to nothing a year and a good chance to get yourself filled with lead once a week."

"Neilan," said the boy, "why didn't I think of it before. I take the job right now."

"Better ask Isabella, first," said the marshal.

"Aye," Grey agreed. "I suppose I had."

ABOUT THE AUTHOR

Max Brand is the best-known pen name of Frederick Faust, creator of Dr. Kildare, Destry, and many other fictional characters popular with readers and viewers worldwide. Faust wrote for a variety of audiences in many genres. His enormous output, totaling approximately thirty million words or the equivalent of 530 ordinary books, covered nearly every field: crime, fantasy, historical romance, espionage, Westerns, science fiction, adventure, animal stories, love, war, and fashionable society, big business and big medicine. Eighty motion pictures have been based on his work along with many radio and television programs. For good measure he also published four volumes of poetry. Perhaps no other author has reached more people in more different ways.

Born in Seattle in 1892, orphaned early, Faust grew up in the rural San Joaquin Valley of California. At Berkeley he became a student rebel and one-man literary movement, contributing prodigiously to all campus publications. Denied a degree because of unconventional conduct, he embarked on a series of adventures culminating in New York City where, after a period of near starvation, he received simultaneous recognition as a serious poet and successful popular-prose writer. Later, he traveled widely, making his home in New York, then in Florence, and finally in Los Angeles.

Once the United States entered the Second World War, Faust abandoned his lucrative writing career and his work as a screenwriter to serve as a war correspondent with the infantry in Italy, despite his fifty-one years and a bad heart. He was killed during a night attack on a hilltop village held by the German army. New books based on magazine serials or unpublished manuscripts or restored versions continue to appear so that, alive or dead, he has averaged a new book every four months for seventy-five years. Beyond this, some work by him is newly reprinted every week of every year in one or another format somewhere in the world. A great deal more about this author and his work can be found in *The Max Brand Companion* (Greenwood Press, 1997) edited by Jon Tuska and Vicki Piekarski. His next Five Star Western will be *Legend of the Golden Coyote*. His Website is www.MaxBrandOnline.com.